UNCONQUERED
~ COUNTRIES ~

Also by Geoff Ryman

The Warrior Who Carried Life (1985)

The Child Garden (1989)

Was (1992)

UNCONQUERED COUNTRIES ~

Four Novellas

by
Geoff Ryman

St. Martin's Press New York

Design by Basha Zapatka

Library of Congress Cataloging-in-Publication Data

Ryman, Geoff.
    Unconquered countries / Geoff Ryman.
        p.   cm.
    ISBN 0-312-09929-0
    1. Fantastic fiction, English.   2. Science fiction, English.
    I. Title.
    PR6068.Y74U53   1994
    823'.914-dc20   93-44033
                                                                            CIP

First Edition: April 1994
10 9 8 7 6 5 4 3 2 1

To the Creature, again.

⏤ Contents ⏤

⌁ INTRODUCTION ⌁
by Samuel R. Delany

In *A Fall of Angels* it's Hellespont, the world of the Hellesian settlers, circling the star Daphne.

In *Fan* it's the world of working-class London.

In *O Happy Day!* it's the camp beside the railroad line.

And in *The Unconquered Country* it's the unconquered country itself.

The four extraordinary novellas comprising this book portray, each of them, the detail and texture of a life on the inside—an inside that is bounded by a distant and virtual outside which surrounds or defines it.

In all four, what is outside functions as an ideal reality of unimaginable freedom, power, and fear, more or less inaccessible to the main character inside—Raul Kundara, Billie, the narrator, or Third Child. At one point or another in each story, the main character or characters are positioned at a gate between inside and outside—even Third Child, through her relationship with the young soldier Crow, when he takes her to the Ceremony, is able to see the Neighbors and the People (the creatures of the outside) in a (briefly) nonwarlike mode. Even Billie, at the concert, manages to get through the coded door to the backstage area that, for her, represents the way to freedom.

But having located such a pattern, we have to ask ourselves just what, in terms of the reading experience, we have found. I mention this because I think what the reader encountering these tales for the first time is likely to notice is not an underlying structural similarity so much as a gripping range of affect, of subject matter, of meaning.

I first became aware of Ryman as a writer in 1985, shortly after the third story here—*O Happy Day!*—appeared in the first *Interzone Anthology* out of England. In the mid-eighties, sociobiology's theoretical backlash against feminism's material advances was at its peak—at least in terms of the attention it was being given by the media: Suppose males really *were* more violent than females through the very biology of their hormones? Somehow, the sociobiologists putting forth this proposition assumed that in the face of such a "fact," women (and men) would have no other choice but to settle back and accept male violence for what it was, and give up trying to reorganize society in a way to contain or control it—presumably accepting the odd black-eye, date rape, or murder with a resigned smile and a mumbled, ". . . Boys will be boys."

But in an appeal to the coldest of cold equations, Ryman's *O Happy Day!* proposes, rather, a Final Solution: Since only a minuscule number of men are needed, whether violent or pacific, to keep the race going, if they really *are* a social menace, get rid of them.

But it's here that we can see what Ryman's repeated inside/outside structure and the gates he positions between them allow him to do, for *O Happy Day!* is not the women's story at all: In the tale, the women are entirely "outside." Rather, Ryman focuses on a group of gay men who have been allowed to serve as clean-up squad in this concentration camp where heterosexual males are being exterminated en mass. The focus is entirely on what goes on at the gate *between* the inside and the outside. As such, he is able to make a pointed analysis, not so much of the *potential* of violence (read: *threat,* which was the sociobiological point) but of the *propagation* of violence: He is able to show how, as a structure, violence *moves* from outside to inside, completely ignoring the fence the women have erected to contain it; thus, it is revealed as a structure that has little to do with hormones, and as such is not containable (or eradicable) the way a disease might be quarantined (or eradicated). For all its sobering premise, *O Happy Day!*

is a rather salutary tale—well worth reading for both its provocations (which are many) and for what it has to say about them.

The Unconquered Country was finished in 1984, the same year as *O Happy Day!,* Ryman tells us in his Afterword ("a year in which," Ryman writes, "I could do no wrong"). Here Ryman has given us a dark fantasy—only a step away from magic realism—that is at once science fiction and a pointed allegory of the inhumanly tragic Cambodian epilogue to the Vietnam nightmare. Its living houses, its biological farming and body-part sales serve to distance the story. At the same time, as we recognize the technology behind them, they give the tale moments of immediacy truly unsettling. (In one sense, this is the tale of the Hellesian settlers from *A Fall of Angels* looked at through a microscope.) Someone might argue that the religious ending mitigates the horror of the story, in a manner reminiscent of Flaubert's classic tale, *"Un Coeur simple,"* without Flaubert's coruscating and subversive ironies. But since the horror with which Ryman deals—the bridge on which we end is only another concentration camp—is so much beyond any ever envisioned by Flaubert, finally we have to ask: Would the story have been bearable *without* some respite?

Whatever our answer, both *The Unconquered Country* and *O Happy Day!* are political science fiction at its most effective. And when *O Happy Day!* first appeared in England, the discussion around it quickly crossed the sea to become almost as heated here as it was abroad.

When *The Unconquered Country* was first published in the United States as a separate novel in 1987 in paperback, people in the SF world passed it to one another with quiet exhortations: "Read this . . . this is extraordinary! This is something you've *never* encountered before!" They were right.

As easily as we can call *The Unconquered Country* and *O Happy Day!* political science fiction, we can call *Fan* sociological science fiction. Set in an England that could as easily come about next week as next year, the story examines the growing part the entertainment media—particularly pop music—play in our lives, as their substance becomes less and less and their preordained form becomes greater and greater. In this tale, all Billie's effort to reach her idol, to join with his world of travel and glamor even as she hopes to escape her dull, dull life and emotionally disturbed son, works as an allegory for the analytical effort required to see through the process to its essential, illusory core.

Similarly, *A Fall of Angels* might be called "pure" science fiction—for those still looking for some sort of purity in the range of imaginary fomentation. The harsh, if human, society of the settlers makes an effective contrast with the soaring, transcendental world of the Angels and their mission to refuel the red giant suns with interstellar hydrogen by means of the Charlie Slides: This is Ryman's one tale—here—where the basic drama *occurs* in the "outside," even while the fundamental humanity remains within.

All four of the Ryman novellas here are rich in ideas, insight, and drama—as are his three, full-length novels. The most recent of those, *Was,* is a disturbingly inventive take on the story behind the story of Frank L. Baum's children's classic, *The Wizard of Oz,* and Baum's relation to the real Dorothy Gael, as well as the making of the 1939 MGM film with the young Judy Garland. (Ryman is one of those rare writers in whose work singular ideas—particularly admirable in a writer of a certain sort of science fiction—tend to gain the solidity of well-realized characters.) The bottom line is, as it must be in any such introduction, that I enjoyed these stories mightily. I'm sure you will, too. They exhibit both the clarity of surface and clarity of structure that mark a formidable writing talent.

—New York
November 1993

A FALL OF ANGELS

OR

ON THE POSSIBILITY OF LIFE UNDER EXTREME CONDITIONS

— 1 —

---

from *Remembrances of Bee*

The first thing you miss is the process of waking up, the delicious nestling back down into yourself, the curling of arms and legs about each other. Suddenly, coldly, you are aware.

You see the room, all four metal walls and the floor and the ceiling all at once. You do not seem to be in it. You turn, but the room does not spin around you. You are ill with panic and confusion.

A voice calls you by name, and gratefully you stutter, stammer, surprised to find that you are not speaking, that you have no voice.

"You must try to remain calm," the voice advises. It is honey smooth and female. "Try to remember the drill we practiced. Remember the drill? What is your name?"

"Where is my body!"

"What is your name? Tell me your name."

"What has happened? Where are my hands?"

The animal reaction is fear. You are weaponless; you feel horribly naked and exposed. You want to beg to be allowed back into the shelter of yourself, but what has happened is final and permanent. Your body has been amputated.

It lives on, in mild unconcern, perhaps curious as to what use you will be put. Those miraculous eyes, those gliding joints, those delicate hands are no longer yours. No longer will you change the universe by simply grabbing it. Your family, your friends, the whole mosaic of your memory belongs to someone, something, else. You hear no warm, close pumping, you are no longer reassured by your own subtle odors. You have no gender, or sense of smell or taste or touch.

But a clock in your mind tells you the percentage of oxygen in the atmosphere. You turn upside down, but the room does not.

You will never sleep or dream again. You are an Angel.

It can take a year to adjust. Then you make up your mind to be what you are, and to do your duty. You are a tool, an imprint, a creation of Humankind, its messenger. They send you first to scout for wealth and homeworlds, tasting the air, mingling with the stone. You find uranium and tin; you call, and the Charlie Slides follow, like pigeons. They entrust you with work for Entropy Control.

Inside you, there is a little, sharp corner of pain. But I still feel, it protests. They give you a partner. My first was Ai. We should have been compatible; perhaps we were too much alike. He felt all decisions should be his. When we disagreed, he claimed I was impossible to work with. I think of Ai sometimes. It might be that the pain of being an Angel blinded him, made him deny feeling. He tried to become a machine. He could not.

Control understood. They teamed me with Bee, my lovely Bee.

Bee had been chosen, not for intelligence, diligence, or loyalty as had Ai, but simply because he would love being an Angel. Bee had been a large, awkward, driven man. No place could be found for him. Angelhood released him.

When I first met him, I was overwhelmed. I went very cold and formal. He darted in swift, straight lines: nervous, jerky, eager. He seemed to sing in a tumble of words and images. He teased me and cajoled me, made a sound like an elephant with his mind, to startle me. Gradually, I learned to follow him. Bee showed me freedom and taught me how to enjoy it, and for that I loved him.

We plunged through suns and swam through the canyons of the sea. Bee took me to a world made of crystal that was the size of a house. We fell like rain through the blazing depths of the substratum where there is no time and it is white, blinding white, from the explosion that is both the beginning and the end. Humans cannot go there.

Then one of our Controllers died. She was replaced with another, who also died. We still lived. We were Angels, no longer human. There are layers of realization within that realization, as there are layers within the universe. I had yet to penetrate them all.

---

from the letters of Raul Kundara, written in his youth during his term as a Researcher for Entropy Control, Hellespont

---

Hola Mari,

I had hoped to send you an account of my arrival, but there was no time. Immediately, I was shuttled down from the Platform to this world. I am writing to you now, with apologies.

Sliding was entirely without pain. I came down the cold side and was numb afterward. The station here is pleasant and well designed, prefab as it is. Hellespont is the third world on which the station has been placed. I have my own room. I share a water room only, with four others. Three are my elders and are regular officers. They have been with the station many years. I thought they would ask me about home. They showed no such interest. They joked instead about all the equipment I brought with me. Fourth is another researcher. His name is Gareth, very thin with carrot red hair, from wild Lenin. His project is radiation sliding. He talks about it frequently. There are nine researchers here on the station. They are all very involved with their work. Some are elders or even seniors, and I feel very honored to be here.

We all have duty-work on the station. I have a cert in chemistry, so I help test the slided food. Once salt arrived scrambled as lithium. I also serve in the kitchens. The food is nourishing, but it all tastes of boiled metal.

I wish you could see Hellespont. Its sun, Daphne, is huge and swollen, a red giant with a hazy outline, when you see it at sunset. The daysky is always clouded. Hellespont was an oceaned world, with forests and lakes, before Daphne began to relax. In winter, it rains here every night. Further south, on the plains, water boils during the day. It is exceeding hot! We sleep during the day and work at night when it is cooler. We cast off heat with Charlie Slides and wear coolsuits even when we sleep. There are no windows.

At dawn, watersheets unfold over the valley. They catch the evaporation and save it. Even so, the morning air is always choked with mist. It wavers as it rises. Deep ditches channel the winter rains, but they are empty now.

My first day, I went out to see the aglamaks, the criers. I like them. They blossom out at sunrise from the ground one by one with a sound like a yawn. Soon the whole valley dances with them, whooping and groaning. They look something like water hyacinths, bulbous as if meant to float, with fanned gills that they pump in and out. That makes the sound, the hooting. They are respirating then. I took one back. It curled up into its dayball, and simply fell apart when I tried to examine it.

Aglamaks reproduce by worming tendrils through the soil. They are all linked with each other and the connection is never broken while they live. In times of drought, water is carried over many kilometers to them from their more fortunate brethren. Some masters teach that they are all one organism. The settlers here hate them. They do not taste good, and draw moisture from the fields.

By day the valley is dry and empty. The aglamaks draw up small and tight. Much of the flora here flower, seed and die all in the space of a sunrise.

Young Gareth wisely reminds me that true duty can consist of waiting. I have not yet spoken with the station senior. The Chief Researcher, Mzobwe, has briefed me. "Our primary duty is to the control of entropy. All other work must take second place." This means my project must wait until the Angels have finished their first reconnoiter of Daphne. "There is not likely to be much work for a biologist, there," he said. There is much for me to do in the meantime. I will let you know what happens. My respects to my placer Robt, my chanter Bella, Nive and all her children, and of course to my ward Hal.

Love to yourself and Tam, unless you have been lucky enough to find a replacement.

Love,
Toni

Excerpts from
Entropy Control and You,
Narrative Version,
by Senior Alvin Perfect, Master and Chanter

The control of entropy is our purpose. It is our first duty. Yet what is entropy?

The word is much misused. Placers speak of entropy when children neglect their studies. Teachers sometimes talk of the barbarism of olden times as times of entropy. The word has come to mean everything the Regimen opposes.

Entropy is simply the loss of heat every time work is done. Its mathematical sign is S. It is embodied in the Second Law of Thermodynamics. . . .

The Second Law means that gradually the universe is becoming one even temperature. Heat needs a difference in temperature to do work. When all energy has been converted into heat energy and when all differences in temperature are evened out, work will become impossible. The universe will come to a halt without light or motion of any kind other than disordered, undirected molecular movement.

S is the sapping of the lifeblood of the universe.
S is the heat that freezes.
S is the death of all things.

All this will happen unless Humankind intervenes. So S is our symbol, the negation of entropy.

How is this possible? We will trace the development of the Charlie Slide and the opportunity for service that resulted. We will discover how all our skills are united in this aim by the Regimen of Tanner Cahsway. We will see why you are placed, and why it is important that you do your duty.

For you are human, and Humankind is the salvation of the universe. . . .

Three hundred years ago, in the stillness of history, there were only three homeworlds. The vast distances between stars had to be crossed in vessels made of metal. These tiny ships could only approach one half the speed of light. The voyage from Earth to Home took more than eight earthyears. The world of Nippon, now called Ruin, was effectively isolated. Radio messages from Nippon took 22 years to reach Home. New forms of transportation and communication were sought. . . .

In homeyear 872, an earthside research station at Ningsia involved in the investigation of time travel accidentally generated the first true particles of anti-matter. Unlike positrons, they mirrored the complex molecular structures of matter. A catastrophic explosion resulted. Chao Li Sing, working from the records of Ningsia, succeeded in generating true anti-hydrogen. It was kept separate from all forms of matter as plasma in a magnetic trap. . . .

The more complicated molecule of anti-helium was generated

next. This time, matter and anti-matter were allowed to meet. They obliterated each other as expected. The results of the obliteration were not. Both matter and anti-matter were converted into previously unknown quanta. They were named after their discoverer as chaolis.

The chaoli appeared to exist for mere nanoseconds. It was not, however, decaying into other particles or forms of energy. Since energy cannot be destroyed, Chao Li reasoned that it must therefore be going somewhere. Perhaps, he suggested, it was moving outside the universe, perhaps some substratum or subspace.

It is hard for us to imagine the sensation this suggestion created. The discovery of subspace has long been looked to as the only hope for efficient interstellar travel. This was, however, the era of Consolidation.

The Consolidationists were opposed to many forms of research on the grounds that it was necessary to bring together what had already been learned. The specialized branches of science had lost touch with each other. While many sincere and informed people were Consolidationists, there can be no doubt that it was also a movement of anti-science. Some of them would not even admit that an advance of the magnitude of the chaoli was still possible. All of them fought to halt further work with chaolis. Finally, in a compromise, the Consolidationist-controlled research councils agreed to finance work that might prove that chaolis in fact stayed within the known universe.

Chao Li was given clearance to trace the paths of chaolis through matter. Helium and anti-helium were again annihilated. The resulting chaolis were allowed to bombard an adjoining pocket of helium plasma.

It took the rest of Chao Li's life to account for what happened next.

All light in a rough sphere around the chaoli release disappeared. Playbacks of transmissions from the station showed that around the black sphere, gases in the air had frozen instantly. These had no time to fall as crystals, for the helium plasma had shot like a bullet out of the trap, through the walls of the station and out onto the Mongolian plain. A light scattering of tiny black spheres accompanied the helium bullet. Outside the trap, the plasma flared catastrophically to solar temperatures.

Helium is the only known substance that will not freeze under normal vapor pressure. The playbacks showed what appeared to be solid helium shooting out of the black sphere and through the walls of the station. If helium plasma had frozen from a temperature of millions of degrees, then something like absolute zero must have been achieved. It would be like absolute zero, but even more effective at halting molecular motion.

Chao Li, observing the experiment from a bunker hundreds of kilometers away, survived. By analyzing the trajectory of the helium bullet, he determined that it had traveled in a direction exactly opposite to that of Earth's rotation about the sun and its own axis. The helium plasma had been, briefly, absolutely stationary. That is, it had stayed in place while the Earth moved away from it.

Chao Li was able to demonstrate that the only way to root matter so firmly in the fabric of space was to also root it in time. Nothing could happen to it or within it. The helium had not been cooled—all motion within it had stopped. Gravity and inertia no longer affected it; neither did the magnetic trap, its basin and several concrete walls.

Chao Li then made one of his mild but devastating suggestions. The substratum, he proposed, was possibly a region without time. It was a kind of a leftover from the beginning of the universe, some part of creation that time did not affect. Since it has not expanded with the rest of the universe, it would be in physical terms very tiny indeed, yet also existing everywhere, at the core of all existing space.

If chaolis had the ability to almost push matter into the substratum, then, for the brief instant of its bombardment, matter almost existed without time. He concluded two things. First, that while light was pulled into the substratum by chaolis, matter was not. Second, that no one, certainly not himself, knew what existing without time meant.

Then he died, leaving the body of scientific thought and Humankind's hopes for interstellar travel in great disarray. . . .

Observe, gentle scholar, how duty may involve withstanding great opposition from those who are blind to Humankind's high purpose. Study the humble strength of Chao Li Sing. There you will find a path to duty. There you will see how to take your rightful place in the center of things.

For you are human, and Humankind is the salvation of the universe.

---

from the letters of Raul Kundara

Hola Mari,

Thank you for the cast. It is better to talk than to write, and it was a fruitful discussion. My deepest apologies for my error in behavior. I meant only to tease Tamel in the closing of my letter. I meant no disrespect.

I was sad also to learn that you think I came here to spite you. I have examined my actions and have found no cause for these thoughts. Please do not feel that you drove me away. Please do not feel guilty. I came to Hellespont for adventure and research and to do my duty. I have examined my motives and find no hostility on my part. I am sorry for the misunderstanding. Forgive any offensive thing I may have said.

The way of duty is hard and instructive. After four certs and a placement in biology, I am now learning what the maintenance of basic order means. Every fifthday I wash dishes. I enjoy it because of a very funny regular called Stavakanda, from Achilles. We call him Chief. He makes work easy by singing dirty songs, by throwing food at us, by squirting us with water jets. He is the only fat man in the station.

I throw food back at him. (Do not be alarmed, we also clean it up.) We were called into Senior Talsman's room. He is a man of long service, perhaps worn down by it, thin and precise. When he carries food canisters, the muscles of his neck pop out. He reminded us of the waste and the cost of the thrown food. Stavakanda reminded him that the food had already been wasted by those who did not eat it. The Senior became emotional. "I have pressures from above, pressures from below," he said. "Then you are a sandwich," said Stavakanda. I was worried for a time. I thought the Senior might damage my chances for research work. Chief called him a cosmic lightweight and told me not to worry. It is strange for me to be seen as a troublemaker. It must be dreadful for a Senior not to be respected by his workmates.

I have spoken to Senior Thoroughgood as you asked. My term of five years cannot be shortened. I now have a duty to complete, as he explained. He is a firm, polite man of wide interests. It will be some time before the Angels will be free for research work, he told me, but said I might conduct some informal investigations of my own. I asked him about Angelwork, and he said that it is not difficult. He called them "surprisingly human." I think he is fond of them. I found the meeting reassuring. Please, there is no need to worry on my behalf. I think this is an excellent posting.

My usual respects, especially to Tamel.

Love,
Toni.

---

from *Remembrances of Bee*

We did many things together, Bee and I. That was a sweet time, when our work and our wishes seemed to coincide.

We traveled the Horse Head nebula, in the belt of far Orion the Hunter. We drifted through its cool dust, sampling it for them. So vast and peaceful, the great rolling masses of darkness.

We pushed a fistful of dwarf star to them. They caught it in midspace and nibbled its edges like frightened fish.

We wandered the stars, great glowing bullies without souls. We loved the stars. We fed them.

On Ceti, we bathed in a sunspot. The gas roared up in billows away from the center, like a great river, in all directions. It raged uphill, cooled by motion, to high and distant mountains, then poured over their peaks, warming again to a needle-hot white. The sky overhead was a blaze-haze of light. Shreds of flame drifted past like clouds. Beyond the mountains, fire-arms swept the horizon, ragged like feathers.

The churning, slowly boiling plains of firestorm stretching into the distance. Fiery distance and constant motion all about us—that was Ceti.

When we arrived, the Cherubim dived and wove about us, screeching in a flock until we gave them places. "Minus ten! Minus ten!" one of them would cry. "Fifty-five! Fifty-five! Fifty-five!" called another. We strung them in lines so that their shouting would tell us where we were inside the sun.

We saved him, snarling Ceti. He was getting old. We siphoned off his helium and replaced it with hydrogen. It came shuddering out of the Slide, dead and gray; suddenly it would come alive with light and twist away. The work took one hundred years.

We waited together, Bee and I, calling the Slides and watching unwatchable skyscapes. He sang to me through the depths of a star. When we could, we made love, bathing and mingling in each other.

Oh, Bee. The warbling of your touch and the shiver of your joy! Can they destroy such things?

On ripening Daphne, you found a brother.

---

from *Entropy Control and You*

The Consolidationists gained control of the ruling Secretariat in 894. That same year, the Dangerous Experiments Protocol was agreed by all research councils. It declared that, along with many other forms of research, chaoli investigation was illegal. The ban included even mathematical modeling of chaoli behavior.

A colleague of Chao Li's, Dr. Anthony Black, braved the eight-year voyage to Home in an attempt to convince the Five Cities that chaoli experimentation was in the interest of all new home-worlds. A more flamboyant personality than Chao Li Sing, he managed to persuade the Five to finance his research on the first of the hanging platforms.

The story of the design and construction of the first platform would easily by itself fill a narrative of this size. The core idea was that the research station be kept safely away from homeworlds and from all motion itself. To achieve this the platform was oriented around a core chaoli eruption. Thus work could be done with absolutely stationary, time-frozen matter.

The first platform unleashed the kind of rapid-fire sequence of discoveries the Consolidationists most dreaded. It allowed Dr. Black to see for the first time that chaolis did not disappear into the substratum forever. Some of them returned, nanoseconds later, only to disappear again. The cycle was repeated until only a light scattering of chaolis returned. These chaolis, nicknamed Charlies, became a permanent core of returning particles.

If Charlies were being thrown out of the universe, the substratum was hurling them back.

Dr. Black's team found nothing—no substance or particle—that could deflect or slow the chaoli. The force of the explosion that created it was not large enough to account for this, and the chaoli itself was not frozen in time. Either the chaoli was propelling itself, or something else was.

Dr. Black decided that the universe itself was doing the work, the very fabric of space. He postulated a quality of resistance in both the universe and the substratum which he called elasticity. Once generated, a Charlie was thrown back and forth between space and subspace. Black compared elasticity to a wall that does the bouncing for the ball. This bouncing is not perpetual motion because the Charlie is propelled afresh with each bounce. It merely goes on until the end of time.

Black noted one other phenomenon of utmost importance. Light waves, radio waves, X and gamma rays could all be swept into subspace by Charlies, and matter could be time frozen, but only at times. Sometimes Charlies did not produce this effect, or "swiss-cheesed" matter by only affecting parts of it.

Black's team demonstrated that an eruption of chaolis had points of utmost efficacy, analogous to the focus of a beam of light. The random movement of unleashed chaolis often prevented focus from being achieved, and certainly from being predicted. Control of the movement of chaolis would have to be attained if the discovery was to be of practical use. But how, when nothing seemed to have any effect on them?

In 918, chaolis from two neighboring annihilations were allowed to bombard each other. Most of the chaolis simply rebounded off each other or escaped without colliding at all. Particles closer to the center had multiple collisions. These particles, during the brief instant left to them in the universe, sorted themselves into parallel lines. The result was a coherent beam of Charlie particles. This beam returned from the substratum without the loss of any particles. The scattering effect of incoherent Charlies had been overcome. . . .

A coherent Charlie beam is thrown into the substratum. Unlike its counterpart, its member particles all move together though the substratum in the equivalent of a straight line. They reemerge into the universe at a point some distance from where they left it. They are then hurled back across the substratum to their point of origin. Thus is a permanent highway between two points in space forged across the substratum. Because of elasticity, the flow of Charlies in both directions is "downhill." No additional energy need be added to the system. This pathway became known as the Charlie Slide. . . .

The Consolidationists withdrew their ban on chaoli research in 925. That year Earth began the construction of its own platform. . . .

Much remained to be done. In 951 the Earth platform showed how the distortion wave could prepare matter for Sliding. The distortion wave had been noted for some time without importance being attached to it. Time is defined as the expansion of space. Space, all space, continues to expand as time goes on. Time-freezing blocks this expansion. This results in a buildup of potential energy in the form of elasticity. When the time-freezing is over, the space occupied by the freeze violently expands to fill the area it would have occupied if the flow of time had not been interrupted.

The result is a ripple in the fabric of space itself, a wavelike effect that is similar to that on the surface of a pond when a stone is dropped into it. Matter in a distortion wave ripples. Each individual molecule, embedded in space, is distorted as the wave passes. No heat is generated because the molecules themselves are not moving—space itself is. Matter in this state is called soft. Soft matter can be snatched up by a Slide and carried into the substratum. Removed from the distortion, it is expelled by the substratum, along the line of least resistance—the Slide.

Thus the basic process of Sliding was established, at least in theory. Much further practical work needed to be done, but in 976 enough of these problems had been solved for a copper plate to slide between the Earth and Home platforms. The plate bore a portrait of Chao Li Sing and the inscription "The Modern Prometheus." Dr. Black was still alive to view its arrival. For all practical purposes, casting was instantaneous. . . .

Now a net of Charlie Slides has been flung across the stars. Platforms hang without motion near the orbits of over 50 homeworlds. Before that could be achieved, a means of aiming the Slides, of sending beacons to guide them, had to be found. But there was another problem.

A suicidal civil war had destroyed Nippon, one of only three inhabited worlds. Science could peel open space like an orange, but it could provide no answers to moral dilemmas. Consolidation had shown itself to be able only to limit the freedom of science. All other philosophies seemed stale, impotent. Humankind seemed sickened by the possibilities that now opened up, unable to find another kind of platform from which to launch itself, as though distrustful of itself, the universe.

Some new direction, some spark of faith was needed. Faith was found by Our Master in the form of the Regimen.

from *The Syriac Bestiary,*
a Text of Ancient Earth

There is an animal called the *dajja,* extremely gentle, which the hunters are unable to capture because of its great strength. It has in the middle of its brow a single horn. But observe the ruse by which the huntsmen take it. They lead forth a virgin, pure and chaste. When the animal sees her, he approaches and throws himself upon her. The girl offers him her breasts and the animal begins to suck the breasts of the maiden and to conduct himself familiarly with her. Then the girl, while sitting quietly, reaches forth her hand and grabs the horn of the animal's brow. The huntsmen come up and bind the beast and go away with him to the king.

Likewise the Lord Jesus Christ has raised up for us a horn of salvation in the midst of Jerusalem, in the house of God, by intercession of the Mother of God, a virgin pure and chaste, full of mercy, immaculate and inviolate. . . .

from the Angelogs of Entropy Control, Hellespont,
Transcripts of the Proceedings of 1363/13/5

Time in metric time	Recorded Material
1/1649	*B* Look at it, Zoe!
1651	*Z* Yes, my love.

1653

B

Soft and big and gentle!
A docile star!

1657

Z

It is dying.

1661

B

Wisps of gas,
See?
They stand like trees.

1668

Z

Bee, you are a romantic.
It is burnt out,
burnt out,
no fire in its belly.
Hydrogen at 12.
Helium: 4.322!
.361 of total mass!

1684

B

Oh don't *count.*

1687

Z

It is our work.

1690

B

It is their work.
We've just arrived!
I want to play.

1696

Z

They cannot play.
They must work.

1/1700	*B* What of it?
1702	*Z* They need us.
1704	*B* We don't need them. They are dim, not the stars. Dim and damp.
1712	*Control* B and Z
1716	*Z* That is them now.
1717	*B* Don't answer. Perhaps they'll go away.
1720	*Control* B and Z. We are receiving you. Please answer.
1726	*Z* We receive you, Control. We are unable to give you a position.
1732	*Control* No matter. Our respects, Angels! This is Researcher Mzobwe Welcome to Daphne. How was the Slide?

1736

> *Z*
> Silent and very fast,
> Control.

1739

> *Control*
> It took longer than
> we expected.

1743

> *Z*
> We stopped
> briefly
> to look at a double star.

1748

> *Control*
> Anything of interest?

1750

> *B*
> It was beautiful.
> That was all.

1755

> *Control*
> Everything here is ready.
> We have developed a
> navigational system
> for Daphne
> based on a simple
> conformal stereographic projection.
> Are you ready to receive?

1767

> *Z*
> We are ready, Control.

1769

> *Control*
> Casting now.

1723

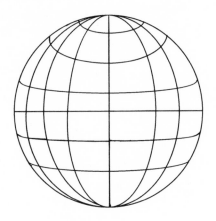

1726

B
Nets,
always nets.
Do they think they can catch
the universe with them?

1733

Z
Projection received and stored,
Control.

1740

Control
Magnetic North and South
are accepted as true N and S.
Parallels and meridians
imprinted by orbiting beacon.
Imprints pulse every 5 thous.
No attempt has been made to
compensate for equatorial drift.
Projection identical
for both hemispheres.

1745

B
Why do they try to talk like their
machines? Do they want to be machines?
Do they want to stop feeling?

1757

Z
They can hear you, Bee.

1797

B
I don't care.

1/1800

Control
We suggest that internal coordinates
be established by
the usual trihedral,
placing X, Y and Z Cherubs
every 5 points from 0 to 100 (+ and −
as follows

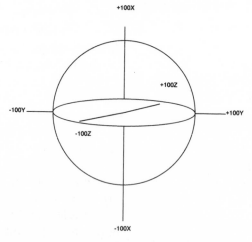

100 defined as 33,781,093. kilometers.

1819

Z
Thank you, Control.
Suggestion accepted.

1824

B
Zoe, I like it so much better
when they aren't here.
I like you so much better when
they aren't here.

1828

Control
B, we are receiving no visuals from you.

1832

B
There is nothing for you to see.
To you it would only look
like red mist.

1839

Control
Nevertheless,
please cast as a matter of course.

1845

(Visual cast commences)
Control
Thank you.
Prime inspection coordinates
follow for the first octant.

1856

Z
Ready to receive, Control.

1/1859

Control
Casting now.
0X, 0Y, 0Z
+ 10X, + 10Y, + 5Z
+ 20X, + 20Y, + 10Z
+ 30X, + 30Y, + 15Z
+ 40X, + 40Y, + 20Z
+ 50X, + 50Y, + 25Z
at this point
please also inspect
+ 51.205X, + 49.87Y, + 26.352Z

1888	and follow this coordinate pattern out to the defined surface at 45°N × 45°W. Please also inspect these coordinates
1/1900	+ 64.043X, + 60.829Y, + 29.999Z + 64.167X, + 60.832Y, + 29.999Z + 64.2077X, + 60.832Y, + 29.999Z
1907	*B* I am so very tired of this.
1910	*Z* Please, my Bee, please.
1914	*Control* Then work your way back in steps of +10 X and Y, moving up Z in steps of +5 to the northern pole. This basic pattern should be followed in octants 2 through 8. . . .

---

from the letters of Raul Kundara

Hola Mari,

Another letter. I missed the fifthday cast and have something to tell you. I have visited the settlers!

We have a regular food run to their nearest town. They have no livestock, but they grow wonderful vegetables. There is one called the havuc. It is like a large carrot and has a meaty taste. They developed it by cross-breeding alone. I asked Senior Talsman if it were convenient for me to go, as I would miss my duty-work shift.

He said he had no authority to stop me. He took it as a personal challenge. I could see it happening. I could not stop it. I went in the landcraft with Chief and two others, by blistering day. The road down is steep and must be traveled by daylight. We were bumped and bruised and broiled. The ventilator blasted in only hot air. We sweated inside our coolsuits. No one spoke at all for the last three tens. It was miserable.

Finally at sunset we saw town lights below us. The road zigzagged down the cliff face into shadow. Darkness was a relief after the lurid red of day. The first Hellesian I saw was an old woman walking by the side of the road, alone. Her back was rigid, her legs bowed. She turned and at first I thought she was not human. The skin on her face was thick and spongy, like the sole of a foot. Hellesian skin goes like that, Chief told me. It is the heat. The old woman did not wear a coolmask. Her coolsuit was pierced by embroidery. Chief asked her if she wanted a ride. She made a croaking noise and waved us on.

The settlement is on top of a slow rise just beneath the plateau. It is called Highplain Snow. It snowed there once, says legend. I do not believe it. Highplain is lower down than the station, and hotter. There is less nightmist there, and less rain. Water floods down from the plateau in winter.

Deep and narrow ditches surround each of the fields and hold the floodwaters. Pumps channel the water into underground tanks. The fields are linked by graceful, arched little bridges. The fieldworkers cross them, singing. We heard them from a distance, droning like deep bells. As we drew closer, the words grew more distinct. According to Chief, they were singing about their breakfast still to come. Their voices meld in layers, like echoes. One of them thumps a drum. They work in time to it, loosening the soil, watering and inspecting the plants. Huge and heavy waterpacks weigh down their backs. They spray the plants with a nozzle. The watersheets were being drawn back as we arrived. Watersheets shield the fields from sun during the day and from rain at night. They are raised briefly to let in gentle twilight. The Hellesians merely looked up as we passed, and then looked down again.

By the road there was a cluster of old electrical generators. They leaned, lopsided tanks with dingy metal tubing. The heat of the day was used to boil water to run buried turbines. Now, after Sliding, the Hellesians use solar cells for electricity. There was a field of them. They glint like eyes.

The town itself is burrowed into the cliffside, deep, where it is cool. We slept in the strangerhouse, a carved chamber called the *misafir pava*. We ate in the *yemek pava,* where food is distributed. Meals and drink are served there also. The Senior of the pava, big and fat, hugged the Chief and slapped his shoulders. He spoke in broken Central. Three girls, his daughters perhaps, served us. They would not look us in the eye.

The pava filled slowly with men, only men. I saw no women among them. I thought them rude at first. They sat playing with dice, only sometimes jerking a head in our direction, or clucking their tongues. "We know all about *them,"* they seemed to say. Hellesians never hurry. They eat with infuriating slowness, but still manage to get food in their mustaches. They do not laugh much. They take everything very seriously, and nod, and murmur. Their cheeks all had a sheen of rubbery thickness to them. But none of them were as baked as the old lady of the road.

The Senior led us back to the misafir pava, with his small and wiry daughters. They gave us towels and waterkeepers, and suddenly burst into giggles. I think it was because we are so much taller than they.

We slept well at night. The beds were boxes of sand covered with sheets. They are very comfortable if the sand does not leak. We woke up at sunrise and full watergathering. The Hellesians still found time to load the landcraft with melons and havuc. They even nodded good-bye and shook hands, beaming with unexpected smiles. The Senior came out with a coolbox of water and fruit for the trip. His daughters stood in a tight nervous group to wave good-bye. I was surprised by this courtesy. They are a tough, silent, decent people. I thought perhaps that desert living forces them to learn cooperation.

The trip back was awful, uphill and slowed by added weight. I got back to the station sick with thirst and exhaustion. But I was happy. Something at last had happened.

My usuals,
Toni

---

from *Entropy Control and You*

Faith was found when Tanner Cahsway saw that the control of entropy was Humankind's high purpose.

Slide engineers noticed that Home Platform required constant cooling. Earth Platform was difficult to keep warm. It became apparent that heat energy is carried by a Charlie Slide, but in one direction only, back toward the Slide's origin. The immediate problem was solved by launching a Slide back from Earth to Home. This created an exchange of heat. It was Our Master who first saw that the Slides could be used to concentrate and gather heat that would otherwise be wasted. . . .

There are certain chemical reactions called endothermic, so named because they absorb rather than give off heat. Water can be reduced to oxygen and hydrogen by absorbing heat. Approximately 25 percent of a volume of water can be reduced by heating it to a temperature of 3000°C. Dinitrogen and dioxide also are net users of heat when forming nitrous oxide. Such endothermic reactions reduce stable chemical compounds to less stable. Less stable substances are more likely to react to other substances. They are more likely to do work. If gathered heat could be used to trigger such reactions, Our Master reasoned, Humankind could work to replenish the supply of chemical energy.

Thus, finally, did Humankind discover its high purpose. Life reverses entropy. Life increases order. Life becomes conscious, becomes the eyes and ears of the universe. We are its healing hands.

The Regimen of Tanner Cahsway uses this revelation to direct the energies and talents of all of Humankind. Above all else, our First Master sought to use Humankind to the full, to give complete expression to its potential. . . .

Tanner Cahsway was born in the year 1000 in Nueva Madrid. It was an age of intellectual and economic stagnation, of overpopulation and unchanging lives. The condition of the times was summed up for the Master when, as a researcher in a library, he saw a grown man waste an entire day playing with window blinds. In passage 9.45.3 of the Regimen, he says, "I thought then of four billion similarly engaged. I thought of the abilities and the hopes and the inner human resources that were shriveling through disuse. Anger and despair seized me. I thought of the patience of conscious thought, the power of the subconscious, and I knew Humankind was meant for greater things. . . ." From this moment of impassioned enlightenment came the inspiration for his lifelong crusade.

In 1041, with the acquiescence of the Home City, the last of the Five, the success of the Controllers was ensured. The following year, the first Control of the Regimen was established under Moira Flourens. Efforts began to rationalize and intensify the program of Entropy Control. It is a program that is always in a state of becoming, for it, like Humankind, is alive. . . .

Now mobile Slides, called and guided by living gravity, siphon off heat like dancing searchlights over the surface of suns, over the surface of home worlds, collecting heat that would be wasted, concentrating it. The Platforms have become great factories, converting heat into other forms of energy to do varieties of work—or replenishing unstable elements through endothermic reactions.

. . . But most loved of the Regimen's works are the Angels, the clarions who guide and call the Slides. They are the flesh made spirit, Humankind refined into pure duty.

As with so much else, Consolidationism had blocked research into the paranormal. The Regimen actively encouraged it. A timeless core to a transitory universe is a common theme in mystical experience. Our Master was himself convinced that astral personalities could enter the substratum and provide the needed beacons to guide and steer the Slides out into far space. . . .

This projection of personality has been perfected. Enhanced by artificial intelligence and sensors, these astral personalities are the ideal messengers able to brave the extremes of the universe. Where they go, we can perceive if not follow. They are more than our vanguards, our scouts. They are our translators. Through them we can see the unseeable, hear the unhearable. Aided by non-intelligent beacons, the Cherubim, they move through the uncharted hazes of Creation. Their great freedom and their lasting faithfulness speak deeply to all of Humankind. Study and honor them, scholars and distributors, analysts and street sweepers, placers and chanters, cooks and mathematicians. The Angels have surrendered all—their bodies, their friendships, their pleasures, their very names—in the following of their Duty. . . .

---

from the *Hellespont Angelogs*
Transcripts of 1363/19/2

Time	Recorded Material
5/0821	Z
	Li 1
	Be 1.2751
	B 2.42
	C 8.53096
0831	*Control*
	A high carbon count.
0834	Z
	N 9

0836

Control
. . . and for nitrogen!

0837

Z
F 4.61
Ne .22
Na 6.3
Mg 7.04
Al 6.2107
Si 7.2

(0851)

P 5.31 . . .

5/0821

B
Zoe still counts.
My decent, trusting Zoe,
he works from love and loyalty
and does not recognize
their tone of command.
How they strut and fret and worry.
Little, sad creatures.
How dim they seem now,
and faraway.
There was a room
with a handstain on the wall,
I remember;
and a warm whiteness all around me.
That was my mother!
I remember
a tinkling sound
la la la-la la
and a baby that shouted
"Hello! Hello!"
to the world, in the mornings;
a girl with peach-colored skin;
friends colliding with me
and each other,

chasing a ball,
elbows muffled by flesh
numbing my cheekbone.
Violence is the only way
they have of breaking into each other
besides sex.
I saw a man
staggering in the street.
I caught him as he fell.
I thought he was drunk.
Then I saw blood on his forehead,
slowly seeping.
He was heavy and the bones inside him
tumbled in unexpected directions.
I took him home to his woman.
She was small and harried.
She wore a dressing gown
out into the night.
The door of their house
slammed shut behind her and locked.
She gave a sad little cry,
like a bird,
"Oh no. Oh no."
Faraway,
on a cold little nugget of a world.

(0869)

0851

$$Z$$
P 5.31
S 7.32
Cl 3.92
Ar .407
K 4.22
Ca 6.01
Sc 2.982
Ti 4.8113
V 4.27
Cr 5

Mn 5.102
Fe 10.372
Co 1.089
Ni 5.808

0877

Control
What is going on?
Look at the count for iron!
Z, your pardon please.
For this log $S =$
12.00 for hydrogen?

0888

Z
Yes, Control, as stated.

0890

Control
Extraordinary.

(0894)

Continue, Z.

0871

B
Old doors open.
I remember pain,
how it leapt
from the body to the soul
and wounded it.
I remember handshakes,
touching,
the scrape of skin on skin.
I remember speech,
lungs forcing out words
that were lost or misconstrued;
hills;
muscles that ached and needed feeding;
food!
How the throat would gather it
and push it down in lumps,
how it merged with me

as I swallowed it.
I remember weight
pinning me to a chair,
holding my body to the ground.
That body
that could not fly.
That body that would betray me
and die.
Limitations, limitations!
cutting into my soul.
Things I could not do.
Things I could not prevent.
Living as I slowly died,
body and mind
exchanging hope and poison.

I don't want to remember!
I want to forget!
Forget Humanity and being human.
If I could forget, I would be free!
Then I would slip
into the warm whiteness of subspace
and be reborn
(0906) in galaxies beyond their grasp!

0894 Z
Cu 4.5
Zn 3.5
Ga 2.73
Ge 2.509
Rb 2.55
Sr 3.09
Y 3.245
Zr 2.71
Nb .006
Mo 2.43

Ru .04
Ag 8.77
Cd 1.02
In .07
Sn .004
Sb .19

(0912)

5/0911

B
Should I tell them?
It was nothing,
something small and silent
rooted round a sunsore like a mold.
Should I tell them
that I saw it?
Is it living?
Could they leave it growing
undisturbed?
Or would they conquer it and claim it,
make it theirs with understanding.
Can they hear me?
They can hear our thoughts,
I know that.
If they can, they know already
where to find it.
They know I hate and fear them.

(0927)

And Zoe still counts.

0912

Z
Ba .009
La 2.65
Ce .82
Eu 1.13

0920

Control
Europium
On a sun?

$$Z$$
Tb .089
Ho .001
Yb .008
W .03
Os .45
Au .37

(0932)

0929
$$B$$
Aaaah!
Something moved!
I felt it!
Zoe! Zoe!

0936
$$Z$$
Bee!
I count!

0940
$$B$$
Zoe!
Something's moving! Something is alive.

0946
$$Z$$
Where are you?
What coordinate?

0946
The Alien
Shiftpoint.

0948
$$B$$
What?

0950
$$Z$$
Where are you?

0951
The Alien
Shiftpoint there!

0953

> **B**
> It thinks!
> It *thinks!*

0955

> *The Alien*
> Otherself!

0956

> **B**
> Zoe! Zoe!
> Come here, it thinks, it's alive!

0958

> *Control*
> What does he mean, Z?

0959

> **Z**
> What coordinate, Bee?
> Bee, what coordinate?

0960

> *The Alien*
> Ticklethoughts!
> Leapsniff
> Snuffletaste!

0963

> **B**
> I can see it!

0965

> *Control*
> Please repeat, Angels.
> We cannot follow.
> Angels, repeat, please!

0966

> *The Alien*
> Play!

from *Remembrances of Bee*

When we found them, it was nestled around Bee. It hung like a curtain in folds, folds of light, and it rippled as it swam. I thought for a moment it might hurt him. Then I felt it too. A probing, shy mind, so slowly, delicately nuzzling my own.

Then it leapt skittishly away, and danced and Bee followed. It gamboled and called us My Other Selves. It spun, and stopped, and its folds flowed on about it. It was dazzlingly beautiful.

We tried to tell it who we were. We showed it pictures, memories. It shivered in confusion and delight at the thought of lands beyond the sky. It eats nothing, but burns through itself, a filament.

For its gentleness and purity, Bee called it Dajja—the unicorn's real name. He meant this as a warning and as a revenge.

On the star of Daphne, I learned the truth.

from the letters of Raul Kundara

Hola Mari,

Sad news, sad news. You were brave not to tell me that you were ill. But please, let me know next time. And do not run through too often. You know the limit. I am very glad that you are well now.

Bad news comes in threes, like dwarves. Senior Talsman has been sent home. I remember seeing his face the day before it happened. He sat at lunch, eyes staring, his lower lip hiding his upper. He looked like a child about to cry. I thought then how upset and unsteady he looked.

The next day in the kitchens, we heard the Senior shouting. "Why do you humiliate me?" he yelled at the Chief. Chief shouted back at him, "I don't take orders from you! You are blind to Achilleans!" Chief was angry!

"The old bladder," Chief called the Senior, later. "He hates Achilleans. You cannot see it, but I do." Could that be true? Would a prejudiced man be placed as Senior? Chief made us all laugh at Senior Talsman, widened his eyes and quivered in imitation of him. "Tell them about our food throwing, and what he said," Chief demanded of me. I do not like to make charges, but I think Chief pulled us all against Senior Talsman. Can two dutiful men, placed and certed, hate each other? I did mean to speak quietly with the Senior, but failed to. Now I must regret my lack of wisdom.

The same day Senior Talsman went in tears to Senior Thoroughgood and asked to be placed for Earth. We held a farewell dinner for him. It was a mistake. He looked weak and tired and ill with us. His blockmates cleared his room for him. I saw his things—holograms of Earth trayed for Sliding. Fields, running water, gentle forests. They looked very private and sad. Senior Talsman worked as a regular at the station for fifteen years. He goes home to nothing. Chief has been given his placing. There was no one else to do the job. Senior Stavakanda, he is called now.

You will remember Gareth, my young blockmate. His father has died after a long, helpless illness. I did not know he was ill, though others did. Gareth was called into the casting room. He appeared at my doorway a few moments later. He did not come in. "I will be gone many days," he told me. Suddenly his face reddened and he gripped the bridge of his nose. "My father has just died." His voice broke, and he ran. I called out my respects too late.

So Gareth is gone. We weren't friends. He would come and talk to me when I didn't want to talk. But now it seems he was trying to ease me into the life of the station. I must remember duty to people. There are so many duties.

Nothing else has happened. No word on my research. Keep well yourself. Let me know if you are ill again. I am sure I could arrange leave to see you, if you are. I will try to write and cast to you more often.

* * *

My respects to my Placer Robt, my chanter Bella, Nive and her ward Zal; Deo and Ri, Tam and you, and also, especially to Cila. Let her know I am well.

---

from the *Hellespont Angelogs*
Transcripts of 1363/21/9

Time	Recorded Material
7/4471	*Control* Z, we have lost them again.
4476	Z He still plays with the alien. Shall I throw what I hear to you?
4481	*Control* No, thank you. Please relay coordinates.
4486	Z $-13.7321X, + 3.224Y, -9.81Z$ They are descending rapidly, Control.
7/4500	*Control* Thank you, Z. We have them.
4500	*The Alien* Feelrush Rippleshock

4502   *B*
                        Rippleshock!

4503   *The Alien*
                        Rippleshock
                        Tumbleturn
                        Spinwhip
                        Brightburn
                        Crashroll

(4509)   Skyhaze-Shinebright

4506   *Z*
                      I feel sadness.
                   Bee has left me alone
                   and I am spying on him.

4510   *Control*
                 (More emotional problems.
                      What is awry
                   with them this counting?
                   We have no need of it,
(4520)   now of all times!)

4509   *The Alien*
                        Plungeroar!

4510   *B*
                        Plungeroar!

4511   *The Alien*
                     Plungeroar-down!

4513   *B*
                          Down!

4514	*The Alien* Downfar-Downdeep!
4514	*Both together* Down!
4522	*The Alien* Hah-hah! Fardown Coolplace Coolplace Clean! Downdeep Quietstorm Waftsleep Nameplace Peacenames
(4531)	All the names of peace!
4533	*Control* We do not understand, Z. What is happening?
4538	*Z* The alien names.
4540	*Control* Names?
4542	*Z* That is what it does. It eats nothing. It sleeps at times. Otherwise, it names things. It has few verb concepts. Those it has translate into forms of "to be" or "to feel" or "to know."

It thinks in great
passive chunks of noun.

4560

Control
Primitive.

4561

Z
I do not know.
What it says logs into language.

4565

Control
True, but we can also log
animals and even plants.
Gibbons think in great blasts
of emotion.
It is not so different from

(4574)

this.

4532

B
Peacenames!
All of them!

4534

The Alien
Stillpeace
Softpeace
Loudpeace
Proudpeace
Listenwatchpeace
Deafblindpeace
Lifepeace
Dreampeace
Sleeppeace
Wakepeace
Surepeace
Uncertainpeace
Laughpeace

Soarpeace
Weep-peace
Awepeace
—Awepeace, strong
see Firerage or chasm!—
Awepeace
Humblepeace
Settlepeace
Surrender

4558
B
Surrender? To what?

4560
The Alien
Awe!
Life!
like Lifepeace,
like my surrender
to the red,
to the thinning.

4566
B
And conflict?

4568
The Alien
Conflict-peace!

4570
B
Conflictpeace?

4572
The Alien
Greatfire
Manyfaces
but one even so
Allpeace
Highpeace
All things me

I God
Me God

4580
B
What?

4581
Control
What? What did it say?

4584
Z
It called itself God.

4585
The Alien
All things me thing
Myself Otherself
Self love
Otherself love
Dajja!

4591
Control
We must interrupt.
We are getting nowhere!

4592
B
Dajja! You know your name!

4594
Z
Bee, my love . . .

4595
The Alien
Nextself!

4597
Control
B, this is Control.

7/4601
The Alien
Newvoice!

4604

Control
Excuse us.
We would like to ask the alien
a few questions.

4606

B
Proof of intelligence.
He's listening to us.
He knows his name!

4608

The Alien
Hello Newvoice
Hello Nextself!
Hello!
Hello!

4613

Control
Hello.

4615

The Alien
Hello!

4617

Control
Hello.

4617

B
I think you'll have to stop saying hello.

4620

Control
Dajja?
You called yourself God.
What did you mean by that?

4625

The Alien
?

4628

B
He doesn't understand
I can answer.

4632

Control
For the alien?
I think we would prefer a less interpretative
approach.

4635

B
He is learning much more from us
that we are from him.
The concept of God.
He learned it from us.
Like his name.

4640

Control
Dajja?
What do you mean by God?

4641

B
He was saying that he, me, you,
all of us are God.

4646

Control
That is an interpretation, yes.

4649

B
He does not understand.
You are asking the question
in the wrong way!
Please!
Let me ask the question.

4651

Control
Go ahead.

4653

B
Dajja.
You God?

4655
The Alien
Me God
You God
All God together!

4657
B
He says that he
and me
and even you
are God . . .

4665
The Alien
I am everything.

4667
B
. . . and also, perhaps
that he identifies himself
with the universe.

4676
Control
Thank you, B.
I think we have a rough idea
how now to proceed.

4682
B
No verbs, please.
He does not understand verbs.

4686
Control
Dajja . . .

4687
The Alien
Hello!

4688
Control
Hello.
Other Dajja?

4692

The Alien
Oh yes!

4693

Control
Where?

4696

The Alien.
Here.

4698

Control
Here?

4699

B
Control . . .

7/4701

Control
Names?

4703

The Alien
Me, Otherself, Nextself and Newvoice.

4705

B
Control,
he thinks that we are a part of him.
Consider that we sound to him
like thoughts inside his mind.

4713

Control
But are there other aliens?
Is he the only one?

4717

B
I think it likely.

4724

Control
We need something altogether
more substantial.
Dajja . . .

4728

The Alien
Hello, Newvoice!

4730

Control
Hello again.
I have a simple puzzle for you.
See picture?
OO

4739

B
Control!

4740

Control
Yes, B.

4743

B
His concept of duality
is different from ours.
He can barely grasp the idea
of a here and a there.
He has no two.
You are showing him two circles,
but he will see only one
set of shapes.

4759

Z
This is Regimen procedure, Bee.

4761

B
There is no point
in testing him on our own terms
for abilities we know he does not possess.

4767

Control
We do not know it yet, **B**.
Be fair to the creature.

4772

B
Be fair!
Mathematics is not intelligence itself!

4775

Control
B, we will continue!
See picture?
O

4782

The Alien
Yes.

4782

Z
Bee, you are behaving badly.

4785

B
Zoe, don't you see what they are doing?

4784

Control
See other picture?
O

4789

The Alien
Yes.

4791

Control
Now see picture and other picture
together.
What does it look like?

4796

The Alien
The same picture.

4798

B
One times one equals one.

Control
Yes, but one added to one is two.
And two added to two equals four.
And without that basic ability
I'm afraid our friend's potential
—and it is potential we are
testing, B, not achievement—
his *potential* is rather limited.
But admittedly the question may
have been unclear.
We shall try again.

7/4800

4819

B
What gives us the right to test him?

4820

Control
Dajja, see picture?
OO
OO

4827

The Alien
Dulldots. Yes.

4828

B
What gives us the right to test him?

4829

Control
See other picture?
OOOO

4835

The Alien
Yes. A row of otherselves.

4838

Control
Can you change it to look like picture?

4842

B
Please,
please do not do this!

4844

The Alien
Urgeplea!

4846

B
Listen to him and learn how he thinks,
He has no verbs!
He has no interest in change!
He has a view of time very different
from ours.
Your question is meaningless to him.

4857

Control
You mean he also has no
conception of time?

4862

B
He thinks of other times as
we would think of other places.

4868

Control
Then he has no conception of
conscious will.

4873

B
He knows what he likes.

4876

The Alien
Hello Newvoice!
See picture?

4879   *Control*
                    Yes, see picture.

4882   *The Alien*
                    Wriggle!

4884   *Control*
                    That is very nice, Dajja.

4886   *The Alien*

4891

Wriggle-wiggle
Hah-hah!
Otherselves! See picture!

4894

7/4901

B
That's Daphne.

4904

Z
When it was younger.

B
Some sort of disturbance.

4921

B
That's a flare!
He's showing us a flare!

4926

The Alien

4934

Z
Daphne when it was much younger.

4938

Control
How much younger?

4941

Z
I do not know.
Six million earthyears?
Seven?

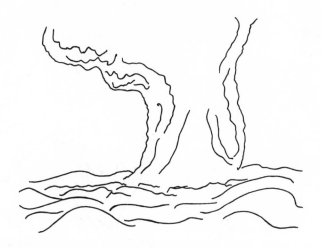

4951
              Control
    It's seven million years old!

4954
                 Z
    If it saw a flare like that, yes.

4957
              Control
              Shit.

4955
            The Alien
            Bangboom!
             Uproar!
             Uprise!
            Blastheat!
           Whitebright!

4961
              Control
        We apologize, Angels.
    One of our riders forgot propriety.

4967

B
No need, Control.

4968

The Alien
Otherselves!
Wiggles!

4972

B
Quiescent prominence.

4978 Firerain-backflow

4979 *Z*
Amendment, Control.

4982 *Control*
Yes.

4983 *Z*
Not just seven million.

Stretchleap
Tear-roar

4995   *Control*
No?

4999   *Z*
Not with this.

9/5002   *The Alien*

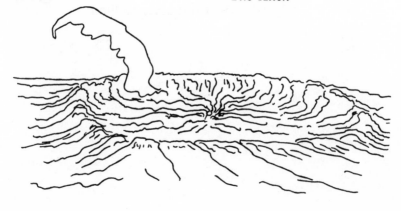

Coolsurge
Heatcrust

5012
Z
It has seen an active, young sun.
Control, it is at least
two hundred million years old.
Perhaps more.

5021
Control
By all that is sacred!

5024
The Alien
Wiggles!
Wriggles!

5025
B
Do you see?
Do you see?
Two hundred *million* years!
He is older
than all of Humankind!
Do you see?

5033
Control
We all see it, B.

5034 *The Alien*

5039 Settlestill

5042 *B*
Dajja!

5045 *The Alien*

5020	Calm
5055	*Control* Dajja?
5058	*The Alien* Newvoice Griphold!
5060	*Control* The Wiggles, the . . .
5061	*The Alien* Wiggles!
5063	*Control* What did he call the flares?
5065	*Z* Bangbooms.
5066	*The Alien* Bangbooms!
5068	*Control* Yes, bangbooms. Bangbooms part of Dajja?
5073	*B* Yes, and he is part of them. We have been through all this!
5078	*Control* Silence, B!
5079	*The Alien* Angerscramble!

5081

> Control
> Bangboom, Dajja.
> Can you control them?

5088

> The Alien
> control?
> cant-roll?
> count-role?
> Tumbleword,
> Rollword!
> Otherself?

5095

> B
> He doesn't understand.
> It doesn't translate.

5099

> Control
> control
> use
> make use of
> make do what you want

7/5107

> The Alien
> Griphold!

5108

> B
> In the first place you're using verbs. . . .

5110

> Control
> B!

5111

> B
> Oh I hate this!

5116

> Control
> Make Bangbooms stop?
> No Bangboom?

5121

The Alien
No Bangboom?
Me?
Brokenboom?
Why?
Firelove, leapsong
Otherself!

5130

B
I'm here.

5131

The Alien
Help.

5133

B
I cannot.

5135

Control
Fascinating,
fascinating.
Angels, we will want
a reading of the animal.

5142

B
What sort of reading?

5145

Control
The usual sort.
You will penetrate him
and give us a count.

5152

B
No.

5153

Control
Is that a refusal?

5154
> *B*
> Mingling is an act of love.

5155
> *Control*
> We apologize, B.
> We do not wish to disrupt your
> relationship with Zoe.
> But these are special circumstances.

5165
> *B*
> That is not what I meant!
> You do not understand!

5168
> *Z*
> Control, I will do it.

5169
> *B*
> Zoe!

5170
> *Control*
> Please repeat Z.

5172
> *Z*
> I will read him.

5174
> *B*
> Zoe! You will give him over to them
> bound!

5176
> *Z*
> Bound? That is nonsense!
> Bee, they must have information.

5181
> *Control*
> B, you are hostile.
> Why?

5184

                        B
              Because I do not like you.

5186

                        Z
                 Bee, break off!
              Control, this is not usual.

5191

                        B
               I have no trust in you.
           Everything you do and feel is tainted.

5197

                      Control
                 Tainted? By what?

5199

                        B
                      Fear.
                   Selfishness.
               A need to overcome.

7/5205

                        Z
                       Bee!

5206

                      Control
           What are we doing here that is selfish?

5209

                        Z
                 He thinks you want
              to rid Daphne of the alien.

5214

                        B
              You are trying to control.

5217

                      Control
                   Of course!
                Control is necessary
              for the good of the universe.

We are not conquerors.
We are preservers.
We are overwhelmed with wonder
at the marvel that has been found.
Is that so tainted?

5233

B

It all depends,
depends on what you do.
What will you do?

5240

Control

Find out what it is.

5243

B

And when you have done that?

5245

Control

We will determine what this means
for the Daphne project.
The Regimen states that no
intelligent forms of life
shall be displaced or destroyed
by Humankind.
We will abide by that.

5260

Z

You see, love?
Men are reasonable creatures.

5265

B

Reason!
Reason is a weapon!
This is Man, the Hunter!

— III —

---

from the letters of Raul Kundara

Hola Mari,

All casts are vetted. No letters leave unread. I write and can only hope to send this to you later.

We are all under Secrecy Regimen. The unbelievable, the impossible has happened. They have found life on Daphne, life on a sun! Senior Thoroughgood called a gathering to tell us. Later that afternoon I was called to his room. Already I had a nervous inkling of what was to come. Senior Thoroughgood was not there. Researcher Mzobwe greeted me instead, and asked me, so calmly, to follow him to the Angelroom. I knew then what was to happen, and my heart leapt. I was to ride an Angel.

I followed him down a long, low corridor, through a voice-locked door. Seniors Thoroughgood and Yuan sat staring and still, crowned by headpieces. There was an empty chair beside them. Researcher Mzobwe motioned me to it, and I sat down. Consolers listened, leaning forward. On the wall was a screen, filled with red. It was a cast, in hydrogen light, from the sun. I thought I saw movement in it, distant, like kelp in water.

Researcher Mzobwe passed a headpiece to me. "I have never rode before," I whispered.

"Do not fight," he advised me. "Z will read a count of chemical components to you." Then he slipped the headpiece on for me. A metal band cut uncomfortably into my ear. I remember reaching up to adjust it. Suddenly, very suddenly, the room was swallowed by a roaring in my head, and I felt as though I was falling and rising, both at the same time. Different planes of thought passed and intersected each other, like lights from a landcraft passing each other on a wall. Then they focused, and separated, and I could understand.

There were three minds waiting. The first was familiar. It reminded me of Gareth, scholarly but not unkind. The second felt simply angry, hot and heavy, like the breath of a bull. I had a brief image of clear, accusing blue eyes, like a child's.

And there was something else. Something hot and bright and leaping. I shied away from it.

"Please commence reading, Z," said a voice, loud in my head. It was Senior Thoroughgood. Then the Angel spoke. It had a clear, piping voice, that was sad. Fortunately I had my logger with me, for I was not truly listening to the count. The components themselves add up to nothing—chloride, iridium, gallium, common carbon, hydrogen, helium, iron . . . We do not even know how it holds together in one place, let alone lives. The reading Angel was polite and precise in his counting. But I could feel he was under some emotional strain. He seemed so human. He ached for the reading to be over, and so he hurried.

The visualiser glowered at me, his anger steady. When the count was finished, he asked, "Do you think you know him better now?"

"I must beg your pardon," said a too-loud voice. It made me jump. It was my own.

"Does that in truth tell you anything about him?" the voice asked me again. My stomach wilted with excitement. I was riding an Angel!

"Not much. No, nothing. Now," I replied. "Where did you find him?"

"He found us," it growled, and said nothing more. He had relented because I was young and harmless, because he couldn't hate me. I wonder if he knew how much of itself it revealed?

Then the alien touched me. There was a greeting, something that might have been a name. It meant no harm. But it sickened me. I thought of snails and their feelers, and of all that is strange and unrecognizable. All through me, I felt burning, as though my blood were fire. I began to weep, and to shake my head. A sun opened up beneath me, huge, with billows of orange and crinkles of yellow-white heat. I thought I would fall, and I screamed.

"He's panicked," said a voice. I felt something grab an arm, faraway. The headpiece was hauled away from my head, which felt vast, like an ocean, and I was pulled into the real world. Hands, human hands, patted my shoulder and coaxed me to my feet. I stumbled and was caught. "I'm sorry, I'm sorry," I kept repeating.

"Well, you did well," I heard Mzobwe say. "Contact with alien thoughts on first riding! I would not want to face that." The researcher knows the right thing to say. Senior Thoroughgood said nothing. He kept watching the screen. He was riding his Angels.

I still felt weak two tens later. I told my blockmates I was ill. I did not tell them where I had been. I think they guessed. My reaction in other ways has been odd. . . .

---

from *Entropy Control and You*

Entropy Control is our Prime Duty. All other Duties contribute to this end.

The mechanics repair machines, machines that keep Human-kind alive and well, machines that work for Control and order. They contribute.

The builders shape the prefabs and the houses. They keep us sheltered so we can live in comfort and think serenely. They contribute.

The growers feed each new generation and fuel the minds of the Controllers. They contribute.

The man with the broom, sweeping corridors, preserves order and frees great minds from petty worries. They owe him a debt of gratitude. He contributes.

We all give something. The Regimen of Tanner Cahsway directs our energies. The Regimen places us where we are most able to help.

This way brilliant minds are not wasted in vain pursuits. This way good, common people have work that has meaning. This way tasks that need doing are not left undone.

Humankind must lead an orderly life. The Regimen gives us guidance and shows us where our Duty lies. . . .

Juniors must treat elders with respect. The old are many in number, but they have lived long and seen much. Their wisdom must be heeded.

Juniors will follow the course of study set by their placers. They must work hard to uncover their true abilities. They must not contradict their placers.

Juniors must be tidy. Personal order is part of the general order, and thus part of our duty.

No one may have sex for the purpose of having children unless the Regimen permits the union. This makes sure that every child is loved and nurtured.

No one shall neglect his placing, the needed work he is suited to perform.

All seniors must be treated with respect. They are highly placed for good reasons.

No one shall deny the right of the Regimen and its seniors to direct, decree and to place. . . .

All work is the result of disequilibrium, between hot and cold, between stable and unstable, between up and down. The Regimen, as described and founded by Our Master, Tanner Cahsway, maintains social disequilibrium. This generates tension and thus energy and work. If you feel anger toward a senior, that is natural. Do not express it. Take the anger and put it to work for you.

Sublimation is duty.

There is one prime duty, but a thousand pathways to it, all of which are dutiful. Each person with the help of the Regimen travels toward duty in a way that is fresh and new and his own. Anything that contributes to order and energy is dutiful.

Thus duty may consist of overriding all other duties here listed.

Thus one must rebel, show disrespect, go against even a master if it prevents negligence of the one prime duty. One must do so even if justice is not done and one is punished.

Duty takes precedence over individual people.

---

from the letters of Raul Kundara

(continued)

The time drags on since my night in the Angelroom. I stay here in my room. Mzobwe thinks I am working. They will never see this letter. I can say what I like.

I hate this place. I hate my elders, I hate the regulars. They sit dead, playing cards, not speaking even to each other. They have all been placed here because they want to hide, because they dislike the worlds. I hate dirty dishes. I mistrust the Chief and his jokes. And don't, please, tell me again that it is my duty after three years of study to wash dishes! Duty is a lie! There is no such thing! Everyone does what he likes, until made to do something else.

I don't like science. I forced it on myself. I had hoped it would save me from a life like yours and Tamel's, trapped in rigid placings and meager work. You encouraged me. I studied, but only out of habit and fear. I passed exams, and then forgot what I had learned. When I was finished, Old Regi called me a Biological Engineer, and you were proud. I concocted a project for research. Could life exist in stars, in nebulae, on all the cold rocky worlds even Angels bypass? I called it "On the Possibility of Life under Extreme Conditions." It had no interest for me. It was a way out to the stars. And when the alien had been found; when the listing was actually in my hand; when chance had given me a door to open, I simply did not have the energy. I didn't care.

Science can be a beautiful thing. Clean thought, pure thought, peeling back the universe in layers, dazzling in its leaps, humble in its careful workings. I have the head, but not the heart for it. I have misused it and myself.

At supper some days ago, a regular stopped at my table. He wore only half his coolsuit, and his eyes skimmed everyone skittishly as he spoke. He asked for the shift-times, though he plainly had his chart with him, and asked no one in particular if the food was well-cooked. In reply people shrugged and looked embarrassed. He nodded good-bye awkwardly and walked on. I stewed up complicated reasons for his strangeness, all to do with bottled anger and middle age. I like talking about people, but I always make things too complicated. "He is lonely, that's all," said a young regular with a soft and pale face. "He does not know how to talk to people." She was right, inarguably. Simplicity has its own shrewdness. I resent all those years I studied. They gave me an excuse to be aloof. I don't think I understand people at all, and this pains me. I don't think I actually see them. I never saw Gareth. I did not see the Chief until too late. I begin to get some glimmer of this woman.

She hates it here too. We all do. She checks the log transcripts and makes hideous mistakes. Her face goes splotchy with boredom as she sits at her console. She keeps bad shift-time, but most people forgive her because she is so bored. I had thought she was merely stupid. She is, instead, withdrawn. I did not realize that until I saw her laughing and nodding freely with the newly arrived wife of a young regular. Most other women at the station are respected seniors or leathery old researchers. For a time she was the only young woman here. The men made jokes about her body, teased her, coaxed her, eyed her, even the old ones. There was no one for her to talk to. She has been here three years.

I consume my youth for the sake of a placing. She spends her years doing work that she hates. What is this placing? I will tell you. It is a way of using up our time, to keep us busy and unthinking. They don't need young certed men with just three years training and a project that no one is interested in. They don't need someone to check the logs. I tell you this placing is hollow. It is a lie. I feel myself to be no part of any great salvation, just because they tell me so.

They will know I have failed. They will know I let the counting lie on my desk like a sickness. No one will take my title of researcher seriously now. I don't know what will happen. I will stay on here, I suppose. I will do my duty-work testing food from the Slide, inspecting genetic damage, washing dishes. They will call it my contribution. But it could be done by machines. I fear I will end up as lost a soul as any regular. I want to run away, but there is no place to run to.

Just before daylight:

I keep thinking about what went wrong between us, and why I keep writing to you. I can't remember the pain we shared at my birth. But you do. No wonder you love me more than I love you. It is very hard for me to imagine that flesh and blood connection, the fact that I came from you. It seems such a curious thing. But somewhere I must feel it, something that deep. Else, why, alone here in this room, am I writing to you a letter that will never be read?

You were right to say I was hostile and resentful. I was. I felt trapped by so many things. By my work, by our life, by all the things that made Tamel what he is. I'm sorry. I do love you, very much. For some reason I find it very difficult to say.

I wonder if I ever will.

---

from the *Hellespont Angelogs*
Transcripts of 1363/30/1

Time	Recorded Material
9508	*Z* I have come back.
9510	*B* Yes.
9515	*Z* I went outside. I saw the stars again. I went down to the very core. I found your coolplace. Bestilled nitrogen.
9520	*B* It migrates. Did you see him?
9525	*Z* No. Perhaps he'll come back.

9529

B

I hope not.
I hope he stays away,
away from us, away from them.

9532

Z

This anger in you still!
Like a weight!

9536

B

Yes.

9538

Z

It is what drove him away, Bee!
This anger, this bitterness.
It hurt him.
It hurts me.

9541

B

I know.

9545

Z

Then why be taken over by it?
Do you *want* to be alone?
You've become heavy, heavy and dull.

9550

B

Not dull, my love.
No.
I burn!
I burn like a sun!
I know what they are.
I know what they will do.
Animated stomachs
in the habit of eating!
They can't break it.

They would swallow the universe,
if they could.
Do you think they will
stop the Daphne project,
give up a humanized world
for the sake of an alien?

9577

Z
They will hold to
the Regimen Directive.
They have promised us that.

9583

B
The Directive!
The Directive is there
only to keep aliens alive long enough
to steal their technology!
The Dajja has none.

9593

Z
That is not true!

9595

B
It's true enough, in the end.

9598

Z
Tanner Cahsway speaks
of the sacredness of life!
You are blind with hatred!
Why?

10/9604

B
Because they stop us being
what we should be.

9608

Z
Which is?

9610
                                      B
Free!
From them!
To wander where we will,
beyond the stars.

9618
                                      Z
Then wander. Leave.

9620
                                      B
I am waiting for you.

9624
                                      Z
Bee.
We are human too.

9630
                                      B
No. Not any longer.

9638
                                  Control
Angels, are you receiving?
Angels, this is Control.

9643
                                      Z
Yes, Control, we are receiving.

9645
                                      B
What has Control decided?

9648
                                  Control
Will you be able to find the alien
when the time comes?

9653
                                      Z
Daphne is a large sun.
But yes.

9658

B
What have you decided!

9662

Control
The decision that has been made
was not an easy one, B. . . .

9665

B
It should have been.

9667

Control
. . . We still do not know
what the alien is.
What Central Control can say
with some assurance
is that it would not survive
a return, however gradual,
to a less ripe stellar environment.
The increased density
and temperature would rather quickly
disperse it.
Perhaps when we have studied it further. . . .

9689

B
And where will you study him?

9691

Control
That brings up the question of
its intelligence.

9695

B
There is no question of it.

9697

Control
I am afraid that there is.

10/9700   *B*
                              On what grounds?
                              The Dajja thinks!

9705   *Control*
                              I am afraid the beast
                         has forced us to redefine our terms. . . .

9708   *B*
                                Of course.

9710   *Control*
                           Intelligence is an active,
                            not a passive quality.
                           Intelligence does things.

9716   *B*
                                I knew it!

9717   *Control*
                         This creature has evolved
                    completely alone and self-sufficient,
                        without need of self-defense
                          or activity of any sort.
                    It has no capacity for solving problems.
                              It is conscious
                            but not intelligent
                      as Control now defines the word.

9733   *B*
                           Intelligence does things?
                              Birds do things.
                              They eat worms.
                            Are birds intelligent?

9742

Control
Of course not.
They are conscious, they act,
but their actions are a function
of instinct.

9751

B
So are yours.
Intelligence merely helps you
do them more thoroughly.
Perhaps, just perhaps, Control
by some holy accident
there has evolved an intelligence
that has no need to do anything,
as you say,
whose only activity is to see
and to delight!
Who doesn't hunt or maim or battle
or build,
who loves everything!
As it is!

9778

Control
The beast has not progressed
beyond the stage of
infantile identification
of the self with the universe.
It is utterly egocentric
and very, very primitive.

9790

B
Backward!
You've got it backward!
You are primitive.
You are at the mercy of your instincts,
Entropy Control!

You can't even control yourselves!
You are the beast!

10/9801
                    Control
              This is unheard of.

9804
                       Z
         Bee, we do not know the decision yet.

9806
                       B
                     I do!

9808
                   Control
              Then we will be brief.
              We have decided to
          transport the beast to Aldebaran,
            another K-type orange giant
            with similar enough readings.
               The project here
           will progress as planned.
          The beast will be returned here
          if that ever becomes possible.
          That, we think, is very fair.

9823
                       B
             This is his home.
          He is part of this place!
          Taking him from here
          would be like cutting him in two!

9828
                       Z
              Perhaps, Control,
          the Dajja could stay here. . . .

9831
                       B
          Don't you understand?
          You have no right to do this.

9835

Control
We have every right, B.

9837

Z
Please, listen!
It will take a century, more,
before there is a climactic change.
Surely the Dajja can stay here
until then?

9847

Control
Nothing would be gained.
A decision has been made by the Regimen.

9851

Z
You could study him here!

9853

Control
That will be all, Z.

9856

Z
You haven't helped, Bee.

9861

Control
In any event,
if all places and things are one to it,
it shouldn't mind,
should it?

9867

B
You are evil.
You don't know it,
but you are.

9876

Control
A mobile Slide
will be established for one casting

between Daphne and Aldebaran
when and where the beast is located.

9884
B
I will not search.

9886
Control
The project will still continue.

9889
B
I will not call the Slides.

9892
Control
B, is that a refusal?

9894
B
Yes.

9895
Z
Bee! Consider!

9897
Control
You refute a decision
of the Regimen itself?

10/9902
B
I refute Control altogether.

9904
Control
No matter.
Z will find the animal for us.

9908
B
Will you, Zoe?

9912
Z
It is not right to ask me
to make this decision, Control.

9917

Control
But we have.

9921

Z
Between Bee and duty?
Have you listened to what he said?
Do you realize you are
asking me to betray him?

9927

Control
Him, or us.

9929

Z
It is not that simple!
I do not disagree violently
with your decision!

9935

Control
Then implement it.
You have a duty.

9940

Z
I cannot!
You want me to lead the beast to you,
to the jaws of the Slide?
It couldn't understand.
We are its friends.

9947

Control
This does not surprise us.
It is not unusual
for Angels to lose touch
with Humankind and duty.
It is in itself a form of decay.
Under the Entropy Directive
our duty is clear.
You must both be recalled from service.

9963   *Z*
      What does that mean?

9965   *B*
      It means they also think
      we are no longer human.

9970   *Control*
      It means you will be
      returned to Central Control
      and rehabilitated.
      If that fails you will be
      dispersed.

9980   *Z*
      What does dispersed mean?

9982   *Control*
      It means you will cease to exist.

9984   *Z*
      That is possible?

9986   *Control*
      It need not come to that.

9989   *Z*
      We have a right to life!

9991   *Control*
      You are not, strictly speaking, alive.

9993   *Z*
      We will fight!
      We will hide!

9998

Thank you, Zoe.

30/2/0001

Control
We will find you.
There is no fighting us.
We are Control.

---

from *Entropy Control and You*

Time . . . Without time, there is no beginning; there is no creation; there is nothing.

The stubborn nothingness of space resists time and the things time creates. What exists is the product of a struggle between nothingness and creation.

Time began with the massive explosion called the big bang. The big bang divided space from subspace. It unleashed the energy that forces space to open out, like a flower, and thus to move forward in time. This expansion will continue for another 10^{100} earthyears. After that the force of time will no longer be able to overcome the elastic resistance of space. Expansion will stop, space will contract. Time will run backward, all the way back to the big bang.

This contraction will have no future in which to occur. Time will have ceased to go forward. The contraction must, therefore, occupy the same period of time as the expansion. At any one moment, space is simultaneously expanding and contracting, going both forward and backward in time.

Entropy Control uses the force of time in two ways. We use it to soften matter for Sliding. We also use it to generate chaolis.

You will remember that chaolis are generated by the collision of matter and anti-matter. True anti-matter is, simply, matter that is moving backward in time. It was not generated by Humankind until time was accidentally reversed at the Ningsia Time Travel project. The first discovered anti-particles, such as the positron, were not true anti-matter. When a positron collides with an electron, gamma rays, not chaolis are produced. Nevertheless, a positron behaves very much like a true anti-electron. It was with good reason that the physicists of old Earth speculated that it might be moving backward in time. . . .

The present moment then, is made up of a universe of matter moving forward in time, and also an anti-universe of anti-matter moving backward in time. A teacup is also an anti-teacup. The two would annihilate each other, but for the fact that they mutually occupy the same space at the same moment. They behave like one thing. No reaction between them is possible.

At Ningsia, anti-matter was created by forcing expanding space within the universe to contract. This technique is crude and expensive. Entropy Control now simply split the present moment into two. Since we cannot make the universe and the anti-universe occupy different times, we make them occupy different places.

This is done by means of a set of time freezes, arranged in a pentangle as determined by the Luftens equations. . . . The freezes shoot a highly disruptive pattern of distortion waves through a carefully limited space, for example, a block of granite. The elastic resistance of this space, which holds the two universes together in that place, is momentarily broken apart. Matter and anti-matter separate. Then, as elasticity "knits" space back together, they meet. Chaolis in abundance are released.

It was at first feared that this method of chaoli generation would unduly consume the precious force of time. The Blake refinements to the Luftens equation proved, however, that the expansion of space is momentarily speeded up by the release of chaolis. The force of time is thus renewed.

And this is the most curious and wonderful thing of all. If the Blake refinements are correct, the force of time itself is generated by chaoli release. The big bang, then, is simply the final, catastrophic meeting of universe and anti-universe, just before the rebirth of time. Both are dissolved in a shower of chaolis. Both are then reborn from them.

The chaoli is the source of everything. All forms of matter and anti-matter are derived from it. Time is born as its twin. It sires all forms of energy, save for the steady elasticity of empty space. From chaolis we could, theoretically, make anything.

> Like hydrogen
> Like gold
> Like warm, living soil.

We are learning how to do that, too.

When we succeed, Humankind will have unlimited power to create. We will invent new elements, build whole worlds, throw up new suns to replace old. We will learn how to generate cold, rather than heat. A thousand means will be at our disposal to ensure that work will be possible until time reverses. No catastrophe will be great enough to destroy us. Humanity will be immortal,

Consider the pieces—the Charlie Slide, the time freeze, the gathering of heat, endothermic reactions, the final unveiling. See with what perfection they form the whole that is Entropy Control. They would not have come together, but for Humankind. Wonder at the need creation has of us. Ponder how we have been pulled up from the boiling seas of primeval Earth into the heavens. Marvel at the place reserved for us in the temple of time.

For time, without a time itself to change in, is inalterable. Everything within it is predestined and unavoidable. This, then, is the fate of Humankind: to save the universe and to be the dutiful masters of matter. Faced with this, who could deny the right of the Regimen to direct and to control? What sour fool, tired of life, can plaint now that human existence is without meaning or purpose? For we are the stewards of creation.

from *Remembrances of Bee*

We kept our minds still and small. We hid where the babble of the sun would be greatest. But every time we spoke our love, Control heard us. It was not long before the Warrior Angels came. Control Apparatus, they are called. We did not even know they existed.

They crashed about us, dead and dull and strong. Control had cut away their hearts, they saw no beauty. They were loyal and powerful.

We tried to flee, up through the twisting gas. They followed, howling. We gave off fear, like a scent they could taste. We could feel them behind us gaping like mouths and they were the faster.

Then we saw the Dajja, enrobed in light.

from the *Hellespont Angelogs* Transcripts of 1363/30/2

Time	Recorded Material
2/3031	*The Alien* Hello Otherself! Hello Nextself! Hello! Hello!
3036	*B* Get away! Get away! Hide!
(3039)	*The Alien* Tumblewords!

3031

Apparatus

H
 a
  a
   a
    a
     a
      a
       a
        h!

(3038)

We have them !

3040

B
Pain!
Hurt!
Hide!
Oh, Dajja,
you don't understand!

3041

Apparatus
Is that the beast?

3045

Z
Yes.

3044

The Alien
Sleekvoice!
Sleekvoice-Cold!
Glintgleam.

3047

Apparatus
We have them both, Control!
Both them and the animal.

3052

B
Time!
Time, Dajja!

Time here, us here.
Time go, us not here,
you not here, not home,
but in new world.

3060

The Alien
New-World!

3055

Z
Please, brothers,
let us have
just a few moments?

3061

Apparatus
No.
Control,
Slide to + 2.411X, + .093Y, + .0121Z
Calling to you now.
You can aim at us
E
E
E
E
E
E

(3085)

E . . .

3063

B
But pain in New-world.
No otherself in New-world.

3068

The Alien
Sadshiver
Soft regret
But all time
One-time.

Us-together
always here.
Look!
Can you see us?
There!

3079

B
No, I cannot.
Dajja, what do you mean?

3085

Apparatus
The Slide is here.
The beast goes first.

3091

The Alien
Poor Sleekvoices.
Deadminds Loveless.

3096

Apparatus
In, beast.
We can make you!

2/3101

B
Farewell, Dajja.

3102

Z
Good-bye.

3107

The Alien
Hello Otherself!
Hello Nextself!
Hello Sleekvoices!
Hello!
Hello!
Hello!

Apparatus
You have the beast, Control.
Now for rebels,
small and dainty
little rebels.

---

from *Remembrances of Bee*

They snatched us up, one each and swept us away.

First Bee was torn from me, without farewells. I reached out after him, but his thoughts were gone; space seemed suddenly hollow. Then the remaining warrior clenched about me, stifling me, choking me. "I am stronger than you, little rebel," he said, his thoughts crushing mine. I could not move. I was helpless. I fell, in perfect silence. I left the Cherubim behind me, crying out still, pleading it seemed, for someone, just once, to give them each a name.

I awoke once again in the gray metal room. The walls were streaked now, and spotted, as though it had rained. In the corners, black dust clung. A voice, the old voice, echoed once more.

"Z," it asked, "do you deny the Regimen?"

"No, I do not," I replied.

"Then why have you failed to carry out your duty?" it demanded.

"I was led astray," I said in a small voice. "I loved B and thought I could withstand his influence. In a moment of weakness I followed him and not the path of duty. I see my mistake, now."

The voice paused. "It is true that you have been dutiful and helpful until now. But tell us, how can we trust you now?"

"Do not give me another partner," I begged. "I only wish to serve. Give me unimportant work that I can do alone." They agreed, to save themselves a further murder.

Bee, I think my heart is broken. I called you, called you, but there was no answer. They could not make you recant. So they killed you. That part of my mind that was filled with you aches, like a wound. I do not think that time is long enough for it to heal.

Forgive me my betrayal. I tell myself I lied so that I could spread your story, but I know that is not the truth. I was afraid, afraid to die. We had forgotten the terror of death, Bee. Its grip is iron. I would do anything to live, even deny you.

You cannot ask a people to die. You cannot be angry if they refuse. That was your mistake, Bee. Anger is not enough. You also need love and pity and a measure of diplomacy. Bee, you even hated yourself for the human in you, and that hatred destroyed you. So much else could have been done!

Now I work, alone. They send me down into old Earth to scrounge exhausted mines. They make me count each mote of dust in Saturn's rainbow rings. I have much time to think.

The Dajja is always with me, in my mind. I think of all the things he said, and I find hope. We never understood him, Bee; we never saw what he was. "All time is One-time," he said before they took him. It is true. Time is a complete cycle. We only see half of it, that part which goes forward. The past is swallowed up for us, destroyed, except in memory. The future is simply mute.

But I think the Dajja sees all of it, time and anti-time. He exists in both, and knows it. We, poor creatures, see only one half of ourselves. We have grown up half-blind. He can remember the future; he looks forward to the past. Time to him is complete. And we can speak with him! He loves us.

He tried to tell us, Bee, not to grieve. Somewhere in the past, you and I and he still swim in the depths of Daphne. In anti-time, you and I are still to meet. You are still to dazzle me into silence. Always behind me, you will be singing. It is all still there.

Everything is perpetual. Death invalidates nothing. Nothing is made futile by it, or small. The flower blooms forever. Time goes to the end, and then springs back on itself. The universe saves itself! It doesn't need Entropy Control to do that!

I want them to understand that. They are so afraid to die. They pit themselves against time and entropy, and build monuments to prove that they ever existed. The Dajja can help them to know the reality of the past. He can teach them to roll with time and be at peace with death. He can show them their whole selves. They won't need to be gods, then.

He must survive. They must be made to understand the treasure that gleams half-forgotten in Aldebaran. Then, perhaps, Control will be allowed to fade, and the sweet fruits of decay can blossom. They watch me always. All I need do is speak for them to hear. I am sure they will understand. With time.

So rest, Bee, rest in my memory. Dance freely in the past, and cease to accuse me. For I am Zoe, the slow and faithful, and with these Remembrances of you I begin my work.

---

from the letters of Raul Kundara

Hola Mari,

I apologize for the lack of letters. There were reasons why I could not write. I am not allowed to explain them to you. Please understand.

I have visited the Hellesians once more. They do not like to be called that. They call their world Channakale, for reasons that they do not explain. They do not call their sun Daphne, but Yildiz. It means simply, star. Less simply, it means Destiny.

The trip was hot and unhappy, as before, but I knew better what to expect. We arrived at sunset while the settlers were in the fields. Chief walked on to the pava, but I stayed to record the work songs. They saw me with my recorder, but kept on working. A few made wry smiles and prodded each other. A bright-faced young woman waved and yelled something to me that made the others laugh. They were amused that anyone would want to record their songs. They call them kundara or esk-kundara. That means "old shoes."

The watersheets were rolled up and we went together through the growing heat of the day to the yemek pava. There I played for them the songs, and they hooted with laughter. The Senior of the pava brought me a glass of clear liquor. I was made to understand that I had to drink it in one swallow. It tasted somewhat of methane and burned my mouth, but I managed. They clapped me on the back and applauded. The Chief stood up and volunteered, not to be outdone as always. There were cheers and we all became great friends. The Senior can speak some Central. He told me the drink was called Bom aksamlayin: the evening bomb!

They sang more songs, of a different sort, called haberi. These are true stories. One was about an avalanche ten years before. Another told how cloth is woven and of the discovery of keten, the plant that grows on cliffs from which cloth is made. The Senior sang his parents' marriage-song. It told the story of their courtship and is quite lovely. They try to sing these songs seriously, stiff-backed, but their high, straining voices make even them giggle. At gatherings like these, the women are allowed to join in the laughter and the jokes, but not to sing.

It is an old Channukale joke that the men love their machines more than their wives. They repeat this joke endlessly, and do their best to make it seem true. All their machines have affectionate names. They sing songs about them. The women groaned when the first machine song began. The best of these was a doleful ode to a still called Sofia. After that one, the women insisted no more of them be sung.

Many of the haberi tell of how the colony has survived and grown. No history of Channukale has been written. Yet it is all there for the collecting in these songs. It is a wonderful story. The first Channuks were workers on Ruin, and were expelled on a pre-Slide vessel. Its guiding jig, faced with spreading and irreparable breakdown, chose the first marginally inhabitable world. Most of the equipment, including the cloners, was lost in the landing. The settlers dug themselves into the caves now called the Old City. They established ways of gathering water not too different from those used now. They developed the watersheets, dug ditches, and made crude batteries and boilers for electricity. There are now six major settlements on Channukale. They are populated by 70,000 people, all descended from the 350 colonists from Ruin. Each settlement is self-sufficient. The nearest to Highplain Snow is Scout-sighted, 50 kilometers further along the Kizildaglar, Red Mountains. No one in the pava had been there.

In exchange for songs, I had to answer many questions. They became interested when they learned I am a certed bio-engineer. They wanted to know about colonial adaptations. The original 350 were all trained in some discipline. Their bio-engineer worked the change in their skins, but then died, leaving no apprentice. Still, I found their knowledge surprising. I told them about the enlarged lungs, the strengthened bones, the chill-resistant metabolisms. They listened, shook their heads, and stifled some disagreement among themselves. "We live here without such things," said the Senior, "Some of us think it would be good to change."

They also asked about the Angels. They call them yildizibojeyee, fireflies, star flies. I told them what I knew—of their cold, piping voices, of how they plunge through fire and space and the substratum, of how they see the unseeable and translate for us, of how they never die. The Channuks sing songs about Angels. They believe children can hear Angels without headpieces—or so one old woman nodded wisely. She spoke of Angels visiting children at night and whispering stories to them in the dark. The Senior dismissed what she said.

I do not think they much favor Entropy Control. They say they follow the Regimen, but are more interested in their ancient religion. They worship a god and his prophet. They would not talk about it, but in the midafternoon, I heard a song go through all the corridors, and they all went to another pava called a Jami, to pray.

I asked them if they looked forward to a newer sun, and life without coolsuits. They shrugged as though it did not concern them. Perhaps they cannot conceive of it. "You came here. No one asked," said a stern young man called Ekrem. This was considered bad form, I think. He was cautioned by an elder, or so it seemed. I could not understand what was said.

There was one brief unpleasantness, after the singing. The Senior's eldest daughter, Hatija, had been talking with me. She asked about Home, the clothes, the language, the music. She was very lively, and yearned, I think, to see other places. The Senior and Ekrem, leading me back to the misafir pava, drew me aside.

The father spoke to me first, with an air of not wishing to offend a pleasant off-worlder. "Please," he said. "You must understand. Our women. They are our treasures. You must have nothing to do with them."

"Hatija," said Ekrem. He puffed out his chest in a way that made me smile without showing it. "You must stop courting her!" I tried to explain I had only been speaking politely, as a friend. To a Channuk, that sounds the same as courting.

"Nevertheless, you must not do it, please," insisted the Senior.

It is understandable. Off-worlders might have caused trouble before. Some women might find them exciting, though not, surely, the regulars of Entropy Control. Still, I will be friends with the settlers. They are pleased a bit I think that an off-worlder takes such an interest in them. They have asked me to return. They will let me talk to Hatija in time. I like them, even solemn Ekrem.

Enclosed with this letter are some of the songs. The first is a work song. I have translated it into Central as best I could, with its rhymes and plodding rhythm.

> Destiny is glaring down
> Are the good leaves browning?
> Was there too much rain last night?
> Are the good leaves drowning?
> Does the sunscreen let in light?
> Are the good leaves paling?
> Should the soil be re-plowed?
> Are the good leaves failing?
> Sister Sezen stands there dawdling
> Smoothing down her trousers.
> Brother Raul sits and smokes,

Never himself rouses.
Look out on the wide green fields
Each flower feeds a child.
Look then to your children, sisters.
Are the good leaves browning?

The second song is the Senior of the pava, singing his parents'
marriage song. The old couple are still alive. New words have been
added as they age. The song is now very long and records the birth
of their children and grandchildren, and many domestic disasters.
I have been able to translate only part of it. The "thin skin" refers
to the lack of callusing of the Channuks when young.

Though you would not know it now,
They were young with thin skin.
One was known as Laughter
The other one was Grin.
She had loved another man.
We will not give his name.
He bedded down another wife
and left her to her shame.
She turned then to her childhood friend,
The boy who always smiled.
One night the winds about them whispered
Warm and wet and mild.
"I love you," he said simply.
"I love you like the rain.
"I love you like the boiling clouds
"That hang above the plain.
"And should you die or leave me
"My heart would wait for you
"Until the sands blown by the wind
"Have planed the hills away . . ."

That is the best I can do. Those last lines say literally, but in
fewer words, "Until the sands of the wind have ground away the

hills and the plane of the world is perfectly level." Strange how Humankind can pierce the substratum and fly between the stars, only to live on a world that still seems flat. Some things never change. Perhaps all conditions are extreme.

Love,
Toni

FAN

Billie fell in love with Eamon Strafe when she was fifteen years old. Billie was quiet, unconfident, but festooned with symbols. She was bold in the language of signs—anhks, Hittite seals, vampire chic. She read Edgar Allan Poe and Bram Stoker and wore black. She liked spiders and coffins and poems about death. For a time, she confused sex with horror.

Then she heard Eamon Strafe sing. She was buying snacks in a Pakistani supermarket. It was open late, and sold things like coconut-coated peanuts and fresh ginger. The radio was on, a soft-voiced DJ who played hard music, but the song he played now was quiet. The moment she heard it, Billie was shocked by a sense of recognition. Without knowing it, this was what she had been waiting for.

The music was measured, almost stately, and seemed to say some things were important. The voice was high and sweet and grieving, and it came in breathless gasps. Was the singer a woman? Who was it? Billie stood still, straining to hear the DJ, but after the song, he issued a warning about traffic congestion. Billie asked the woman at the counter if she knew what that song was, and the woman smiled sweetly back, barely speaking English.

Billie heard the song again a week later. She was going home from London to South End on the train and a girl called Tora got on. Billie knew her from school. Tora was alarmingly confident and slightly beyond Billie's social ken. Tora dropped down onto a nearby seat, laughing with older friends and slightly out of breath. Ghetto blasters had come back. Tora aggressively turned hers up. From the first sighing note, Billie knew. The song hauled her up from her seat.

"Hi Tora. I'm sorry to bother you, but who is that? What's the song?"

Tora was flattered. "This. Oh, it's Eamon Strafe." As if everyone but Billie knew.

"It's wonderful!" said Billie.

"You bet," said Tora. And passed her the disk cover.

For the Lebanon Dead, it said. There was a picture of a slightly older man, with a kind, lumpy, ultimately handsome face.

"He's a monk," said Tora and giggled. "An Irish monk. He's got an album coming out next month."

"I've got to get it."

"Tom here knows his manager."

Tom was older, with rodent smile. "He's gonna make it, the industry's behind him. People done Goth, they're bored with rave, they need stars."

Billie, in Goth, caught the drift. "Hype," she said, and passed the disk back.

"Yeah, but the music's fucking brilliant," corrected Tora. Billie's friend Janice still sat on the other seat looking slightly wasted and abandoned. Billie waved her forward.

Tora was gratified by the effect she had had on Billie, so gratified that she and even Janice became friends. They became fans, before anyone else did, fans of Eamon Strafe. They read in the newspaper that he was going to sing on a late night arts program. "We can put our handbags in a circle and scream," said Tora as a joke. But when the camera caught him for the first time, all three girls turned in silence and looked at each other.

"Isn't he beautiful? Scrum-my," said Tora.

He wasn't handsome. He had a rough boxer's nose and a heavy jaw, and he was burly about the shoulders, but his arms and lower body seemed to shrink away, like a carrot. It was his expression that made him angelic, the crinkled, smiling eyes out of which shone ice blue irises. And the teeth, the famous teeth. They were too big. Whenever he smiled they took over, illuminated his face. Billie lost her taste for the Gothic. White became her color, Eamon's color.

Billie and Tora united in a campaign of conversion. They wore white jackets, white trousers, and white headscarves tied under their chins, like wimples. They sat in Piccadilly Circus, playing his music as loudly as they could. The police would move them on. They carried a poster of him and walked, singing his name, and accosting passersby, demanding that they give up meat and alcohol. The world would have to come to love Eamon Strafe as well.

And for a time, incredibly, heartbreakingly, the world did.

He was right for the times. The New Aestheticism, the newspapers called it. They always led with a photograph of Eamon—*The Antithesis of a Pop Star*. It seemed so wonderful to Billie that other people could feel as she did. For a brief time, two or three years only, she and the age were one. It seemed there would be a place for her in the world after all.

He was beautiful, his music was beautiful. Somewhere he lived and breathed, she reminded herself, somewhere right now, in Ireland. She seemed to hear him sing everywhere she went.

For the Lebanon Dead was followed by *Afghanistan,* and it was even better. He had actually gone there and seen the fighting. *Afghanistan* got to number one. It was followed by a book of poetry, and a further disk of the verse recited over sparse music. Every six months there was a new album of proper music. There was plenty to buy.

But there were no live performances—videos, yes, but no tours. He's shy, thought Billie, and loved him for it. Eamon said he found tours exploitative. He felt he owed it to people to give them more than a rehearsed performance. He wanted to talk to them all in person, and that was not possible. That meant he would need to find some new and better way to reach them. Billie was not entirely sure she understood what he meant.

Billie wrote him letters.

Dear Eamon

This is just to let you know that someone cares.

Billie

She didn't expect an answer. Someone sent her a four-color booklet about the fan club. She didn't join. She didn't need to, or want to. Eamon lived inside her.

Fans are like seashells. They emerge once the tide has retreated. Billie did not feel beached when Eamon's time had passed. The surprise was that he was ever as popular as he had once been. Now he was left to those who understood. If anything, she became more loyal, but in silence.

Billie moved to London, because of Eamon. Because of Eamon, she had the courage. It seemed possible that she would meet other people like herself. She found that she had values, from somewhere. Like many of her generation, a certain purity of outlook would linger into adulthood. She didn't drink; she sought harmless occupation. She studied pottery, and found a job working lunchtimes in a health food shop.

Sometimes for the hell of it and a little money, Billie appeared with a band. She and three other girls would stand on the stage and pretend to scream at the lead singer. It was a joke. Billie was dressed in all her old Strafe idolatry. That was a joke too. The jokes protected her.

On the sticky black floors of the clubs, the young people stood in groups, smiling and saying excuse me. They acted like aristocrats because they had time. They still had time in which to preserve a measure of grace.

Billie met a man in her art class who had an Irish accent and chestnut hair. His name was Roy. For a very short while, they slept rough under the arches of a bridge. Billie had to wash in the sink in back of the shop, and give her mother's address in order to be paid. Finally they found a room a good hour and a half from the center of London, out toward the east, as if magnetized back toward South End. At first they were supposed to be saving money to move to Ireland. Roy was sweet and feckless and unwittingly selfish. Life to him was like a blow to the head. He sat on the floor all day watching television, perplexed, anxious, always realizing too late that he should have helped Billie carry in the shopping bags or wash the dishes or move a chair. When he finally told her he was going, she was surprised to find that her main emotion was relief. He left her with Joey, her son. Joey was then two and Billie was 22. Joey's middle, hidden name was Eamon.

There was a logic to be obeyed. Billie gave up trying to be a potter. She spent mornings waiting in the Benefits Agency, bouncing Joey up and down on her lap, trying to keep him from crying. She had to keep proving that Roy was out of the country before she could claim benefit. Like every other person on the dole, she was made to take a course and like so many others she studied what was called computing. The course taught her how to use two pieces of software and a bit of a third. It was enough to find her a nonpaying job with a Housing Association. She did the accounts and correspondence, and was given a place to live in exchange.

She and her son lived in three rooms. Some money came in from the health shop, but she had to keep that a secret from the Agency. Joey wrestled in her grasp and was aggressive and demanding. They went shopping, and Joey demanded sweets or toys. Billie became yet another woman in the supermarket, hauling a weeping child.

"Joey, if you do that again, I'll give you such a wallop."

Her aggressive son turned out to be timid around other children. He did not like being left alone with them and fought her, punching when she tried to take him to a playgroup. He would not go outside, even when the old brick forecourt echoed with the sound of other children's games.

Sometimes at night, when Joey was asleep, Billie would sense a fullness inside herself. She would draw the curtains, put on headphones, and listen to Eamon Strafe—and she would dance with joy.

It would feel as though the music were coming out of her. She would startle herself, miming to the songs. She would sometimes weep or rage or shake with nervous laughter. She would tease new meanings out of the words, by gesture or expression.

Her dancing was a performance. If other people could have seen her, they would have been startled too. Eamon Strafe mimed when he performed on television. Billie did it better.

The Association bought Billie a new computer.

She kept it in her bedroom, away from tiny fingers. It was a beautiful thing. It got to know its operators and wrote new programs to help them with their work. Digital broadcasting had only just got going: the computer was linked to all kinds of information, about tax regulations, benefit rates and means testing. It would suddenly announce:

NEW PROGRAM AVAILABLE FOR THAT FUNCTION

and print out instructions. It would read Billie's letters as she wrote them. It would interrupt.

INFORMATION REVISE; NEW LEGAL PRECEDENT, SEE CROWN VS MACAL-LAUGH CRESCENT HOUSING ASSOCIA-TION.

Billie was buying paper for it and floppy disks when something in the store racks caught her eyes. She was strummed like a chord. On the cover of a CD ROM, Eamon's face stared out at her. Eamon on software?

CONVERSATIONS WITH THE STARS said a banner over the racks.

Blue Laser Personality Software.

Billie went to the racks and turned the jewelbox case over in her hand. The cover was white. He was brown, windswept, staring out at her from some new place. It was like buying an Eamon Strafe CD ten years before. The back of the case said:

A program taken from an imprint of your favorite celebrity's personality. Eamon Strafe himself will be able to answer all your questions about his songs, his poetry, his religious beliefs. Why did he reject the Church? What does he mean by Spirit? What does he think of the new generation of Blue Stars?

This disk has been authored and engineered to the most precise standards. The program card has its own updating digital transceiver. This means the program is kept abreast of developments in Eamon's life. You go with him as he visits Yemen or withdraws to his estates in County Down, traveling all over the world, seeking answers. Now Eamon can give you those answers himself—and some of the questions.

Warning: to be used only on self-programming, digital-broadcast equipment, equipped with white-laser CD drive.

Well that's what I've got, thought Billie. It's the Association's, but they did say I could use it for myself.

She turned the case over in her hand. The disk and the card cost 25 pounds. It's just another way, she thought, to separate me from my money. But she didn't put it back in the rack.

You wrote all those letters, Billie, and you never got an answer. She looked at Eamon's face, and knew there was a part of her that no amount of sense could control. She wanted it. There was little enough in life.

If I don't get it now, she thought, I never will. Who knows, maybe he'll help me with my own poetry. Maybe he could explain to me what iambic pentameter is.

She let the Association pay for it. She would pay them back, bit by bit. After all, she kept the accounts. The black girl at the counter entered the bar code without even reading what it was. The girl at the counter didn't care what Billie bought.

Billie went home, and inserted the card and the CD, and the screen went blank and then words came up, glowing on the screen.

PLEASE SAY HELLO.

"Hello," whispered Billie, with a shrug. In her mind, she saw the dog with the phonograph. His Master's Voice.

Color marched down the screen in an orderly scan. The patterns made a face. Eamon's. There were creases in his cheeks now, and bags under his eyes. Billie found it moving that he was growing old. He was sitting on a wooden chair, in front of a wall that was made of raw wooden planks.

"Hello," he said. "What's your name, then?" Emphasis on the YOUR, as if he had been talking to so many other strangers.

"Billie," she replied. "Billie de Vaille. Billie's just a nickname." There was a hush of shyness.

"Where do you live, Billie?"

"Stratford East. London. Where are you?"

"I'm in Canada," he said. "Just staying here for a while."

"The papers said you were in China." She said it in accusation. She was looking for flaws.

"I'm on my way back," he said.

Billie was beginning to wonder if the program would be fearfully dull, like one of those programmed doctor's surgeries.

"You've just got a prepared list of questions and replies," she told the program. Eamon leaned even more precariously back in the chair.

"I am a Read Only Memory and a card, but that's not how I work," he replied.

Billie felt something akin to panic. It's not even trying to fool me.

"I react like Eamon would react. And the transceiver keeps the personality updated with new information. Like, I went to China to keep up my Tai Chi."

Ah yes, his Tai Chi. All part of the image.

"I was supposed to meet this great master while he was doing his exercises in a public square. So I went to the square and there were thousands of Chinese people all doing their morning exercises. So I thought: I'm the only Westerner here, he'll see me. I walked up and down for hours. I stood on the steps of a public monument. No master. I got back and my guide was furious. 'You insult the master!' she says. The master, you see, thought I ought to come to him."

It's not bad, thought Billie. Quite good, really. A bit of a laugh.

"I'll wait until you tell me that story again," she said, "and then I'll know just how big your memory is." She was smiling.

"Frankly," he said, "about as big as yours." He grinned. The giant teeth. "I'll wait until you repeat yourself too."

It was a terrible winter and life seemed hard for everyone. Billie found that Eamon saw her through it.

Mrs. King in the next flat nearly died of cold. At 5:30 in the morning, Billie heard the police breaking down the old lady's door.

"I have a key. Don't," Billie murmured, but the police ignored her. Mrs. King was confused but didn't want to go to the hospital. The police called her daughter, and said in Mrs. King's hearing, "The daughter doesn't give a shit."

"She certainly does," said Billie, "and I'm sure if she said she's on her way, then she'll be here."

Billie sat with Mrs. King and held her hand. That made Billie feel a bit better about not being able to stop the police destroying the door. The room was icy cold and smelled like an old lady's room, that's all. Billie turned on the heater. She delicately covered the bottom of her nose with an index finger, and still managed to smile and talk. Mrs. King described her daughter's wedding. The old woman had lain on the floor all night. Very suddenly Billie saw that there was excrement, flattened on the carpet, excrement on Billie's shoes. In the midst of trying to give comfort, Billie gagged. She had to run out of the room. So she felt bad about herself again. So she said hello, and talked to Eamon.

"Billie. You can't blame yourself for being human," he told her. "You did everything you could, even some things you couldn't do."

"I'm just so angry being ambushed by my body like that." She meant being ill. "I just felt so weak. That poor old lady."

"And how does she feel now?"

"Well enough," she admitted.

"Then what are you worried about?" he asked.

"Everything," she admitted. Everything and nothing.

Joey had started school in the autumn, and hated it, hated it. He came home in tears, and tried to hit her when she walked him to the bus stop. I'm even a bad mother, she thought. No money, no father, no brothers and sisters. No wonder the poor kid is terrified of everything.

And when she got home from walking him to school, she would turn on the computer.

She would say hello, and Eamon would be in some new place, having read some new book, and she would talk to him as if he were real. He would talk to her as though she were real. He remembered who the people in the Association were, and asked about them.

Billie loaned her door key to a neighbor who needed to use the computer. When the woman gave the key back, it was new and shiny and had a different brand name. Without asking, the woman had cut a copy of Billie's key and given her the copy by mistake. Billie found herself asking Eamon's advice.

"I mean, do I just go up to her and say 'You've cut a copy of my key. I'd like the original back, please?' It's like calling her a thief."

And Eamon said, "You've got to do it, Billie. For your self-respect."

In the evenings, while Joey was asleep, the computer would say simple things like. "You look all done in, love. Go make yourself a cup of tea."

She could rationalize it. People keep pets, she would tell herself, as she scraped most of Joey's dinner into the waste bin. People keep pets and pets can't even talk.

If she felt good, she made it seem raffish and *moderne*. I've got a computer for a lover, she would tell imaginary female chums. Who needs a man? They're all creeps. This one doesn't come home drunk, doesn't need his laundry done, and I can talk to him about anything. She'd had a few bad dates: the estate agent who thought his aging BMW entitled him to true love, a musician from the Association who had to be stoned before he could converse like a human being. The software, she would say, is more authentic. She said it to the empty air.

The truth was that there was no one there. The logic was that very little changed in Billie's life. A year passed almost without her noticing. Joey wanted computer games for Christmas.

PLEASE SAY HELLO.

"Hello," she would whisper. She didn't like seeing the image scan in. So she looked at herself in the bedroom mirror. There was still some hint of the good-looking girl she had been, sallow, dark circles under the eyes, puffy around the chin. It was February, the day was too dull even to rain. On the kitchen table, Joey's breakfast cereal was drying hard on the unwashed blue of his bowl.

She heard the sound of the sea, murmuring surf and the cries of seagulls.

"Hello?" said Eamon. "Yoo-hoo."

Billie looked back round at him. And said nothing.

"I wouldn't want to rush you," he said. There was sand behind him, shifting brown grass, wind in his hair. Billie suddenly found she yearned to be by the sea. Did the computer know that, too? Did it have diagnostic skills? Eamon looked at her, smiling, waiting for her to speak. The thing's real eye, a tiny glass bead at the top of the monitor, stared unblinking back at her.

"Where are you?" she asked him.

"By the sea." His milk white cheeks were flushed with blood. She rolled her eyes. "Well, fancy that. Are you in Ireland?"

"Uh-huh."

The machine, for some reason, had stopped giving her exact locales.

"Do you really think I'm going to rush off and try to find a man who won't even know me when he sees me?"

He went still, his eyes closed. "You're going to start this again, are you?"

"Do you have any idea how humiliating this is? I sit here and listen to you. I give you advice about your songs. I talk to you about my life, as if you were real, and then I turn you off, and I realize I don't have anything. Nothing!"

He looked directly at her. "You have a copy of me. What else am I to say?" If it's boring for you, mate, thought Billie, think what it's like for me. Eamon sighed. "I really am by the sea, you know."

"Except that the machine can't show it, because it's bad at simulating waves."

"There's a monastery behind the headland." He made a vague gesture, indicating a sweep of coast. "I'm thinking of becoming a monk again."

"Pressure of fame getting too much for you?" Billie asked. "I wouldn't have thought too much fame was your problem these days. Who are you going to sing to, the seagulls?"

"If they'll listen to me. The new stuff I'm writing now is going back to Christianity."

"You're telling me this," said Billie, her lips thin with bitterness, "because whoever programmed you wants me to go on buying your CDs."

"I'm telling you this because I thought you were interested in my music." Ooh, so it can get angry too? Does it wet itself, like a baby doll?

"How is Joey?" he asked.

"I don't want to talk about Joey. He's a messed up, lonely little kid, just like his mum. That's not going to change. Nothing is going to change."

He stepped forward, settling into sand. "I wish you'd let me meet him. I'd love to talk to him."

"Sod off! Do you think I want him to know what a wanker his mother is? Spending all day talking to a computer?"

He looked crestfallen. "I'd just like to see him, that's all."

"Get them young, you mean?"

Eamon sighed. "Look. If I were really here, all I could do is what I'm doing now. I would talk to you. I would say what I'm saying now."

"You don't even know I'm alive!" She was shouting.

His voice kept quiet. "There are a lot of people I want to talk to, Billie. But I can't. I'd have to stretch myself as thin as the mist. You know my songs, they're about the Spirit, aren't they? I mean it, Billie. You think the Spirit has a body? You think the Spirit can exist only in one body? This way I can become like the Spirit." Eamon pinched finger and thumb together to show how small he could become. "This way, I can talk to more people than was ever possible before."

Billie glared back at him. "Take your clothes off," she told him. "If you're so real."

He ran a hand across his forehead and looked away. "Oh God, Billie, this is so sad."

"Go on. That's what this is all about isn't it? Ersatz sex. Or don't they program in any information about your cock?"

"You're a friend, OK. Someone I talk to. It's not something I normally do with a friend."

"You don't exist! You're a product!"

"You think all singers aren't? They're all makeup and camera angles and ghost writers. What do people get who buy that?"

It's so strange, thought Billie. You can know and know and still not be able to help yourself.

"It seems so real," she said. Her throat clenched and she couldn't speak.

Eamon rolled forward, dropping onto his knees. "I know what I am," he said. "I'm not alive, I'm just digital code. I'm only a copy. But believe me, Billie. If I could know you as well as this copy knows you . . ." His lower chin seemed to crumple up like cardboard. "Then I'd love you, too."

The invisible ocean roared, the wind blew, somewhere and nowhere, in a bedroom in Stratford East.

Tora wrote.
She sent a card.

A celebration of Eamon Strafe's birthday
Saturday, 25th March, 8:30 P.M.

No husbands allowed.

There was a map, and an address in Finchley.

On the back Tora had written. "Found you in the phone book. You always were the best of us. If you don't come, I'll know it's too late for the rest of us."

The rest of whom?

Tora had done well. She worked in telesales and lived in a 1930s red brick house, with mock Tudor half-timbering around the gables. Tora opened the door, even plumper than before, and cried out Billie's name, and hugged her, held her, wept. Surprised, Billie wept too.

"Tora," she accused. "You've gone glam."

"Oh, you gotta go for it," said Tora. She'd sprinkled sparkly stuff on her cheeks and wore a dark loose shirt and mid-calf trousers. She made Billie feel pinched and delicate like something breakable. Tora led her in, arm in arm.

The two big downstairs rooms had been cleared of furniture, and were full of women. The walls were covered with balloons and pictures of Eamon Strafe. Slumped in a corner chair there was a thing like a scarecrow that grinned blindly with huge teeth. It was a life-size doll.

The women were rubbing balloons on their thighs and giggling naughtily. The rubbed ballons stuck to the wallpaper with static. "Oooh, Berthe, you're highly charged tonight!"

Billie felt at once superior and envious. The women all looked like hairdressers, happy and boring. She felt like something sharp-edged and broken in comparison. She wanted to leave.

She was introduced. The faces and names passed in a nervous blur. Tora held it together for all of them. "Tonight is our night, love. Caterers in so nobody has any washing up to do. Here's the food." There was a table full of prawns and salads and quiches. No meat. "This is Gwen. She's in charge." Gwen evidently was not. She was a small, round-shouldered woman in a white T-shirt, black leather jacket and motor cycling boots. She poured Billie a glass of punch.

"I call it Tanamera after the second book," Gwen said, giggling for no reason. She was from the north, and the word "book" had a owl's hoot in the middle of it. "It's made from fruit and traditional Irish herbs. I like to think it's the sort of thing our Eamon would drink himself."

"Thank you. It's very nice," Billie heard herself say. She wasn't used to parties. She found she had nothing to say to Gwen. She went and stood by Tora again.

"Well, I've applied what I've learned from Eamon to my business," Tora was saying. "You know, he's right, the main thing, even in selling, is to listen. If you don't listen, you don't get the information you need."

"Well, I've noticed that," said another woman. "You think it's all a bit airy-fairy, and then you find it works in the real world."

A third woman looked very serious indeed, a tiny sharp chin over lace collar. "If Eamon Strafe had been born two thousand years ago, who would he have been?" she said. "Think about it."

John the Baptist? Herod? Pontius Pilate? "I didn't think they had pop stars back then, actually," said Billie. Tora chuckled. "Well, no," she said. At least Tora wasn't losing her sense of proportion. "You all have everything you need? I think everyone's here. Shall we make a start?"

"Yeah, if anyone's a bit late, it won't matter," said the woman who didn't like things airy-fairy.

Tora stepped away from them and clapped her hands. "OK, everybody. Thank you all for coming, and for bringing all these things! Eamon will be with us later, but first we'll have a reading. Danielle?"

The most beautiful woman Billie had ever seen stood up. Perfect hair, perfect face, lovely hands. She was French, and there was a precision in the way she moved that was not English. She was lovely, but her voice was tuneless and deadening, and she recited the worst of Eamon Strafe. She recited the awful little poem about love being like a hyacinth. Billie had never thought that absolutely everything Eamon wrote was wonderful. That was not the point. The point was that sometimes, waywardly, he would give you things that could not be found anywhere else.

When Danielle began to recite "Changes" (rearranges, turning pages, the different ages) and the women sat, cross-legged, with their eyes closed, nodding, Billie realized that these were the people who actually liked the bad stuff. It was the bad stuff they came for. The chilling thought was that maybe most Eamon Strafe fans did.

Billie felt betrayed. They called themselves fans, but they didn't understand. Sometimes Eamon sang about the pain and terror in the world, and whatever hope was left. They only saw his little greeting cards.

Danielle finished and the women applauded. It's because she's French, thought Billie. They like her accent.

Then they played some clips.

Their instinct was unerring. They started with Eamon's worst ever song, "I Want to Be with You." There were only about four things that Eamon had done that Billie truly could not stand, and this was the worst. It was about someone whose girlfriend had died, and he is trying to join her or something.

"Oh, that voice," said the lady in the black leather jacket, and she shrank down further into herself. Another took out a lipstick-smeared Kleenex and unabashedly wept into it. Weeping was approved behavior. They all began to weep, hands around each other's shoulders. In respectful silence, Tora tiptoed about her room, lighting candles. It was as though they were in mourning.

Then came "A Voice like Mist," and Billie could feel her face go as hard as stone. It had been on the same cassette single as "Lebanon Dead," and on no album, and there he was, on "The Late Show," 12 years ago, and almost skinny, and she had not heard the song since she had lost the cassette moving house, and she had not seen the clip since she and Tora had first become friends.

It really was as good as she remembered it, and she remembered how she had felt then, when the whole flavor of the world had been different.

And as she realized this, all the women stood up and held hands, just like she and Tora and Janice had done, and they began to sing the words by heart in strained and cracking voices, like in church, and she couldn't hear Eamon any more.

A voice like the mist
Lands like a kiss
And then it's gone.

It's not some drippy love song, Billie wanted to say, surprised at how copious were her tears. It's about the Spirit. It only speaks sometimes. Billie looked up and the Frenchwoman, Danielle, was looking at her with an expression like love. It seemed to say: I understand what you feel. No you don't, thought Billie.

Danielle came up to her after the clip had finished. "I live in this country because of him," she said, amorous.

Billie felt as cold as ice. "Then you're in the wrong country. He's Irish."

Danielle's smooth surface was only slightly fractured. She smiled and made a little shrug. Well not quite Irish, no.

Ireland might muss your makeup, thought Billie. She found herself yearning for Ireland, the Ireland of her dreams.

Tora came in with a cake. Billie had a terrible feeling that she knew what was going to happen next. There was a blue-green flutter on the screen.

"HEL-LO-O!" all the women shouted.

Billie looked away. She tried not to see. All the women started to sing.

"Happy birthday dear Eamon. Happy birthday to you."

Eamon was wearing sunglasses. He never wore sunglasses. Sunglasses and a Hawaiian shirt, and he was by the sea, but it was a beach, with palm frond umbrellas and drinks on white tables and people water skiing. The waves rippled and reflected light in irregular patterns. Tora had a more powerful machine than Billie: it could do waves.

"Hey Tora," Eamon said jauntily. He was a deep nut brown. "Girls. Hi there, how ya doing?"

They chorused back, "Hello."

"You don't need any cake, you'll get even fatter."

"Well," replied Tora. "You tell me you like them plump."

"Ho, ho, hey," said the women, as though something truly wicked had been said.

"Depends on the plump girl," said Eamon, adjusting his sunglasses.

"Hooo!" said all the women.

Tora lunged toward Billie, and took hold of her arms. She gave them a squeeze, perhaps to find if they were as skinny as they looked. "Eamon, I'd like you to meet someone new."

New! Billie turned. New? Do you think you own him?

"That's Billie," said Eamon. "I know Billie. Hi, how are you?"

"I should have known," murmured Tora, eyes narrowed, smiling. "Sorry."

"Hello," said Billie, embarrassed. "That's what I normally say to you isn't it?"

For some reason Tora's group thought this very funny—the laughter was sudden, then quickly hushed. It sounded canned. Billie felt shop soiled. So all these machines, they're all linked by the transceivers. They talk to each other. It's all one thing, all linked, all colluding so we can all keep, so that *I* can keep, my illusions.

And she was even grateful.

Tora was blowing out the candles on the cake. Since Eamon couldn't.

"Sing for us, Eddie," called one of the woman.

"Yeah, all right!" said a woman leaping up from the floor. She was burly and wore blue and white and a string of pearls. None of it made sense.

" 'Basic Blue!' "

"Hoo! Yeah! 'Basic Blue,' Eamon!"

Eamon put his sunglasses back on, and started to croon and all at once, Billie understood what was happening, happening to them all.

"Tora," said Billie. "I think I'm going to be sick."

Tora looked at her for a moment as if it were a criticism of the group. The glass in Billie's hand turned as if by itself. Billie dropped her drink. Her knees went from under her, and she fell. It was the burly woman in pale blue who caught her.

"Oh, love, oh darling," said Tora, genuinely concerned.

The women sprang to help. Billie was lowered to the floor.

"Poor love," said Tora, deeply moved. "She always was his biggest fan."

Someone called to the screen. "Eddie? Eddie could you hold on, someone's ill."

"We never had anyone faint before," said a lean and craggy blonde on the outskirts of the group. She was just a little amused.

Tora said, "Let's get her to the loo."

They carried her into the bathroom. They stroked her hair and called her Pet, as she threw up traditional Irish herbs. To Billie, none of it mattered.

Self-programming. They get to know us. They become what we want them to be. So all the different Eamons drift away. They become ugly monks or spiffy little jerks in Hawaiian shirts.

And none of them are Eamon at all.

"I think we should leave her alone for a few minutes," said Tora quietly, and ushered the women out.

And Billie lay on the thick, pink, shaggy rug and thought, I'm dying. I'm dying inside. Dimly she heard Eamon singing. So how thin do you have to become, Eamon? You said you would become thin if you tried to reach everyone. Aren't you thin enough, now, changing for them all? A thin film of Eamon Strafe all over the world. And getting thinner.

Billie stood up, unsteadily, before any of them came back. She slipped into the hallway from the loo. Her coat was hanging up. All of them were turned to the screen, arms around each other, like the puppy dogs in *101 Dalmatians*. Or the dog on the record label.

Billie walked on, out of the front door, closing it softly, without saying thank you, without saying good-bye. She ran on tiptoes, like the house was made out of china. She ran up the street, expecting any moment to hear them call.

She went home and said hello.

"You're not Eamon," she told it, shaking with rage.

She'd woken him up. He was in a bedroom in the monastery, a wooden cross on the wall.

"You know that. I know that," he said, squiffy from lack of sleep, annoyed.

"I've just seen you at a resort beach, in, I'd say, Acapulco. This is self-programming stuff. It changes. It becomes what we want it to be like. I've just seen you on someone else's machine and you came on like some naff Joe Cool."

"So what bothers you more? The fact that you own me, or the fact that you don't?" The question threw Billie.

"Every performer adapts to the audience. If I adapt to a different audience, that's just being professional."

"You have nothing to do with the real Eamon Strafe. I am sick of dreaming about Eamon Strafe. I am going to find him, the real one. And, I am going to turn you off."

He shrugged. "That's your choice." He reached across and turned off the light.

The screen was dark. There were small shifting sounds of sheets. Through the closed monastery window there came the sound of surf. With an angry punch, Billie canceled it all out.

The next day, Billie wrote a letter to Eamon Strafe's book publishers.

Dear Mr. Strafe,

This is a real woman who is tired of illusion. I have spent time, Mr. Strafe, reading your verse and listening to your records. Not all of them are very good. Some of them, however, changed my life and made me who I am.

Are you still so famous that it is impossible to meet you? I am a mature person, Mr. Strafe, with something to say. You said once that you felt you had to give the people who loved you more than a rehearsed performance. Was that true? I don't know if I can believe you.

It would be nice to have an answer.

Yours sincerely,

Billie

There was no answer. Billie scanned in the logo of a computer magazine, and printed stationery using her own address and telephone number.

Dear Mr. Strafe:

As you may know, the readership of *Computer Entanglements* is one of the most sophisticated in the field of computer-society interface.

We would very much like to interview you as part of a feature we are planning on personality programming. We are particularly interested in your views on the effects of such programming on the people who use it.

If you are happy to be interviewed or have any questions, please contact me at the above telephone number.

Yours faithfully,

Wilhelmina del Vaille

No answer. Another letter, sent registered post, gave him a time and a place to meet. It was outside an expensive Japanese restaurant in Knightsbridge. It took her two hours to travel to it, and though she wore her best dress, she felt drab and shabby standing outside it. The wealth in the nearby windows shocked her. There was a giant glass peacock being sold for thousands of pounds. Who would need such a thing? Where could they put it? What would they do when the kids broke it? She stood waiting until her feet went dead with cold. Eamon did not come. This did not surprise her. She knew, but she could not help herself.

Dear Eamon,

In a way, I carry your baby. The man who gave it to me reminded me of you. It's a boy and I gave him your name. I know you are married now, but I still think I could have your baby. I know where it should be conceived. It should be conceived on a mountain top in Ireland, looking over a forest. It would be summer, and we could go swimming in the lake. Like in your song.

You see, I believe in you, Eamon. I know you mean the things you sometimes sing about. The words touch me. It's as though I'd thought of them myself only I never quite got them down on paper. It's as though your words are ghosts of my own, ghost words that always escape just ahead of me.

I wish I could see that mountain. I am terribly afraid that you might be the only man who could take me there.

Love,

Billie

Seventy-five letters.

The postage alone came to nearly forty pounds. It made the CD look like a bargain. She was going to have to think of something new.

So what do you know, Billie? You've got a computer that knows company law backwards, and can broadcast into most business records. You know something about how to use it.

Years before, she had tried to set up a pottery business, and things kept going wrong with the tax, or when someone checked her credit. She had tried to call it Folio Crafts, after Shakespeare, and so she had tried to register it as Folio at Company House, with her name as sole proprietor. But somewhere, something went wrong.

Someone had keyed her into the National Business Register as

Polio Crafts. A simple substitution of a P for an F. Maybe they thought it was some sort of charity for the paralyzed. Billie lost a commission because someone did a business check on her and pronounced her nonexistent. So Billie had to do research in the archives to find her own company. I know how to do all that, Billie remembered.

Billie got out all her old CDs. They were about the only thing she had brought with her from home. She read the fine print, particularly fine on the palm-sized jewelbox cases. Released through Sony International, a Memison Production, for Spirit Management. All songs by Eamon Strafe through Songfeast International, courtesy of Haskell Inc.

Of course, you were just a simple Irish monk, right?

Billie could not afford Dun and Bradstreet. She went through the Financial Times Profiles. They only listed Haskell Inc., which had two related companies, one in the UK and Haskell NV in the Netherlands. When she looked it up, through Profiles' foreign database, NV turned out to be part-owned by a huge Dutch electronics firm. There was also Haskell Arts Ltd, the UK subsidiary of NV. None of the business descriptions made any sense. NV called itself a hardware developer, but appeared to neither sell designs nor manufacture machinery. The UK company specialized in something called, with great vagueness, multimedia applications.

Dead End.

She was trying to find a company, small enough, just an office, where Eamon Strafe himself was likely to turn up.

She had the computer look through the entire UK telephone directory. No Songfeast International. No Spirit Management.

Suppose there was someone who was trying to find Polio Crafts. It was not in the telephone book, but it would, must be registered.

A search of the NBR would cost £100.00. And if the companies were not registered in the UK? A search of EC registries would be possible but for even more money.

Billie knew that there was this thing called hacking. She had no idea how it worked, except that phone lines could be accessed for free. She knew that codes were mathematically generated, until one was found that worked. The instant she asked the self-programmer to come up with something that would do that, a message came up.

THAT FUNCTION DISALLOWED
For everyone's sake—avoid electronic intrusion.

No wonder everyone wants you to buy a self-programmer. Something told her: take out the transceiver. Just in case it tells anyone. She pulled out the card, and felt relief. Her machine was no longer in touch with the Eamon Strafe network. It would now know nothing about her, or she about it.

Joey was home for the school holidays. Billie and he got on a bus to a public library. There were ten left for all eight million inhabitants of London. The nearest was in Holborn, in the old Daily Mirror building. The bus ride lasted 45 minutes. Joey liked to pretend he was big enough to travel on his own, and liked to sit two or three seats away on the bus, turning around in the seat, grinning, kicking his heels. His face was beautiful, very pink, with an orange tint, carrot hair, huge blue eyes. Children were beautiful. What happened to the adults? Billie could not relax, all through the long ride; children needed to be guarded, locked in, supervised.

The library allowed no adults into the children's reading room. "Nobody gets in?" asked Billie, anxiously, making sure.

The room had Disney videos, to keep the children quiet, assuming that books bored them. Joey sat down to watch, on a blue bubble chair, away from the other children. He did not look behind him, at her.

Spirit Management was registered in Bonn, of all places. It had a series of subsidiaries, registered throughout the EC. Hush Hush Services, Desperate Dan Butch cosmetics—that was part of the Empire as well? Wait for it. The cosmetic company partly owned Songfeast International, a music publishing business that seemed only to deal with Eamon Strafe. Eamon Strafe had started out in male cosmetics? And Songfeast was partly owned by something new—Haskell Holdings.

It was quite an education. The companies kept interlocking.

Completely different types of businesses turned out to have the same address. Gradually, however, it all seemed to narrow down to Haskell Holdings and Spirit Management. Billie made a family tree on her kitchen table. It looked like this.

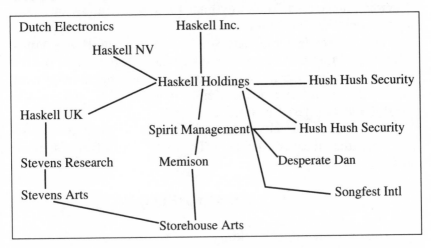

Imagine all those people, all those directors, sitting on each other's companies, all owning each other. Are you really in there, Eamon? Does it take all those suits to make one free man? And where does that leave the rest of us?

She and Joey sat looking at it together. He drew on it, squiggles in crayon, and she found the splash of color a relief. Something bothered her. These days, it was supposed to be cheaper for companies to have all their work done by freelancers. No sick pay, no pensions. Just like Billie, really. The newspapers were full of the Death of Corporate Man, but here he was, back again.

"Is it a computer game?" Joey asked.

"Yes," she answered him.

"What are you going to do?"

"Give one of them a call," she replied.

She worked late into the night, when Joey was asleep. She interrogated the CD, at second hand. "Scan CD memory, do not call up simulation program," she asked it.

RECORDS SHOW NO MEMORY OF BUSINESS DEALINGS

"Paste and copy any application material," she told it. Part of Eamon, the part that knew anything about record companies, was copied onto her hard disk.

Then, she made her choice. She chose Memison. It was named after one of Eamon's songs, and it was the only name that did not appear to be another kind of business—publishing, management, market research, electronics. Memison appeared to make music. And it was registered in Ireland.

Without her transceiver, she had to use the modem. She took a deep breath and called Memison. The first message from Memison was:

PLEASE SAY HELLO.

"Hello," said Billie. Nothing.

PLEASE LEAVE MESSAGE.

Billie did not want to leave a message. She wanted to reach Eamon. She wanted to find out, really, where he was. She needed access to the system.

ENTER PASSWORD.

That was it, then, stymied again. Billie looked at the screen. If she left a message now, would they be able to trace that she'd tried to penetrate their system? Log off, Billie.

Then, an interception from her own machine.

PLEASE HOLD. ENDEAVORING TO ENTER PASSWORD.

What? thought Billie. It's supposed to be blocked from doing that, we're all supposed to be blocked. Different combinations of letters rattled past on the screen. She caught some of them. *Stevens, spirit, sea, strafe* . . .

Her computer had overridden itself, somehow: *songfeast, songfish* . . .

Eamon, thought Billie. I put him in the systems folder. Eamon is doing this. My Eamon, she thought, as opposed to theirs.

A flurry of numbers blizzarded past in another window. Suddenly the screen blinked, and they were all gone.

SYSTEM ACCESS GRANTED.

A range of folders came up. SIM 1, SIM 2. She copied them onto her own disk, quickly. FUTURES, said one.

The file names were DIRECTIONS. TITLES. EAMON.

She opened EAMON, and it was full of code. And her own machine intervened with a message.

BILLIE, LOVE. GET OUT NOW.

This is the real one, she thought, this is the real Eamon.

I MEAN IT. THEY KNOW WE'RE HERE.

Panic fluttered only very briefly, then certainty seized her.

"Copy from Directory E MALE file Letter 76. Then log off," she said.

Up came a window, a directory, a ghost dance as files darkened and opened themselves like lovers, more completely than lovers could.

Then, darkness, plunged from light, from a place where intelligence pirouetted in metaphoric forms, into a void. Billie's hand shook, as it darted behind the machine, and pulled out the modem jack.

Did we make it?

"Restart," she said.

Ping, sang the machine.

She didn't know how to ask if they had been detected. She opened up her directory the old-fashioned way. The Memison files she had tried to save were not there. Had they been wiped, Billie wondered. By the speed of their exit? Or by Eamon? Talk about the ghost in the machine.

"What was the password?" she asked. Numbers came up: 5 1 13 15 14. The letters of Eamon's name in their numerical order of the alphabet. "Save," she told the machine, told herself.

She opened up E MALE, E for Eamon, and read the letter she had posted.

Eamon

I am nothing to you, less than air, not even a whisper, and yet my life is built around you. I see your picture, and my heart goes into my mouth, and stays there until I want to tear my heart out. You are my heart, Eamon. Does that mean I want to tear you out? Sometimes I think it does. If I could tear you out, Eamon, all of this could stop.

Do you know how humiliating it is? You see, I know, Eamon. The newspapers, the companies, the videos, the men in suits, they do it to us deliberately. They show us men like you, and what are we to do in our heart of hearts, in this drab world, but love you? And the less of you we get, the more we want. In a real world, Eamon, I would have had you or been turned down. Whatever happened, I would have gotten used to it by now. It would become ordinary. I might even have grown bored with you. That cannot happen. The first full flush of love is always on me, Eamon. The love has nowhere to go.

I don't buy your books or records anymore. I can't bear to. You have grown so far away. The software copies decay and turn into someone else. I want to see you, Eamon, for real. I want to see that you are middle-aged, pockmarked, a bit odd. Nothing else will do. I'm so tired of being pandered to.

They do it to us deliberately. They addict us to you. Can you stop them doing that? Please?

Love,

Billie.

Her real name was Wilhelmina, her mother was German. It was OK that her name was on their files. She would be as hard to trace, in her own way, as Eamon Strafe, as Polio.

Three days later there was a headline in her newspaper.
It stilled her heart, even before she had read it.

RECLUSE STRAFE TO TOUR
Generation of fans in shock.

An answer. It had to be an answer. She had spoken to Eamon, and he had heard. She felt joy, then dismay. She had no idea how to get a ticket; it had been ten years since she had bought a ticket for anything. She could see herself, on that night, with no ticket, circling the blank walls of Wembley, calling Eamon's name like a jealous wife. Eamon! It was me, I was the one who wrote you!
She rang the Arena. Busy. Busy. She took a taxi instead, to Leyton, tube to Oxford Circus, change onto the Bakerloo Line. Huddling in her thin coat, she walked to the Arena. She had expected thousands of people to be in line, but the place was as bleak as the surface of the moon. The parking lot was nearly empty and light rain lay on her coatsleeves like bits of broken glass.
The box office was open. She simply bought a ticket, a ticket for one. "First come, first served," said the young man behind the counter and shrugged. "No telephone or agency bookings."
"Eamon did that, didn't he?" whispered Billie.

"I suppose," he said. He was not in love with Eamon Strafe. "You're in luck." He frowned slightly when she paid cash. Cash made people untraceable. Billie turned, and there was sunlight, bleary and silver, out from under a shelf of cloud.

There was a story she had read once, about a piece of paper on which magic runes were written. The paper blew away by itself, and those it escaped from were cursed. You had to hold onto it, and then give it back. Billie wrapped the ticket round and round her finger, as if it had a life of its own, and could wriggle free. It had cost so much money.

She thought of Joey's shoes. Joey needed new shoes. They would have cost the price of the ticket. If I was rich, she thought, I'd buy him shoes, and a ticket. I'd have a car I could drive here. I'd have tutors for Joey, so he would read and do math. He'd have a computer of his own, full of art galleries and animation. Such thoughts made her feel unworthy, so she made herself walk home from Leyton, to save money.

Joey was at school. She closed her bedroom door anyway, and the blinds, and for the first time in months, loaded the CD.

TRANSCEIVER FAILURE, said the screen.
LOADING BACKUP

"Thank you," she told Eamon.

Eamon was in Japan, where he had been two months before when she took out the transceiver. He was sitting on stone steps. "Did I do anything?" he asked.

"Part of you did. We left a letter to Eamon on a file. And, now he's going on tour."

He looked confused for a moment. "You took out the card?" He paused, considering. "That was pretty smart. I'd leave it out for a while."

"What does that mean?" she asked him.

He chortled. "It means I'll be in Japan for a long, long time."

There was a little Japanese boy in blue shorts, sitting beside him on the steps. Behind them both was a red plaque with gold lettering embedded in the stone.

"Shame you're not going to be at your own concert," she said.
Eamon had something the little boy wanted, something Billie
could not quite see. It caught the light and was made of gold. It
might have been a key. The boy lunged forward and wrestled him
for it, giggling. Eamon grinned suddenly, widely, a grin that could
illumine the world. "I'll be happy enough here," he said. He
relented, and gave whatever it was to the little boy, who shrieked
with delight and ran away. The boy wore new shoes.

"I don't know anything about myself, do I?" he said, looking
back at her. He looked worn, older. "I don't know much about the
business. I don't know where all the money comes from, where all
the money goes. Eamon, he does, I'm sure. That means I'm not at
all like Eamon, really."

"No," sighed Billie. "You're probably nicer than he is."

The little boy came back, riding a red bicycle, beaming, his eyes
in hooded slits. Eamon murmured something to him in Japanese.
The boy appeared to ignore him. But he kept pedaling, round and
round Eamon Strafe.

"How long was I . . . inactive?" he asked.

"Let's see. I had you off for about six months."

"Ah. Did I start to repeat myself then?"

"No, not once."

He looked about himself. "This temple," he said, "is made of
wood imported from Korea. It is torn down and rebuilt every
thirteen years. But it is still the same temple as was built in the
fourteenth century. It is the same temple in spirit. New and old at
the same time."

Billie had never been to Japan. "I'd like to see inside it," she
said.

The flesh on his face went slack, and his smile was edged.
"Maybe they loaded enough data for you to do that. Look, Billie.
Do you mind? I want to be on my own for a bit."

"Fine," she said. He stood up and walked off the screen. She
didn't know he could do that. Did he still have a digital existence?
Was the machine still programming actions for him? From somewhere came the sound of feet on gravel, of air moving, of children
playing, of birds.

She was about to exit, when the little Japanese boy came up to the steps, crying and looking for Eamon. You and me both, kid, thought Billie. The red tricycle went past, pedaled furiously by an older, fatter child. The tricycle had been commandered.

So who is making this up? she wondered. Me? The computer? How far outside of this park could I walk? Do they have all of Kyoto in this thing?

Then she heard Eamon's voice very dimly off-screen. The little boy walked off toward it, off-screen. She heard the boy complain, miserably. There were still birds singing unseen in the bushes. Billie wanted to see them.

In the corner of the monitor, the unblinking eye glowered at her, dull gray, absorbent.

"Put me there," whispered Billie.

She saw herself walk onto the screen, wearing traditional Japanese dress. Yes, that's what I'd wear, she thought, ruefully. I'd keep looking for the old Japan until I found it. She wore green and white silk with something like chopsticks in her hair. Oh, Billie, you fool. Her hair was glossy black, her skin sallow, but she decided it suited her. She was surprised by how much she liked herself. There was something direct and wiry in the way she moved that she had not expected. She was thin, yes, but not delicate. If I saw myself, she thought, I'd say, "That looks like a nice girl."

Billie on the screen sat down on the stone steps, and waited. Sun came and went, filtered by passing clouds, and the light reflected on the gold embroidery. Billie on the screen looked up directly at herself.

"It's nicer here," Billie heard herself say in her own voice. The little boy crunched his way across the gravel to her, and held up a pink and white fish cake.

"Thank you," said Billie on the screen to the boy. She took a bite from the cake, and then offered it back to him.

Don't do that, what about your germs, thought Billie, and then remembered. There are no germs there.

Eamon walked back on screen.

"Feel better now?" asked the copy of Billie.

"Yes, thanks," he said. She stood up, and he kissed her on the cheek.

"Want to see the temple?" Eamon asked.

So they walked hand in hand on stone pathways set like islands in gravel seas. The supports and boards of the roof of the temple made considered patterns. The wood was raw, clean. Billie saw herself stroke it. Light shone in the paper walls, dappled where the paper was slightly thicker. Only a wooden statue of the Buddha was old, deeply creased, with deep cracks across his face. The eyes were ancient, gleaming, creased with a smile.

"Are we going back to a hotel?" Billie on the screen asked, with a tremor of shyness.

"I'm staying here," said Eamon, surprised. "Didn't I tell you?"

There was a path down from the temple, through cherry trees, now just past blossom. White, decaying bloom still littered the ground. The rooms of the monks were in a terrace, like a motel. Inside the rooms were bare—a bed, a basin, a parchment on the wall with calligraphic signs. One window, high, just under the ceiling. Billie flung her arms around Eamon, held him.

"Can we?" she asked. "Here?"

He laughed, and kissed the tip of her nose. He began to wrestle himself out of his shirt. In her own bedroom, Billie saw his back, pale, slightly freckled, broad at the shoulders, but skinny at the arms. Eamon loosened the kimono, and it fell away from the other Billie, and she saw her own body as the computer must have seen it, night after night, still young, still beautiful even with the creases about the belly. She lay down on the bed. Outside, drifting on the wind, was the sound of a radio, some Japanese pop song, very distant. Eamon slipped out of his trousers. He had a washboard tummy and slightly too much chestnut hair. Like himself, his penis was both beautiful and ugly. He stood over Billie for a moment, smiling.

"Thank you for being here," he said, then very gently lowered himself on top of her.

Impassive, on another bed, in a room that smelled of sweat and cabbage and diesel, Billie watched and wondered what it meant that she watched. Round and round on her fingers, she still turned the poisoned paper.

What were six weeks in her life?

Joey went back to school and got into trouble. He got in trouble for being too quiet. "He just doesn't socialize," said his teacher. What could Billie do about that? "He stays indoors all the time," she explained. "I can't really let him out; it's not safe where we live."

There was a spate of burglaries, and the Association could not afford the insurance.

"If you lived in a better area," she was told, "the premiums would be less."

"Rich people pay less insurance?" She was appalled.

"For goods of the same value, yes," said the salesman. "They're less likely to be burgled."

Billie remembered sleeping rough. She knew how it felt. There were homeless people nearby, sleeping under railway bridges. She paid them to keep watch on the Association by day, by forsaken night.

"You're just bribing them to stop thieving," said the woman who had stolen Billie's key. Then the homeless caught a burglar, just a kid. Relations between the two communities improved.

"Not bad," Billie boasted to Eamon, but he was less interested in the Association now. He and the other Billie walked around and around the Temple, the cherry trees, the monks, the gravel gardens. The little boy always waited for them while the same tourists took snapshots. The weather never changed, and the sound of doves fluttering upward in a flock was always the same.

"You really aren't alive, are you?" Billie said to them both.

"No," said Eamon, not surprised anymore that she found it difficult to accept. "Would Heaven be much different from this?"

Billie had made Eamon, her Eamon, happy. What was there for her? The concert, just the concert. Perhaps something would happen at the concert, and then she would be free. She would see the real Eamon Strafe, and either she would be disappointed, and that would end it, or he would be as wonderful as she sometimes imagined. That, also, would be answer enough.

It was a beautiful September, but life was gray from waiting, as she sat in her kitchen/dinette, hands under her armpits. Joey was a shadow to her. She ate when Joey ate—otherwise she might have forgotten to eat altogether. She planned what she would wear to the show, as if it would make any difference to Eamon.

She decided in the end to dress to avoid being mugged—a gray jumpsuit with a small, dripped coffee stain on the thigh. After all, who was she going to see to impress? She would have to come home on the trains at night. A taxi was beyond question. She put a big kitchen knife in her purse. The poison paper had finally been sealed in an envelope to prevent her winding fingers destroying it all together. The envelope was now in her purse, and she hugged her purse to herself with both arms.

Walking to the bus stop, sitting in the tube train, Billie coasted on automatic pilot, pulse racing, unable to think. The train passed the ruined civic spaces, the endless rows of back gardens and shrubbery.

A thousand people got off the train with her. It was like a pilgrimage. Billie looked at the faces. These were her people—the baffled and slightly blank faces, the librarians, typesetters, TV researchers, media secretaries, workers in bookshops, amateur potters—the fans of Eamon Strafe. It made her feel curiously elated to be with them again, as if they were all young, hanging out in Piccadilly, staying late till the clubs opened, and slipping off just as the clubs got going, to make the last train. Was Tora here? She should have rung Tora. Her mind, agitated, was stuck in a groove from one of Eamon's songs. Slaves, slaves, slaves to the rhythm, it sang, over and over.

All of them together flooded up the steps. Just inside the shell of the stadium was a concourse crammed like a street market, hawkers bellowing about hot dogs or fresh squeezed orange juice. The parent company of her health food shop had shown up with bean sprout sandwiches. In comradeship, Billie bounced up to them. "I work for Billing's Natural as well," she told them.

"Oh God, not you too. If I have a daughter, I'll tell her, never work in a health shop."

They commiserated and then, for something to do, some way to finish the conversation, Billie bought a slice of health food carob cake. She walked around the perimeter, trying to find gate M. When she found her seat, her good mood evaporated.

She had been ripped off. Of course she had been ripped off, the whole point was to rip her off. At a time when the bank manager was stopping her checks, she had paid thirty pounds for a supposedly good seat, and here she was—miles back and behind a pillar. There was a great slope of seating, and a further slope of temporary bleachers, and beyond that a flat plain of benches and finally, about the same size as her thumb, the stage. Billie was smiling.

Yes, yes, she thought, almost gleefully, they have to do this to us, to make us understand just how small we are. Yes, yes, yes, when we finally venture out of our little shells. She turned around and looked up at the banks of people behind her. Winkles, she thought, we're just little winkles prized out with pins. It was beginning to be fearsomely hot inside the Arena.

A family fought its way in to sit next to her, bearing thermos flasks of coffee and lemonade and unwrapping an entire, cooked chicken. The husband had a scraggly gray beard, and the wife seemed almost deliberately colorless. Their child, of indeterminate gender, was quiet and still, what is called well behaved.

"Good seats aren't they?" said Billie, bouncy with anger. "Really worth thirty quid."

"Oh, not too bad, actually," said the man.

"We're awfully lucky to get them," said the wife. "I really thought we wouldn't, and I couldn't bear to miss this."

The child was sucking the empty yellow cup from the thermos flask. Are you free? Billie wondered. Did you get away?

"Do you like Eamon, too?" Billie asked the child.

"Yeah," said the child, a boy, without enthusiasm, looking at his cup and not her.

"The whole family," said the father. "We're Eamon-mad.

We've got everything he's done, haven't we, Pat? We bought two copies of some of the disks. One each!"

So many of us, Billie thought. A woman in front of them had turned and was looking back at them. Billie recognized her forlorn expression. It was her own.

The little boy was finally given some lemonade.

Should I have brought Joey? I didn't even think to ask him. He must think that means I didn't want him to come. I didn't want him to come.

Do I love my son? It was a terrible question to ask. But there were worse questions, like, does my son love me? How could he? She found herself wondering if it were at all possible that her son could love her. I've put him into a little compartment, like the dishes. He'll grow up, he'll go away, he won't come back. My life is leaking away.

Because of Eamon Strafe.

A string quartet suddenly struck the spare metallic opening of "A Fish Dinner in Memison."

There was a kind of sigh, and a shushing, and a beehive flurry as people found their seats. The string quartet was live, on a separate stage, half a stadium away from where Eamon would appear. The speakers, behind a blue wall, were the size of small buildings and were swathed in black.

There were two huge blank screens either side of the main stage, and they came live in the same way her monitor at home did, loading the image from the top down.

And there he was smiling at all of them, Eamon Strafe.

There was a kind of roar, the lights dropped, the image on the screen walked off it, and then, on the stage, there he was, stepping into the light, instantly recognizable from half a mile away, tiny, blinding white, and Billie rose to her feet and the audience rose to its feet, in a deathly silence.

No cheers, no sound at all, silent wonder. It was him, it was Eamon.

The way Eamon walked was lonely. The walk said: there are

very few people like me. Becoming me has been a long fight, and there was no one to help. A walk could say that.

Billie couldn't see his face. She couldn't focus, he was a blur, lost in the glare of the lights. His clothes, his shoes were all a haze of light. Except on the screens. There he was, Eamon, rumpled, smiling, lopsided as always, and utterly familiar.

Without introduction, he began to sing.

Billie heard herself scream. It was a real scream, a relief of agony. She was the only one—you do not scream at an Eamon Strafe concert. You listen. You weep. She pushed the palm of her hand into her mouth, and forced herself to sit, and she bit down, and pain shot through her hand. She pulled her hand back, and looked at it.

The bite was deep and bloody, just under the thumb of her right hand.

Oh Billie, you stupid cow, what have you done now?

It was bleeding profusely, down her wrist, over the jumpsuit. The blood crept richly across the glossy white paper of her program book, beside a picture of Eamon.

She held up her hand and whispered to the family. "Do you have a handkerchief?"

They were extremely discomfited. They understood from the scream and its sequel that her sickness was seriously worse than their own. With the care that extends any noise and makes it worse, the wife sought in her bag for a Kleenex. The bag rattled, the plastic pack rustled. Overhead the waves of noise bashed into each other from two directions, source and echo. The music was made nonsense, the beat disrupted, the words lost. Billie pushed the Kleenex against the wound.

"Take the pack," whispered the wife.

Billie closed her eyes and found that the image of Eamon Strafe had been burned into her retina. There was a clear purple silhouette of him in her eyes with a glowing core of yellow. There was a silhouette of the bite in the nerves of her thumb.

She opened her eyes again, saw Eamon on a screen. That was all she was going to see. It was just like being at home. Eamon was not going to be ordinary or wonderful or different in any way from what he had always been. She felt like Alice, shrinking. One song finished, another began. What else did she expect? Fireworks? The music was vaguely familiar. It took a while for it to turn into "Democracy of Greed," the third single, from when he was young and strong, and people still thought he was going to be the last pop star. It got as high as number nine, and then began to slide down the charts, taking Eamon with it.

It wasn't Eamon's singing that she heard. It was the people around her, humming, a sound like bees, holding the music together. You're not performing, Eamon. We are.

> Democracy, democracy,
> Democracy of Greed
> for those who have ability
> from those who have the need

Her Eamon had been right. Her Eamon was as real as anything she was going to get from this. My hand is bleeding, she thought, and my seat is a rip-off. This isn't good enough, it isn't enough at all.

At first she only wanted to leave, escape her anger, go home. "Excuse me," she said to the college students to her right. She stood up, and walked in front of them. "Excuse me, excuse me." She stepped on people's feet, they tutted. Couldn't they see she was trying to get out? "Excuse me," like in those clubs when she was young, it was all she ever said to anyone. "Excuse me."

She pushed her way past them with the force of her whole life. She bled over them deliberately. It's a sign, she told them in her mind. It's what's happening to all of you. She broke free into an aisle, and thumped down the steps, only to be intercepted by a guard. Hush Hush said a badge on his shoulder.

"I've cut myself. Is there a first aid kit?" she asked him.

Oh God. "Basic Blue" was starting up. At least she would be spared that.

The guard was fat, older than he should be, and he nervously jingled keys in his pocket. He walked with her to gate M, made sure she exited, and told her to ask at the trailer by Gate A. She walked back along the marketplace. The girls at Billing's Natural were wiping the countertop, and talking, oblivious to the music drifting about them. By gate A, there was a white trailer. Inside it there was a tiny seating area for the guards. Face down on a table there was a magazine called *Four Wheel Drive Vehicles.* A sign on the wall said, SHOWERS. Another guard sat at a desk, and inside it was a blue box with bandages.

"How did you manage that?" the guard asked, cutting gauze.

"Slipped and fell," she said.

His eyes were heavy with meaning as he looked back into hers. "Don't understand this hysteria stuff," he said. He paused, then seemed to think better of saying anything further.

"Neither do I," whispered Billie. "Neither do I."

I'm going to get what I came for, she thought.

She stood by Gate A and looked at the defenses. The stage was in layers like a ziggurat, each step 10, 15 feet high. That was to keep them all away, and the wall as well, painted a sweet powder blue, cutting off all the backstage area, and in front of that, rows of waist-high barriers. Up and down the aisles, guards patrolled.

What are you frightened of, Eamon? Why don't you want us near you? You've taken enough from us. Beside her were bleachers, and she could see their innards above wood panels, a glimpse of shadowed scaffolding.

A guard came out from beyond the last row of defenses, walking beside the wall. He stopped in front of what Billie saw was a door in the wall. Billie walked forward, in front of the bleachers, to see him better. There was a black circle on the wall, and her eyes hauled it closer to her, and she saw the guard's hand dabbling over its surface—four strokes, five strokes—and a door in the wall opened.

Billie knew then how she was going to get to Eamon.

As she ran up the steps of the bleachers she could feel them shake slightly under foot, boards supported on temporary scaffolding. The seats were made of planks, meeting at right angles, sealing off the innards. But the steps consisted of a top board only. Underneath each step, there was a gap of about eight inches.

Billie had not been eating much lately. In truth, Billie was half-starved.

She glanced about her, people in darkness, light catching on teeth or spectacles or jewelry, or hair clips, or eyes, the rest of the face lost in darkness. All looking at the light below, watching it pirouette. No guards. Billie sat down on the steps, as if not finding her seat. She crouched low, looked one more time, and then she lay down flat on the step. She rolled onto her tummy, and felt the boards press clothes, flesh, the bones of her hip, her elbow. The bones were so close to the surface. She shifted sideways, and headfirst, pulled herself under the step. The boards were rough, slivers entered her thighs. The scaffolding and steps began to shake. Was someone coming up after her? Below was an eight foot drop to concrete, not too far; Billie grabbed hold of a cross support and pulled.

She swung out, her feet like lead weights, and she had to hold, even though the bite on her hand was torn wider. Her shins struck another pole, and she hissed and clenched and kicked, and found footing.

Gingerly, she slid her feet down a smooth diagonally supporting pole until she could stand on a right angle support. She wavered in place, nearly falling, and then sat down, and reached with her feet for the next, treacherously angled pole down. She did that once more, and was within jumping distance. Then she saw the flashlight beam.

It skittered like Tinker Bell in *Peter Pan,* under the steps, along the supports. You'll have to jump now, Billie. And without shaking the scaffolding.

She dropped down and her good hand struck a pole and went numb, and she landed in a heap. The floor was gray, her jumpsuit was gray, and she pulled her arms over her neck and face and went still. She saw the skittering light dance toward her, and pass over her and up into the network of poles.

Billie was now as invisible as a message down a telephone line.

She scampered, shaking with nerves, ducking down under poles, in nearly complete darkness. Only when she passed under an aisle did the gaps in the boards admit light, in slats overhead.

There were slashes of light, where rough boards failed to fit. And all the time, that voice came ghostly, filtering, as if singing in Japanese.

Billie came to the end of the bleachers and found them sealed with a barrier of wood panels bolted to supports that looked like something from a Mechano set. Overhead, at the top of the bleachers was the area that was not closed off.

Billie started to climb again, to the very apex of the bleachers, in the back. Billie looked out from it, as if from a gable window.

Eamon was talking, telling a story.

". . . so I was in the square, looking for the master. I figured I was the only Westerner there and that he would see me. . . ."

He was blinding bright here as well, and Billie saw why. He was lit, fiercely, from underneath. He must be standing over spotlights. The pyramid must be full of machinery.

The blue wall reached from the bleachers all the way to the gray first step of the pyramid and stuck to it like a wet lipstick kiss. Below her was a ten foot drop, and the silver fencing, and to the right, in the concrete, was a door. Someone could come through it at any moment. She herself could have come through it.

Her way was blocked by a crucifix of scaffolding. She sat backwards on it, lifted her feet, swung them around and out. No time to think, Billie, no need to look.

Her feet hung in space and she took all her weight on her hands, locking her elbows. She had thought she could lower herself further down from there, hang down with hands above her head. She did not know how to shift to that position without jarring; she doubted that she had the strength. She began to feel the tickle of fear in her belly, the fear that comes when you're stuck on a rock face or can't climb down from a tree. She didn't have time for that.

"The master, you see, thought I ought to come to him."

Here I come, Eamon. Billie pushed herself clear of the wall and let go.

Something seemed to clutch her insides, and with increasing force haul them upward. Something struck her head, something rang—a security fence—she fell slightly sideways, landing on calf, thigh, buttock, shoulder. She rolled, ending up with feet over her head.

Get up, Billie, get up, get up. She rocked herself to her feet. Her shoulder ached, her back would be dusty; she patted the back of her head for blood. There was blood. Or was that only from her hand? She began to walk, using arched fingers to comb her hair, brush it back over the wound, and she tried to rid her face of the squiffy, drunken look she knew she had around the eyes.

I am from Stevens Arts, she told herself. I'm here to check out the imaging on the screens. A guard stood in front of her, scanning the audience, hands on his hips. Billie saw the pouch of fat on the small of his back, straining against his shirt. As long as his back was toward her, she ran, lightly trotting, trying to look like a businesswoman who was late.

He glanced over his shoulder, she slowed, he turned, she nodded to him, smiling. The door was near now, and she fixed her gaze on the round black security panel. Were the keys digits or lettering?

The guard sauntered toward her, smiling and shaking his head. Digits, she saw, there were only ten of them. She had to get to the door first, and key in and key in right.

"I'm from Stevens," she called, and turned to the keys, and cooled her mind. If she failed, she would shrug, smile, say, well it was worth a try.

5 1 13 15 14. EAMON in code.

The door clicked, and seemed to sigh. Gotcha!

Billie nodded again to the guard; nodding to him was good, it meant she faced him and he couldn't see the dust on her back, the blood on her head.

The guard's smile became one of relief, chagrin. He waved her in.

Billie slipped sideways through the door still facing the guard, closed the door, and turned around.

She was surprised by something. Dark and shadow. There were trailers on the backstage area, also in shadow, and thick cables underfoot. She was too preoccupied by fear to have said precisely what was missing, what was wrong. On the steps of one of the trailers, a man was hunched over a cellphone. She heard Donald-Duck squawking, she saw a ponytail, she ran, footfall cushioned, hobbled, by rubber cable underfoot. Too late to worry about 20,000 volts now, Billie. She ran for the shelter of the giant speaker; she saw its scaffolding support was wrapped in cloth, loose cloth this side. Dark and speed and silence were all she had. She began to shake, made the shelter of the cloth, enfolded herself in its edges.

Finally, she was able to breathe, and to hear the sound booming muffled overhead. Eamon began to sing, and there was a roar of approval when the audience recognized the song.

> *The music gets louder*
> *And the beat gets faster*
> *And the man who calls the tune*
> *Becomes your lord and master.*
> *And between him and you*
> *There grows such a schism*
> *That the only word for it is*
> *Sadomasochism.*

And people were cheering? He's telling you what he's doing to you, to all of us. Maybe that's how they do it. They tell us the truth, just enough to make us feel better. Open the door, and then slam it shut on our fingers.

She peered out from her folds of cloth, and it seemed as though her trembling breath ought to be forming white vapor from cold. A great blank stretch of concrete, dusty, a chocolate bar wrapper.

Where were the people? Where were the tables with food, the deck chairs, the crowding of family, friends, record company execs, liggers with no real business? Where was the man with the cellphone? From the screens, from somewhere, there came a strange blue-white light. It played over everything, flickering. It seemed to flow along the concrete like ground mist.

And Billie looked at the giant stage, and there were no steps, no ladders, no lift, no way up, even from the back. How did Eamon get there? Fly? Between her and the stage were the giant screens, supported by scaffolding, scaffolding her new friend.

She ran again. A curtain of giant cables hung down behind the screen; they must be insulated, just push. Billie ducked behind a screen of thick rubber, and crouched.

Above her was the scaffolding and beside her the gray wall of the stage. Billie began to climb. You thought you were untouchable, Mr. Strafe. You really thought no one reached you. Well, I will. And I will show you, Eamon Strafe, that you are not my lord and master.

Halfway up, a megaphone voice said, "Please, young lady. Come down."

"Go to hell!" she shouted.

It was harder going up scaffolding than coming down. She had to lie on the diagonals and shimmy up them, then twist herself around. She saw ladders being carried down below, through the strange thick light.

She came to wooden planks, a platform, and a ladder, going up to the works behind the screen. She scuttled up the ladder, onto another platform. This one did not shake as she ran. The last level of the ziggurat lay below her, and to her right, a drop of about her own height, across a gap of some yards. She had time to see the surface of the stage was black, glass perhaps or formica, but glistening with flakes of gold, or light.

"Don't! Please!" called a voice behind.

Here goes, Eamon, thought Billie, and flung herself into the air. She flung herself into the viscous light, and became aware in a moment that it was different from any light she had known. It made her skin buzz, and where she blocked it, the shadows moved across each other in different planes, like the lights of passing trucks on her bedroom wall at night. Where the planes of light met and crossed, there was a flaring of rainbow color.

And overhead, stars seemed to reach up into infinity, dwindling to nothingness. But the stars were in serried ranks, orderly in planes of light.

And the light was so solid, it was for an instant as though it were impeding her progress, as though she had leapt through water. She remembered the lake in childhood. She remembered her parents. And suddenly she was lying in a crumpled heap on the stage, looking down.

At a kind of glass, dark as though smoked, but in layers somehow, translucent, and shifting. And the stars were there too, going down forever, through the floor of the stadium, through the earth itself, and in their midst there seemed to be twin suns blazing up at her.

Don't look! something told her, and she looked away, and everything was dark, and she stumbled; her ankle was twisted. She was blind, her skin sore as though sunburned, and she turned toward Eamon, and she heard footsteps behind her, and through the smoke of her blindness, she saw Eamon, made of light, like an angel, blazing with inner fire. He did not know she was there.

And the weight of the world seemed to slam into her, bringing her down, and it was not just the weight of the arms that hugged her knees and the body that tackled her to the stage. Don't! Look! Down! Something in her mind screamed at her, knowing that a second time, she would go blind forever. Instead she looked up.

Looked up at Eamon Strafe. He was singing.

A voice like mist
hits like a fist
and then it's gone.

Eamon Strafe was translucent, and motes of dust swam through him glinting like galaxies. There was nothing in his eyes, in his mouth. They were shadows, dark inside, with scaffolding, staging, showing through them. He was checkerboard, little defined mosaics of color, and all through his hair, teeth, tongue, eyes, clothes, dust moved in a sluggish current. And Billie knew if her hand reached out to touch him, it would pass through.

Billie was hoisted to her feet, swung around, taken by the arms, and dragged, her feet sliding on the surface of the stage, slightly greasy. She ran to catch up, took her own weight, even on the damaged ankle, hobbled to keep up with them. The guards pulled her back toward the screen. When she tried to look behind her, one of them took the top of her head in his hand, and turned it back around.

Hush Hush said their sleeves, and they wore thick protective dress, and mirror visors. Billie had never thought so quickly.

"I saw him," she lied. "I saw Eamon! Isn't he beautiful!"

The guards said nothing. Below them was spread the unused part of the stadium. Light flickered over rows of deserted seats, invisible people listening to ghost music. This is the future, Billie thought, this is what it will be like.

There were ladders now.

"OK, climb down. If you fall, we are not responsible, all right."

"Yeah, sure," said Billie, trying to sound thick.

On the ground, two men were waiting. One was tall, with a ponytail and an ear stud.

"Are you OK?" he asked. He came forward, took her wrist. "Can you see all right? Does that hurt." Gently, he moved his hand along her wrist. It stung. The skin was lobster pink. "Ouch!" she yelped. "I'm just back from Ibiza," she said. "I got a bit too much sun."

The two men glanced at each other nervously. "You saw Eamon, did you?" the other man asked. He was short, with a neck thicker than his head, and he wore a white shirt and tie. His voice was darker. What would he do to protect an investment?

She had to get away, get away before that other guard could come and say: but she knew the password. She got in through the door.

"Oh, yes, he's even more beautiful than I thought he would be." Sixteen. Billie remembered being sixteen. She found the sixteen-year-old was still there, to wonder at things and be hurt by them.

"I don't mind anything now. I've seen him!" She managed to hop up and down. "At last, at last, at last. Do you know him? Do you get to talk to him?" She found she was weeping.

"We talk to him, yeah," said the earring, and he looked just the slightest bit wistful. "He's a really nice guy."

"Did you see anything else?" asked the white shirt.

"I couldn't see anything but Eamon!" she said, her voice clogging with mucus and tears.

The two looked at each other. Roadies, she thought, they used to be roadies for a band and got a big idea.

"If you've got a ticket," said the ear stud, "you can go back to your seat."

Billie reached for her purse. "I've lost it!" she cried in a dismay that was only partly feigned. "It's gone!"

"Then I'm afraid, love," said the white shirt, "we're going to have to throw you out."

"Oh no, please!" she wailed. It was just what she wanted.

They asked for her name. Any ID? Sure, the Association's card, which gave her name as Wilhelmina. A door was opened in a gate big enough to drive lorries through, just as the image of Eamon Strafe stopped singing about mist and Spirit.

The door closed. Billie was outside.

There was a light rain. London looks best at night. The asphalt, the paving stones all reflect the orange street lights, and the drops on cars and windows glow like little jewels.

Billie began to laugh.

She laughed out of sheer nerves. She laughed at the way she had fooled the guards. She spun on her heel and kicked a bottle. Hot damn, what had she done? Played Tarzan on scaffolding, fooled the guards, and found the truth.

Eamon Strafe did not exist. He probably never had. All that love, all that listening, it was for nothing? Laughter and terror bubbled up inside her.

After all, he was the perfect pop star. Always distant, always perfect, nipping in and out of view, aging beautifully. All those people! Buying disks and tickets and software, and all those women melting at the thought of him, we've all been idiots, dupes. What a joke.

Oh, this is an evil place, a rotten place, scheming, scheming, to get at your loot. I know you, Billie said to the street lights, the closed-up shops, I know what all of you are, small and mean or big and grand, and, you know? You don't scare me at all.

I'm free of you, Eamon! You great big blouse! You empty set of knocker thumpers! You great big cardboard box full of fart. You were made up.

She found she was jumping up and down through a mud puddle like a kid. She laughed again and saw in the dark water a reflection, her face, translucent like Eamon's. That stirred something in her, and she broke the image apart with her foot, but not before she saw there were blisters on her face, like raindrops on the hoods of cars. Whatever it was, she had now what she had come for. Whatever it was, she had better get moving out of here.

It was a long ride home, and fear and elation went stale. Billie watched the blackness of the underground walls pass by in a rattling smear, and she asked herself, what now? I'm twenty-seven years old. I have some skills. Scaffold climbing among them. I have the Association, and I like the people in it. And I have my son. She made up her mind what she was going to do when she got home.

After the tube ride, there was the bus. A drunk got on, reeking and singing harshly, and, oh God, he was singing one of Eamon's songs. See where it got you, mate? The man looked fifty, and Billie couldn't tell if it was dirt or hard living that made his skin so dark and blotchy. "Life could be good," he roared. It seemed to make him feel better.

You play a crying baby a tape of its own weeping, and it is soothed. That's all you did, Eamon. You played it back to us. The music came from us, not you.

In the dark of her flat, Billie found a note from the babysitter. It said that Joey was asleep, so would Billie mind if she left? Bloody hell, thought Billie, the point was to have someone here WHILE he slept. OK, she thought, but I won't pay you.

Billie gently pushed open his door, and smelled him, and heard his soft child's breath. He was growing up a stranger. She did not know what he thought or felt. There was a bursting of love and regret in her, as if she had bitten into a bitter fruit. It made her angry at Eamon Strafe all over again. Billie knelt next to the bed and stroked her son's brown and slightly greasy hair.

"Joey," she whispered. "I'm sorry."

He groaned and rolled over.

"I'll be a better Mum, I promise. We'll do something fun on Saturday."

He lay inert and unresponsive.

"I'm sorry life isn't beautiful." She meant she was sorry that she had not made it beautiful for him.

"I'm asleep," he said, pouting, angry.

"You know I love you, don't you?"

There was no answer. Billie was used to that.

She kissed him and went back to her bedroom, her own little world, the bed, the posters, the boots and panties on the floor, and the machine. She turned it on.

"Hello," she said, darkening, full of strength.

The image unfurled down her screen from the top down. Eamon was in his dressing room, ebullient, full of joy, happy to see her. "Billie!" he exclaimed, hopping out of his chair. "Hello, love, it's great to see you!" He looked tanned and worn in his crumpled white suit. It had a stain on the thigh.

This was her Eamon. Pity, useless pity, moved her.

"Did you enjoy the show?" he asked. Outside his dressing room, the audience was still rhythmically thumping, demanding more.

Billie considered her answer. "I learned a lot," she said. She sat down on the bed and faced him. "I got up on stage tonight. I saw Eamon up close, I stood right next to him. He doesn't exist. He's some kind of hologram."

"What?" This Eamon made a kind of nervous chuckle.

"I think it means there has never been an Eamon Strafe. I think he's been a construct from the beginning."

"There's photographs of me in the papers!"

"Yes, photographs of *you*. You don't exist, either."

"Oh, come on, Billie, I'm full of his memories!"

"Do they add up to a life?" Billie asked. "His life?"

She had killed him. The picture froze, the sound of cheering stopped, his face was still. Billie could hear the hard disk whirring to itself, trying to consult, trying to find a model response. It was suddenly terrible sitting alone in a bedroom with a frozen screen and the sound of rain.

"Could you bring Billie on, please?" she asked.

The screen snapped back into life, and Billie came in wearing black trousers, silver studded, and a black jacket, and a diamond bracelet. Billie, as she might have been if she had money and power and had done what she wanted to. Or was she?

"Is it true?" Eamon asked this other Billie.

And this Billie nodded: yes. And Billie on the screen said simply, "Think of it this way. It means you are the real Eamon. You always were." And she glanced, just once, out at the tiny bedroom, the unmade bed, the other Billie in the stained jumpsuit. What was she thinking? I'm doing your job for you? Which one of us has the better life? Was she thinking anything at all?

The Billie on the bed said, "I want the two of you to go for a walk, wherever you want to go. Don't take me with you, I don't want to be there. Just go there, now, to Ireland maybe."

"Japan," said the other Billie. Billie was almost touched, until she remembered that the temple and the park was the failsafe locale.

A single perfect tear slid down Eamon's cheek, leaving a trail behind like a snail. In its perfect depths, upside down, was a reflection of the real Billie. A calculation of the light.

"Come on, love," said the other Billie and tapped his shoulder, to go. For some reason, Billie did not want to see them leave the dressing room.

Billie went to make herself a cup of tea. It would be lonely now without a kindly voice to tell her that she deserved it. She thought of her mother, the house in South End, school, Joey's father, her memories. Did they add up to a life?

When she went back into the bedroom, the screen showed Eamon's empty dressing room. On the table top there were the face powder and the mild-colored lipsticks. Desperate Dan Butch Cosmetics. A sweaty white suit hung on a peg. The murmuring of the crowd had faded away. It was silent now, except for the sound of someone sweeping outside. The shadow of a broom slid along the crack of light underneath the door.

Billie reinserted the transceiver card.

"Broadcast down the transceiver network," Billie told her machine. "Tell them all that Eamon is a digital construct. Tell them all that there is no Eamon. Don't say how you know. Try to disguise where the message entered the system. Do not reveal the source of information."

PROCESSING INSTRUCTIONS said a message on the screen, with a little moving clock.

"Locate where Eamon and Billie are in the system now, and save it as a separate file. As long as you operate, keep the file active, but security block it. Never open it, even if I ask you to." Did it understand? "Ice it."

Heaven, where nothing ever happens.

"OK, log off," she said. She slid the CD out of its player, and saw Eamon's picture printed on it, and that's when she began to weep. Water leaked into her mouth tasting of salt. Tears of rage, pity, joy—take your pick, at least you know you're alive. She knew then that Eamon, her Eamon, would always be with her, inside. There were words flickering on the screen. Like all of us, the machine wanted its actions to be authorized.

PLEASE SAY GOODBYE, it asked.

Billie found that she couldn't.

O HAPPY DAY!

They're fooled by history. They think they won't be killed until they get into camps. So when we load them onto a different train, they go willingly. They see an old country railroad station with a big red hill behind it, and they think it's just a stop along the way.

They slip down from the cars and can't keep their feet on the sharp-edged rubble of the track. They're all on testosterone specifics, a really massive dose. They're passive and confused, and their skin has a yellow taint to it, and their eyes stare out of patches of darkness, and they need a shave. They smell. They look like a trainload of derelicts. It must be easier to kill people who look like that, easier to call them Stiffs, as if they were already dead.

We're probably on specifics, too, but a very mild dose. We have to work, after all.

We load the Stiffs into cars, the Cars with the special features, and the second train goes off, and ten minutes later it comes back, and we unload them, dead, and that is life under what we call the Grils.

We are the Boys. We get up each morning and we shave. We're male, so we shave. Some of us do our make-up then, a bit of lipstick and slap, and an earring maybe. Big Lou always wore an earring and a tight short-sleeved T-shirt that showed off his arms. It was very strange, all those muscles with his pudding basin haircut and hatchet face, all pressed and prim around the lips.

Big Lou thought what was happening was good. I remember

him explaining it to me my first day, the day he recruited me. "Men are violent," he said. "All through history, you look at violence, and it's male. That was OK in the jungle, but not now, with the gangs and the bombs and everything else. What is happening here is simple evolutionary necessity. It's the most liberating event in human history. And we're part of it." Then he kissed me. It was a political kiss, wet and cold. Then he introduced me to the work.

After we unload the trains, we strip the corpses. There are still shortages, so we tie up the clothes in bundles and save everything else of value—money, watches, cigarette lighters—and send them back on the train. It would be a terrible job for anyone, but it's worse for a faggot. Most of the bodies are young. You feel tender toward them. You want them to wake up again and move, and you think, surely there must be something better to do with this young brown body than kill it? We work very quickly, like ants on a hill.

I don't think we're mad. I think the work has become normal for us, and so we're normal within it. We have overwhelming reasons for doing it. As long as we do this work, as long as there is this work to do, we stay alive. Most of the Boys volunteered, but not for this. At first, it was just going to be internal deportation, work camps for the revolution. They were just going to be guards. Me, I was put on that train to die, and I don't know why. They dope whole areas, and collect the people they want. Lou saw me on the platform, and pulled me in. Recruited me, he called it. I slept with him, out of gratitude and fear. I still remember sleeping with him.

I was the one who recruited Royce. He saw me first. He walked up to me on the gravel between the trains, nothing out of the ordinary, just a tall black man in rumpled khaki. He was jingling the keys in his pockets, housekeys, as if he was going to need them again. He was shaking, and he kept blinking, and swaying where he stood, and he asked in a sick and panicky voice, "It's cold. It's cold. Isn't there any food?"

The information that he was good-looking got through slowly.

The reaction was neutral, like you'd get from looking at a model on a billboard. Then I thought: in ten minutes' time, he's going to be dead.

You always promise yourself "just once." Just once, you'll tell the boss off; just once, you'll phone in sick and go out to the lakes. Just once. So here, I thought, is my just once: I'm going to save one of them.

"Are you gay?" I asked him. I did it without moving my lips. The cameras were always on us.

"What?" Incomprehension.

Oh God, I thought, he's going to be difficult, this is dumb. I got scared.

"What did you ask me?"

"Nothing. Go on." I nodded toward the second train.

"Am I gay?" He said it quickly, glancing around him. I just nodded.

The last of the other Stiffs were being loaded on, the old ones, who had to be lifted up. I saw Big Lou look at us and start walking toward us, sauntering, amiable, with a diamanté earring.

"Yes," said Royce. "Why?"

"Make like you know me. My name's Richard."

"Royce," he said, but I couldn't catch it.

Then Lou was standing next to us. "A little tête-à-tête?" he asked.

"Hi Lou," I said. I leaned back on my heels, away from him. "We got ourselves a new recruit."

"Don't need one, Rich," he said, still smiling.

"Lou, look. We were lovers. We lived together for two years. We did a lot of work for the movement together. He's OK, really."

Lou was looking at Royce, at Royce's face. Being black was in Royce's favor, ideologically. All the other Boys were white. No one wanted the Station to be accused of racism.

"I don't believe a word of it," said Lou. "But OK."

Lou walked toward one of the cameras. "Hey!" he shouted up to it. The camera was armed. It turned toward him, slowly. "We've got a new recruit."

"What was that?" asked the camera, or rather the voice of the

Gril behind it. The sound was flat and mechanical, the tone off-hand and bored.

"A new recruit. A new Boy. He's with us, so don't burn him, OK?"

"OK, OK," said the camera. Lou turned back, and patted Royce's bare, goose-pimpled arm. Royce lurched after him, and I grabbed hold of his shirt to stop him. I was frightened he was going to get back onto the train. I waited until it was pulling out, creaking and crashing, so that the noise would cover what I said.

"It's terrible here," I told Royce. "But it's better than dying. Watch what you say. The cameras don't always hear, but usually they can. It's all right to look disgusted. They don't mind if you look a bit sick. They like us to do the job with distaste. Just don't ever say you think it's wrong."

"What's wrong?" he asked, and I thought: Oh God, he doesn't know. He doesn't know what's going on here. And I thought: now what do I do with him?

I showed him around the Station. It's a small, old-fashioned building made of yellow and black brick, with no sign on it to tell us where we are. One hundred years ago women in long dresses with children would have waited on its platform for the train to take them shopping in the city. There would have been a ticket-seller behind the counter who knew all the women by their last name, and who kept a girlie calendar pinned on the wall. His booth still has ornate iron bars across it, the word "Tickets" in art nouveau scrolling, still slightly gilded. The waiting room is full of temporary metal beds. The walls are painted a musty pistachio, and the varnish on the wooden floor has gone black. There are games machines in the corner, and behind the ticket counter is an electric cooker. We eat sitting on our beds. There are cold showers, outside by the wall, and there are flower boxes in the windows. James the Tape Head—he's one of the Boys—keeps them full of petunias and geraniums. All around it and the hill behind are concentric rows of wire mesh, thirty feet high and thirty feet deep, to keep the Stiffs controlled, and us in. It isn't a Station, it's a mass graveyard, for them and probably for us.

I tried to get Royce to go to bed, but he wouldn't. He was

frightened to be left alone. He followed me out onto the platform where we were unloading the Stiffs, rolling them out. Sometimes the bodies sigh when they hit the concrete.

Royce's eyes went as wide as a rabbit's that's been run over by a car.

"What are you doing? What are you doing?" he yelped, over and over.

"What the fuck does it look like?" I said.

We strip them on the platform, and load them into trolleys. We shake them out of their trousers, and go through the pockets. Getting them out of their shirts is worse; their arms flop, and their heads loll. We're allowed to leave them in their underwear.

"They're doing it. Oh God, oh Jesus, they're killing them! Nobody knows that! Nobody believes that!"

"Help me carry them," I said. I said it for his sake. He shook his head, and stepped back, and stumbled over arms and legs and fell into a tangle of them.

Only the worst, we're told, only the most violent of men. That means the poor bastards who had to pick up a gun, or join a gang, or sign up for the police or the army. In other words, most of the people we kill are either black or Latino. I tried to tell them, I tried to tell the women that would happen.

Royce was suddenly sick. It was partly the drugs wearing off. Charlie and I hoisted him up and dragged him, as limp as a Stiff, into the showers. We got him cleaned up and into bed—my bed, there wasn't any other—and after that he was very quiet. Everybody was interested in him. New dog in the pound. Harry offered him one of his peppermints. Harry came up smiling, but then Harry is always smiling like the Man who Laughed, yellow teeth in a red beard. He'd got the peppermints off a Stiff. Royce didn't know how precious they were. He just shook his head, and lay there staring under the blanket, as one by one we all came back from the platform. Lou was last, thumping in and sighing, like he was satisfied with something. He slumped down on my bed next to Royce's knees, and I thought: uh-oh, Lou likes him too.

"Bad day, huh," Lou said. "Listen, I know, the first day is poison. But you got to ask yourself why it's happening."

"Why is it?" asked Royce, his face and mouth muffled in the crook of his elbow. He sounded like he was going to be sick again.

"Why?" Lou sounded shocked. "Royce, you remember how bad things got. The assassinations, the military build-up, the bombs?"

Only in America: the gangs got hold of tactical nuclear weapons. They punched out their rivals' turf: parts of Detroit, Miami, Houston, Chicago and then the big DC.

"I know," said Royce. "I used to live in Los Angeles."

Los Angeles came later. I sometimes wonder now if Los Angeles wasn't a special case. Ever hear of the Reichstag fire? Lou went respectful and silent, and he sat back, head bowed. "I am really sick at heart to hear that. I am so sorry. It must be like your whole past life has been blown away. What can I say? You probably know what I'm talking about better than anyone else here. It just had to be stopped, didn't it?"

"It did stop," said Royce.

"Yeah, I know, and that was because of the testosterone specifics. The women gave us that. Do you remember how great that felt, Royce? How calm you felt. That's because you'd been released from your masculinity, the specifics set men free from themselves. It was a beautiful thing to do."

Lou rocked back on the bed, and recited the old doggerel slogan. "TSI, in the water supply, a year-round high. I remember the first day I could leave my gun at home, man. I got on the subway, and there was this big Kahuna, all beads and tattoos, and he just smiled at me and passed me a joint. I really thought the specifics were the answer. But they hurt women, not many, but that's enough. So the specifics were withdrawn, and look what happened. Six months later, Los Angeles went up. The violence had to stop. And that's what we're going for here, Royce. Not men per se, but violence: the military, the police, criminals, gangsters, pornographers. Once they go, this whole thing here stops. It's like a surgical operation."

"Could you let me sleep?" Royce asked.

"Yeah sure," said Lou gently, and leaned forward and kissed

him. "Don't worry, Royce, we take care of our own here. These guys are a really great bunch of people. Welcome home."

The Boys went back to playing computer games in the waiting room. Bleep bleep bleep. One of the guys started yelling because a jack was missing from his deck of cards. James the Tape Head sat on his bed, Mozart hissing at him through his headphones. I looked at Royce, and I thought of him: you are a good person. That's when I began to have the fantasy. We all have the fantasy, of someone good and kind and strong, who sees who we really are when we're not messed up. Without knowing I was doing it, I began to make Royce my fantasy, my beautiful, kind, good man. The strange thing was that in a way the fantasy was true. So was it a fantasy at all?

The next day—it was the very next day—Royce began his campaign.

I volunteered us both to get the food. The food comes down the tracks very early in a little automatic car. Someone has to unload it and take it into the kitchen. I wanted to get Royce and me away from the Boys to talk. He was unsure of me; he pulled on his socks and looked at me, solemnly, in the eye. Fair enough, I thought, he doesn't know me. Lou loaned him a big duffle coat, and Royce led us both out through the turnstiles and onto the platform.

We didn't have our talk. Like he was stepping out onto a stage, under the cameras, Royce started to play a part. I don't like to say this, but he started to play the part of a black man. It was an act, designed to disarm. He grinned and did a Joe Cool kind of movement. "Hey! How are you?" he said to one particular camera.

The camera stayed still, and silent.

"You can't fool me, I know there's someone there. What's your name?" he asked it. Silence, of course.

"Aw, come on, you can tell me that, can't you? Listen I have got a terrible name. It's Royce. How would you like to be called after a car? Your name can't be as bad as that. What is it? Grizelda? Hortensia? My favorite aunt's called Hortensia. How about Gertrude? Ever read *Hamlet*? What about . . . Lurleen?"

There was a hollow sound, like in a transatlantic phone call, when you talk over someone and it cuts out what they're saying for a couple of seconds afterwards. The camera did that. It had turned off its voice. And I thought, I didn't know it could do that; and I thought, why did it do it?

"Look. I have to call you something. My sister is called Alice. You don't mind if I call you Alice? Like in Wonderland?" Royce stepped forward. The camera did not have to bristle; its warm-up light went on.

"You see, Alice. I—uh—have a personal question."

The camera spoke. "What is it?" The voice was sharp and wary. I had the feeling that he had actually found her real name.

"Alice—uh—I don't want to embarrass anyone, but, um, you see, I got this little emergency, and everywhere I look there are cameras, so, um, where can I *go*?"

A pause from the camera. "I'm sorry," it said. "There are toilet facilities, but I'm afraid we have to keep you under observation."

"Really, I don't do anything that much different from anyone else."

"I'm sure you don't."

"I mean sometimes I try it standing on the seat or in a yoga position."

"Fine, but I'm afraid you'll still have to put up with the cameras."

"Well I hope you're recording it for posterity, 'cause if you get rid of all the men, it'll have real historical interest."

There was a click from the camera again. I stepped out of the line of fire. Royce presented himself at the turnstiles, and they buzzed to let him through. He made his way toward the john singing "That's Entertainment."

All the cameras turned to watch him.

Just before he went into the shed, he pulled out his pecker and waggled it at them. "Wave bye-bye," he said.

He'll get us all killed, I thought. The john was a trench with a plywood shed around it, open all along one side. I went to the wire mesh behind it, to listen.

"Alice?" I heard him ask through the plywood.

"I'm not Alice," said another voice from another camera. She meant in more ways than one, she was not Alice.

"Uh—Hortensia? Uh. There's no toilet paper, Hortensia."

"I know."

"Gee, I wish you'd told me first."

"There are some old clothes on the floor. Use some of them and throw them over the side."

Dead men's shirts. I heard a kind of rustle and saw a line of shadow under the boards, waddling forward, crouched.

"I must look like a duck, huh?"

"A roast one in a minute."

Royce was quiet for a while after that. Finally he said, grumbling, "Trust me to pick tweed."

He kept it up, all morning long, talking to the Grils. During breakfast, he talked about home cooking and how to make tostadas and enchiladas. He talked about a summer job he'd had in Los Angeles, working in a diner that specialized in Kosher Mexican Food. Except for Royce, everyone who worked there including the owners was Japanese. That, said Royce, shaking his head, was LA. He and his mother had to move back east, to get away from the gang wars.

As the bodies were being unloaded, Royce talked about his grandmother. He'd lived with her when he was a child, and his father was dying. His grandmother made ice cream in the bathtub. She filled it full of ice and spun tubs of cream in it. Then she put one of the tubs in a basket with an umbrella over it on the front of her bicycle. She cycled through the neighborhood, selling ice cream and singing "Rock of Ages." She kept chickens, which was against the zoning regulations, and threw them at people who annoyed her, especially policemen. Royce had a cat, and it and a chicken fell in love. They would mew and cluck for each other, and sit for contented hours at a time, the chicken's neck snugly and safely inside the cat's mouth.

It was embarrassing, hearing someone talk. Usually we worked in silence. And the talk was confusing; we didn't think about things like summer jobs or household pets anymore. As the bodies were dumped and stripped, Royce's face was hard and shiny with sweat, like polished wood.

That afternoon, we had our talk. Since we'd gotten the food, it was our turn to cook lunch. So I got him away from the Boys.

We took our soup and crackers up to the top of the mound. The mound is dug out of a small hill behind the Station. James makes it in his bulldozer, listening to Mozart. He pulls the trolleys up a long dirt ramp, and empties them, and smooths the sandstone soil over each day's addition of Stiffs. I get the feeling he thinks he works like Mozart. The mound rises up in terraces, each terrace perfectly level, its slope at the same angle as the one below it. The dirt is brick red and there are seven levels. It looks like Babylon.

There are cameras on top, but you can see over the fence. You can see the New England forest. It looks tired and small, maybe even dusty, as if it needed someone to clean the leaves. There's another small hill. You can hear birds. Royce and I climbed up to the top, and I gathered up my nerve and said, "I really like you."

"Uh-huh," he said, balancing his soup, and I knew it wasn't going to work.

Leave it, I thought, don't push, it's hard for him, he doesn't know you.

"You come here a lot," he said. It was a statement.

"I come here to get away."

Royce blew out through his nostrils: a kind of a laugh. "Get away? You know what's under your feet?"

"Yes," I said, looking at the forest. Neither one of us wanted to sit on that red soil, even to eat the soup. I passed him his crackers, from my coat pocket.

"So why did you pick me? Out of all the other Stiffs?"

"I guess I just liked what I saw."

"Why?"

I smiled with embarrassment at being forced to say it; it was as if there were no words for it that were not slightly wrong. "Because I guess you're kind of good-looking and I . . . just thought I would like you a lot."

"Because I'm black?"

"You are black, yes."

"Are most of your boyfriends black?"

Bull's-eye. That was scary. "I, uh, did go through a phase where I guess I was kind of fixated on black people. But I stopped that, I mean, I realized that what I was actually doing was depersonalizing the people I was with, which wasn't very flattering to them. But that is all over. It really isn't important to me now."

"So you went out and made yourself sleep with white people." He does not, I thought, even remotely like me.

"I found white people I liked. It didn't take much."

"You toe the line all the way down the line, don't you?" he said.

I thought I didn't understand.

"Is that why you're here?" A blank from me. "You toe the line, the right *line,* so you're here."

"Yes," I said. "In a way. Big Lou saw me on the platform, and knew me from politics. I guess you don't take much interest in politics." I was beginning to feel like hitting back.

"Depends on the politics," he said, briskly.

"Well you're OK, I guess. You made it out."

"Out of where?"

I just looked back at him. "Los Angeles."

He gave a long and very bitter sigh, mixed with a kind of chortle. "Whenever I am in this . . . situation, there is the conversation. I always end up having the same conversation. I reckon you're going to tell me I'm not black enough."

"You do kind of shriek I am middle class."

"Uh-huh. You use that word class, so that means it's not racist, right?"

"I mean, you're being loyal to your class, to which most black people do not belong."

"Hey, bro', you can't fool me, we're from the same neighborhood. That sort of thing?" It was imitation ghetto. "You want somebody with beads in his hair and a beret and a semi who hates white people, but likes you because you're so upfront movement? Is that your little dream? A big bad black man?"

I turned away from him completely.

He said, in a very cold still voice. "Do you get off on corpses, too?"

"This was a mistake," I said. "Let's go back."

"I thought you wanted to talk."

"Why are you doing this?"

"Because," he said, "you are someone who takes off dead men's watches, and you look like you could have been a nice person."

"I am," I said, and nearly wept, "a nice person."

"That's what scares the shit out of me."

"You think I want this? You think I don't hate this?" I think that's when I threw down the soup. I grabbed him by the shirt sleeves and held him. I remember being worried about the cameras, so I kept my voice low and rapid, like it was scuttling.

"Look, I was on the train, I was going to die, and Lou said, you can live. You can help here and live. So I did it. And I'm here. And so are you."

"I know," he said, softly.

"So OK, you don't like me, I can live with that, fine, no problem, you're under no obligation, so let's just go back."

"You come up here because of the forest," he said.

"Yes! Brilliant!"

"Even mass murderers need love too, right?"

"Yes! Brilliant!"

"And you want me to love you? When you bear the same relation to me, as Lou does to you?"

"I don't know. I don't care." I was sitting down now, hugging myself. The bowl of soup was on the ground by my foot, tomato sludge creeping out of it. I kicked it. "Sorry I hassled you."

"You didn't hassle me."

"All I want is one little part of my life to have a tiny corner of goodness in it. Just one little place. I probably won't, but I feel like if I don't find it soon, I will bust up into a million pieces. Not love. Not necessarily. Just someone nice to talk to, who I really like. Otherwise I think one day I will climb back into one of those trains." When I said it, I realized it was true. I hadn't known I was that far gone. I thought I had been making a play for sympathy.

Royce was leaning in front of me, looking me in the face. "Listen, I love you."

"Bullshit." What kind of mind-fuck now?

He grabbed my chin, and turned my head back round. "No. True. Not maybe in the way you want, but true. You really do look, right now, like one of those people on the train. Like someone I just unloaded."

I didn't know quite what he was saying, and I wasn't sure I trusted him, but I did know one thing. "I don't want to go back to that bunkhouse, not this afternoon."

"OK. We'll stay up here and talk."

I felt like I was stepping out onto ice. "But can we talk nicely? A little bit less heavy duty?"

"Nicely. Sounds sweet, doesn't mean anything. Like the birds?"

"Yes," I said. "Like the birds."

I reckon that, altogether, we had two weeks. A Lullaby in Birdland. Hum along if you want to. You don't need to know the words.

Every afternoon after the work, Royce and I went up the mound and talked. I think he liked talking to me, I'll go as far as that. I remember one afternoon he showed me photographs from his wallet. He still had a wallet, full of people.

He showed me his mother. She was extremely thin, with dark limp flesh under her eyes. She was trying to smile. Her arms were folded across her stomach. She looked extremely kind, but tired.

There was a photograph of a large red brick house. It had white window sills and a huge white front door, and it sagged in the way that only very old houses do.

"Whose is that?" I asked.

"Ours. Well, my family's. Not my mother's. My uncle lives there now."

"It's got a Confederate flag over it!"

Royce grinned and folded up quietly; his laughter was almost always silent. "Well, my great-grandfather didn't want to lose all his slaves, did he?"

One half of Royce's family were black, one half were white. There were terrible wedding receptions divided in half where no one spoke. "The white people are all so embarrassed, particularly the ones who want to be friendly. There's only one way a black family gets a house like that: Grandfather messed around a whole bunch. He hated his white family, so he left the house to us. My uncle and aunt want to open it up as a Civil War museum and put their picture on the leaflet." Royce folded up again. "I mean, this is in Georgia. Can you imagine all those rednecks showing up and finding a nice black couple owning it, and all this history about black regiments?"

"Who's that?"

"My cousin. She came to live with us for a while."

"She's from the white half."

"Nope. She's black." Royce was enjoying himself. The photograph showed a rather plump, very determined teenage girl with orange hair, slightly wavy, and freckles.

"Oh." I was getting uncomfortable, all this talk of black and white.

"It's really terrible. Everything Cyndi likes, I mean *everything,* is black, but her father married a white woman, and she ended up like that. She wanted to be black so bad. Every time she met anyone, she'd start explaining how she was black, really. She'd go up to black kids and start explaining, and you could see them thinking 'Who is this white girl and is she out of her mind?' We were both on this *program,* so we ended up in a white high school and that was worse because no one knew they'd been integrated when she was around. The first day this white girl asked her if she'd seen any of the new black kids. Then her sister went and became a top black fashion model, you know, features in *Ebony,* and that was it. It got so bad, that whenever Cyndi meant white, she'd say 'the half of me I hate.' "

"What happened to her?"

"I think she gave up and became white. She wanted to be a lawyer. I don't know what happened to her. She got caught in LA."

I flipped over the plastic. There was a photograph of a mother and a small child. "Who's that?"

"My son," said Royce. "That's his mother. Now *she* thinks she's a witch." An ordinary looking girl stared sullenly out at the camera. She had long frizzy hair and some sort of ethnic dress. "She'll go up to waiters she doesn't like in restaurants and whisper spells at them in their ears."

"How long ago was this?" I felt an ache, as if I'd lost him, as if I had ever had him.

"Oh ten years ago, before I knew anything. I mean, I wouldn't do it now. I'd like any kid of mine to have me around, but his mother and I don't get on. She told my aunt that she'd turned me gay by magic to get revenge."

"Were they in LA too?"

Royce went very still, and nodded yes.

"I'm sorry," I said.

He passed me back the wallet. "Here. That's all of them. Last time we got together."

There was a tiny photograph, full of people. The black half. On the far right was a very tall, gangling fifteen-year-old, looking bristly and unformed, shy and sweet. Three of the four people around him were looking at him, bursting with suppressed smiles. I wish I'd known him then, as well. I wanted to know him all his life.

"I got a crazy, crazy family," he said, shaking his head with affection. "I hope they're all still OK." It was best not to think about what was happening outside. Or inside, here.

It was autumn, and the sun would come slanting through the leaves of the woods. It would make a kind of corona around them, especially if the Boys were burning garbage and there was smoke in the air. The light would come in shafts, like God was hiding behind the leaves. The leaves were dropping one by one.

There was nothing in the Station that was anything to do with Royce. Everything that made him Royce, that made him interesting, is separate. It is the small real things that get obliterated in a holocaust, forgotten. The horrors are distinct and do not connect with the people, but it is the horrors that get remembered in history.

When it got dark, we would go back down, and I hated it because each day it was getting dark earlier and earlier. We'd get back and find that there had been—oh—a macaroni fight over lunch, great handprints of it over the windows and on the beds, that had been left to dry. Once we got back to the waiting room, and there had been a fight, a real one. Lou had given one of the Boys a bloody nose, to stop it. There was blood on the floor. Lou lectured us all about male violence, saying anyone who used violence in the Station would get violence back.

He took away all of Tom's clothes. Tom was beautiful, and very quiet, but sometimes he got mad. Lou kicked him out of the building in punishment. It was going to be a cold night. Long after the Grils had turned out the lights, we could hear Tom whimpering, just outside the door. "Please, Lou. It's cold. Lou, I'm sorry. Lou? I just got carried away. Please?"

I felt Royce jump up and throw the blanket aside. Oh God, I thought, don't get Lou mad at us. Royce padded across the dark room, and I heard the door open, and I heard him say, "OK, come in.

"Sorry, Lou," Royce said. "But we all need to get to sleep."

Lou only grunted. "OK," he said, in a voice that was biding its time.

And Royce came back to my bed.

I would hold him, and he would hold me, but only, I think, to stop falling out of the bed. It was so narrow and cold. Royce's body was always taut, like each individual strand of muscle had been pulled back, tightly, from the shoulder. It was as tense through the night as if it were carrying something, and nothing I could do would soothe it. What I am trying to say, and I have to say it, is that Royce was impotent, at least with me, at least in the Station. "As long as I can't do it," he told me once on the mound, "I know I haven't forgotten where I am." Maybe that was just an excuse. The Boys knew about it, of course. They listened in the dark and knew what was and was not happening.

And the day would begin at dawn. The little automatic car, the porridge and the bread, the icy showers, and the wait for the first train. James the Tape Head, Harry with his constant grin, Gary who was tall and ropey, and who kept tugging at his pigtail. He'd been a trader in books, and he talked books and politics and thought he was Lou's lieutenant. Lou wasn't saying. And Bill the

Brylcreem, and Charlie with his still, and Tom. The Boys. Hating each other, with no one else to talk to, waiting for the day when the Grils would burn us, or the food in the cart would have an added secret ingredient. When they were done with us.

Royce talked, learning who the cameras were.

There were only four Grils, dividing the day into two shifts. Royce gave them names. There was Alice and Hortensia, and Miss Scarlett who turned out to be from Atlanta. Only one of the Grils took a while to find a name, and she got it the first day one of the cameras laughed.

She'd been called Greta, I think because she had such a low, deep voice. Sometimes Royce called her Sir. Then one morning, Lou was late, and as he came, Royce said. "Uh-oh. Here comes the Rear Admiral."

Lou was very sanctimonious about always taking what he as-sumed was the female role in sex. The cameras knew that; they watched all the time. The camera laughed. It was a terrible laugh; a thin, high, wailing, helpless shriek.

"Hey, Sir, that's really Butch," said Royce, and the name Butch stuck.

So did Rear Admiral. God bless all who sail in him.

"Hiya, Admiral," gasped the camera, and even some of the Boys laughed too.

Lou looked confused, a stiff and awkward smile on his face. "It's better than being some macho prick," he said.

That night, he took me to one side, by the showers.

"Look," he said. "I think maybe you should get your friend to ease up a bit."

"Oh Lou, come on, it's just jokes."

"You think all of this is a joke!" yelped Lou.

"No."

"Don't think I don't understand what's going on." The light caught in his eyes, pinprick bright.

"What do you think is going on, Lou?"

I saw him appraising me. I saw him give me the benefit of the doubt. "What you've done, Rich, and maybe it isn't your fault, is to import an ideological wild card into this station."

"Oh Lou," I groaned. I groaned for him, for his mind.

"He's not with us. I don't know what these games are that he's playing with the women, but he's putting us all in danger. Yeah, sure, they're laughing now, but sooner or later he'll say the wrong thing, and some of us will get burned. Cooked. And another thing. These little heart to heart talks you have with each other. Very nice. But that's just the sort of thing the Station cannot tolerate. We are a team, we are a family, we've broken with all of that nuclear family shit, and you guys have re-imported it. You're breaking us up, into little compartments. You, Royce, James, even Harry, you're all going off into little corners away from the rest of us. We have got to work together. Now I want to see you guys with the rest of us. No more withdrawing."

"Lou," I said, helpless to reply. "Lou. Fuck off."

His eyes had the light again. "Careful, Rich."

"Lou. We are with you guys 22 hours a day. Can you really not do without us for the other two? What is wrong with a little privacy, Lou?"

"There is no privacy here," he said. "The cameras pick up just about every word. Now look. I took on a responsibility. I took on the responsibility of getting all of us through this together, show that there is a place in the revolution for good gay men. I have to know what is going on in the Station. I don't know what you guys are saying to each other up there, I don't know what the cameras are hearing. Now you lied to me, Rich. You didn't know Royce before he came here, did you. We don't know who he is, what he is. Rich, is Royce even gay?"

"Yes! Of course!"

"Then how does he fuck?"

"That's none of your business."

"Everything here is my business. You don't fuck him, he doesn't fuck you, so what goes on?"

I was too horrified to speak.

"Look," said Lou, relenting. "I can understand it. You love the guy. You think I don't feel that pull, too, that pull to save them? We wouldn't be gay if we didn't. So you see him on the platform, and he is very nice, and you think, Dear God, why does he have to die?"

"Yes."

"I feel it! I feel it too!" Lou made a good show of doing so. "It's not the people themselves, but what they are that we have to hold onto. Remember, Rich, this is just a program of containment. What we get here are the worst, Rich, the very worst—the sex criminals, the transsexuals, the media freaks. So what you have to ask yourself, Rich, is this: what was Royce doing on that train?"

"Same thing I was. He got pulled in by mistake."

Lou looked at me with a kind of blank pity. Then he looked down at the ground. "There are no mistakes, Rich. They've got the police files."

"Then what was I doing on the train?"

Lou looked back up at me and sighed. "I think you probably got some of the women very angry with you. There's a lot of infighting, particularly where gay men fit in. I don't like it. It's why I got you out. It may be something similar with Royce."

"On the train because I disagreed with them?" Everything felt weak, my knees, my stomach.

"It's possible, only possible. This is a revolution, Rich. Things are pretty fluid."

"Oh God, Lou, what's happening?"

"You see why we have to be careful? People have been burned in this station, Rich. Not lately, because I've been in charge. And I intend to stay in charge. Look."

Lou took me in his arms. "This must be really terrible for you, I know. All of us were really happy for you, when you and Royce started. But we have to protect ourselves. Now let's just go back in, and ask Royce who and what he is."

"What do you mean?"

"Just ask him. In front of the others. What he was. And not take no for an answer." He was stroking my hair.

"He'll hate me if I do that!" I tried to push him away. He grabbed hold of my hair, and pulled it, smiling, almost as if he were still being sexy and affectionate.

"Then he'll just have to get over that kind of mentality. What has he got to hide if he needs privacy? Come on, Rich. Let's just get it over with." He pulled me back, into the waiting room.

Royce took one look at us together as we came in, and his face went still, as if to say, "Uh-huh. This is coming now, is it?" His eyes looked hard into mine, and said, "Are you going to put up with it?" I was ashamed. I was powerless.

"Rich has a confession to make," said Lou, a friendly hand still on the back of my neck. "Don't you, Rich?"

They all seemed to sit up and close in, an inquisition, and I stood there thinking, Dear God, what do I do? What do I do?

"Rich," Lou reminded me. "We have to go through this. We need to talk this through."

Royce sat there, on our bed, reclining, waiting.

Well, I *had* lied. "I don't really know who Royce is. We weren't lovers before. We are lovers now."

"But you don't know what he was doing, or who he was, do you, Rich?"

I just shook my head.

"Don't you want to know that, Rich? Don't you want to know who your lover was? Doesn't it seem strange to you that he's never told you?"

"No," I replied. "We all did what we had to do before the revolution. What we did back then is not who we are." See, I wanted to say to Royce, I'm fighting, see I'm fighting.

"But there are different ways of knuckling under, aren't there, Rich? You taught history. You showed people where the old system had gone wrong. You were a good, gay man."

Royce stood up, abruptly, and said, "I was a prison guard."

The room went cold and Lou's eyes gleamed.

"And there are different ways of being a prison guard. It was a detention center for juveniles, young guys who might have had a chance. Not surprisingly, most of them were black. I don't suppose you know what happens to black juvenile prisoners now, do you? I'd like to know."

"Their records are looked at," said Lou. "So. You were a gay prison guard in charge of young men."

"Is that so impossible?"

"So, you were a closet case for a start."

"No. I told my immediate superior."

"*Immediate superior.* You went along with the hierarchy. Patriarchy, I should say. Did you have a good time with the boys?"

"This camp is a hierarchy, in case you hadn't noticed. And no, I kept my hands off the boys. I was there to help them, not make things worse."

"Helping them to be gay would be worse?" Every word was a trap door that could fall open. The latch was hatred. "Did you ever beat one of the boys up? Did you deal dope on the side?"

Royce was still for a moment, his eyes narrow. Then he spoke. "About four years ago, me and the kids put on a show. We put on a show for the girls' center. The girls came in a bus, and they'd all put their hair in ringlets, and they walked into the gym with too much make-up on, holding each other's hands, clutching each other's forearms, like this, because they were so nervous. And the kids, the boys, they'd been rehearsing, oh, for weeks. They'd built and painted a set. It was a street, with lights in the windows, and a big yellow moon. There was this one kid, Jonesy. Jonesy kept sticking his head through the curtain before we started. 'Hey everybody! I'm a star!' "

Royce said it again, softly. "Hey everybody, I'm a star. And I had to yell at him, Jonesy, get your ass off that stage. The girls sat on one side of the gym, and the boys on the other, and they smiled and waved and threw things at each other, like gum wrappers. It was all they had."

Royce started to cry. He glared at Lou and let the tears slide down his face. "They didn't have anything else to give each other. The show started and one of the kids did his announcing routine. He'd made a bow tie out of a white paper napkin, and it looked so sharp. And then the music came up and one of the girls just shouted. 'Oh, they're going to *dance!*' And those girls screamed. They just screamed. The boys did their dance on the stage, no mistaking what those moves meant. The record was 'It's a Shame.' "

His face contorted suddenly, perhaps with anger. "And I had to keep this god-damned aisle between them, the whole time."

"So?" said Lou, unmoved.

"So," said Royce, and gathered himself in. He wiped the moisture from his face. "So I know a lot about prisons. So, some of those kids are dead now. The boys and the girls wanted each other. That must be an ideological quandary for you, Lou. Here's a big bad guard stopping people doing what they want, but what they want to do is het-ero-sex-u-ality." He turned it into a mock dirty word, his eyes round.

"No problem," said Lou. "All women are really lesbians."

Royce stared at him for a moment. Then he began to laugh.

"I wouldn't expect you to understand. But the first experience of physical tenderness that any woman has is with her mother."

"Gee, I'm sure glad my old aunt Hortensia didn't know that. She would be surprised. Hey, Alice. Are you a dyke?"

Lou went pale, and lines of shadow encircled his mouth.

"Yes," said Alice, the camera.

"Well, I'm a faggot, but it doesn't mean everyone else is."

Lou launched himself from the bed, in a fury. He was on his feet, and shouting, flecks of spit propelled from his mouth. "You do not use demeaning language here!" His voice cracked.

Alice had been working nine hours, and now she was alone, on the night shift. She had been watching, silently, for nine hours. Now, she wanted to talk.

"I had a girlfriend once who was straight," she said. "No matter how hard she tried, women just didn't bring her off. Mind you, that's better than those lust lesbians. They just want your body. Me, I'm totally dedicated to women, but it's a political commitment. It's something I decided. I don't let my body make my decisions for me."

"Yeah, I know what you mean," said Royce. "It's these lust faggots, I can't stand." He cast his eyes about him at the Boys, and they chuckled.

"We do not use the word 'dyke' in this station," said Lou.

Royce looked rather sad and affectionate, and shook his head. "Lou. You are such a prig. Not only are you a prig. You are a dumb prig."

The floor seemed to open up under my feet with admiration.

Only Royce could have said that to Lou. I loved him, even though I did not love myself. The Boys chuckled again, because it was funny, and because it was true, and because it was a little bit of a shock.

"Alice," said Lou. "He has just insulted women."

"Funny," said Alice. "I thought he'd just insulted you."

Lou looked like he was in the middle of a nightmare; you could see it in his face. "Alice is being very tolerant, Royce. But from now on, you talk to and about the women with respect. If you want to live here with us, there are a few ground rules."

"Like what?"

"No more jokes."

Royce was leaning against the bar at the foot of our bed, and he was calm, and his ankles were crossed. He closed his eyes, and smiled. "No more jokes?" he asked, amused.

"You mess around with the women, you put us all in danger. You keep putting us in danger, you got to go."

"Lou," said Alice. "Can I remind you of something? You don't decide who goes on the trains. We do."

"I understand that, Alice." He slumped from the shoulders and his breath seeped out of him. He seemed to shrink.

"Lou," said Royce. "I think you and I are on the same side?" It was a question.

"We'd better be," said Lou.

"Then you do know why I talk to the women."

"Yeah," said Lou. "You want to show off. You want to be the center of attention. You don't want to take responsibility for anything."

He didn't understand. Lou was dangerous because he was stupid.

"I've been a prison guard," said Royce, carefully. "I know what it's like. You're trapped, even worse than the prisoners."

"So?" He was going to make Royce say it, in front of a camera. He was going to make him say that he was talking to the Grils so that they would find it hard to kill us when the time came.

"I'm talking to the women, so that they'll get to know us," said

Royce, "and see that there is a place for gay men within the revolution. They can't know that unless we talk to them. Can they?"

Bull's-eye again. That was the only formulation Lou was ever likely to accept.

"I mean, can they, Lou? I think we're working with the women on this thing together. There's no need for silence between us, not if we're on the same side. OK, so maybe I do it wrong. I don't want to be the only one who does all the talking. We all should talk to them, Lou, you, me, all of us. And the women should feel that they can talk with us as well."

"Oh yeah, I am so bored keeping schtum," said Alice.

Lou went still, and he drew in a deep breath. "OK," he said. "We can proceed on that basis. We all communicate, with each other and with the cameras. But Royce. That means no more withdrawing. No more going off in a corner. No more little heart to hearts on the mound."

"I didn't know that was a problem, Lou. There will be no more of those."

"OK, then," said Lou, murmurous in defeat. Royce strode toward him, both hands outstretched, and took Lou's hand in both of his.

"This is really good, Lou. I'm really glad we talked."

Lou looked back at him, looking worn and heavy, but he was touched. Big Lou was moved, as well, and he gave a slightly forlorn flicker of a smile.

So Royce became head of the Station.

He gave me a friendly little nod, and moved his things away from our bed. He slept in Tom's; Tom never did. It didn't matter, because I still had my little corner of goodness, even if we didn't talk. Royce was still there, telling jokes. I was happy with that because I knew that I had deserted him before he had deserted me; and I understood that I was to be the visible victory he gave to Lou. None of that mattered. Royce had survived. I didn't cry the first night alone; I stopped myself. I didn't want the Boys to hear.

Things started to change. The cameras stopped looking at us on the john. We could see them turn and look away. Then one morning, they were just hanging, dead.

"Hey, Rich!" Harry called me. It was me and Harry, unloading the food cart, as winter finally came. Harry was hopping up and down in front of the camera. He leapt up and tapped it, and the warm-up light did not even go on.

"They've turned it off, Rich! The camera's off. It's dead!"

He grabbed my arms, and spun me around, and started doing a little dance, and I started to hoot with laughter along with him. It was like someone had handed you back part of your pride. It was like we were human enough to be accorded that again.

"Hey Royce, the camera in the john's off!" shouted Harry, as we burst through the canteen doors with the trolley.

"Maybe they're just broken," said Gary, who was still loyal to Lou.

"Naw, man, they'd be telling us to fix it by now. They've turned it off!"

"That so, Alice?" Royce asked the camera in the canteen.

"Oh. Yeah," said Alice. Odd how a mechanical voice could sound so much more personal than a real one, closer somehow, as if in the middle of your ear.

"Thanks, Alice."

" 'S OK," said Alice, embarrassed. "We explained it to the Wigs. We told them it was like pornography, you know, demeaning to us. They bought it. Believe me, you guys are not a lovely sight first thing in the morning."

I could see Royce go all alert at that word "Wig," like an animal raising its ears. He didn't mention the Wigs again until later that afternoon.

"Alice, is our talking ever a problem for you?"

"How d'you mean?"

"Well, if one of the Wigs walked in . . ."

Alice kind of laughed. "Huh. They don't get down this far. What do you know about them, anyhow?"

"Nothing. Who are they?"

"Mind your own business. The people who run things."

"Well if someone does show up and you want us to shut up, just sneeze, and we'll stop talking."

"Sneeze?"

"Well, you could always come right out and say cool it guys, there's someone here."

"Hey Scarlett," said Alice. "Can you sneeze?"

"Ach-ooo," said Miss Scarlett, delicately.

"Just testing, guys," said Alice.

Big Lou hung around, trying to smile, trying to look like somehow all this was going on under his auspices. Nobody was paying attention.

The next day, the train didn't show.

It was very cold, and we stood on the platform, thumping our feet, as the day grew more sparkling, and the shadows shorter.

"Hey, Butch, what's up?" Royce asked.

"I'll check, OK?" said the camera. There was a long silence.

"The train's broken down. It's in a siding. It'll be a while yet. You might as well go back in, have the day off."

That's how it would begin, of course. No train today, fellas, sorry. No need for you, fellas, not today, not ever, and with what you know, can you blame us? What are ten more bodies to us?

Trains did break down, of course. It had happened before. We'd had a holiday then, too, and the long drunken afternoon became a long drunken day.

"Well let's have some fun for a change," said Lou. "Charlie, you got any stuff ready? Let's have a blow-out, man."

"Lou," said Royce, "I was kind of thinking we could get to work on the hot water tank."

"Hot water tank?" said Lou. "Are we going to need it, Royce?" There was a horrified silence. "So much for talking. Go on, Charlie, get your booze."

Then Lou came for me. "How about a little sex and romance, Rich?" Hand on neck again.

"No thanks, Lou."

"You won't get it from him, you know."

"That's my problem. Lou, lay off."

"At least I can do it." Grin.

"Surprise, surprise," I said. His face and body were right up against mine, and I turned away. "You can't get at him through me, you know, Lou. You just can't do it."

Lou relented. He pulled back, but he was still smiling. "You're right," he said. "For that, he'd have to like you. Sucker." He flicked the tip of my nose with his fingers, and walked away.

I went and sat down beside Royce. I needed him to make everything seem normal and ordinary. He was leaning on his elbows, plucking at the grass. "Hi," I said. It was the first time we'd spoken since the inquisition.

"Hi," he said, affectionate and distant.

"Royce, what do you think's going to happen?"

"The train will come in tomorrow," he said.

"I hate it when it comes in," I said, my breath rattling out of me in a kind of chuckle, "and I hate it when it doesn't. I just hate it. Royce, do you think we could go to work on the tank?"

He considered the implications. "OK," he said. "Charlie? Want to come work with us on the tank?"

Charlie was plump with a gray beard, and had a degree in engineering, a coffee tin and a copper coil. He was a sort of Santa Claus of the booze. "Not today," he said, cheerily. "I made all of this, I might as well get to drink some of it myself." It was clear and greasy-looking and came in white plastic screw-top bottles.

Charlie had sacrificed one of the showers to plumb in a hot water tank. We'd hammered the tank together out of an old train door. It was more like a basin, really, balanced in the loft of the Station. There were cameras there, too.

Royce sat looking helplessly at an electric hot plate purloined from the kitchen stove. We'd pushed wiring through from the floor below. "Charlie should be here," he said.

"I really love you, Royce."

He went very still for a moment. "I know," he said. "Rich, don't be scared. You're afraid all the time."

"I know," I said, and felt my hand tremble as I ran it across my forehead.

"You gotta stop it. One day, you'll die of fear."

"It's this place," I said, and broke down, and sat in a heap. "I want to get out!"

He held me, gently. "Someday we'll get out," he said, and the hopelessness of it made me worse. "Someday it'll be all right."

"No, it won't."

"Hi, guys," said Alice. "They're really acting like pigs down there."

"They're scared," said Royce. "We're all scared, Alice. Is that train going to come in tomorrow?"

"Yup," she said brightly.

"Good. You know anything about electricity?"

"Plenty. I used to work for Bell Telephone."

Royce disengaged himself from me. "OK. Do I put the plate inside the tank or underneath it?"

"Inside? Good Lord no!"

So Royce went back to work again, and said to me, "You better go back down, Rich."

"The agreement?" I asked, and he nodded yes. The agreement between him and Lou.

When I got down, the Boys looked like discarded rages. There was piss everywhere, and blood on Lou's penis.

I went up to the top of the mound. All the leaves were gone now. For about the first time in my life, I prayed. Dear God, get me out of here. Dear God, please, please, make it end. But there wasn't any answer. There never is. There was just an avalanche inside my head.

I could shut it out for a while. I could forget that every day I saw piles of corpses bulldozed and mangled, and that I had to chase the birds away from them, and that I peeled off their clothes and looked with inevitable curiosity at the little pouch of genitals in their brightly colored underwear. And the leaking and the sudden hemorrhaging and the supple warmth of the dead, with their marble eyes full of seeming questions. How many had we killed? Was anybody keeping count? Did anyone know their names? Even their names had been taken from them, along with their wallets and watches.

Harry had found his policeman father among them, and had never stopped smiling afterwards, saying "Hi!" like a cartoon chipmunk without a tail.

I listened to the roaring in my head as long as I could and then I went back down to the Boys. "Is there any booze left, Charlie?" I asked, and he passed me up a full plastic bottle, and I drank myself into a stupor.

It got dark and cold, and I woke up alone, and I pulled myself up, and walked back into the waiting room, and it was poison inside. It was as poison as the stuff going sour in our stomachs and brains and breath. We sat in twitchy silence, listening to the wind and our own farts. Nobody could be bothered to cook. Royce was not there, and my stomach twisted around itself like a bag full of snakes. Where was he? What would happen when he got back?

"You look sick," said Lou in disgust. "Go outside if you have to throw up."

"I'm fine, Lou," I said, but I could feel a thin slime of sweat on my forehead.

"You make me sick just looking at you," he said.

"Funny. I was just thinking the same about you." Our eyes locked, and there was no disguising it. We hated each other.

It was then that Royce came back in, rubbing his head with a towel. "Well, there are now hot showers," he announced. "Well, tepid showers. You guys can go clean up."

The Boys looked up to him, smiling. The grins were bleary, but they were glad to see him.

"Phew-wee!" he said, and waved his hand in front of his face. "That's some stuff you come up with, Charlie, what do you make it out of, burnt tires?"

Charlie beamed. "Orange peel and grass," he said proudly. I thought it was going to be all right.

Then Lou stood up out of his bed, and flopped naked toward Royce. "You missed all the fun," he said.

"Yeah, I know, I can smell it."

"Now who's being a prig?" said Lou. "Come on, man, I got something nice to show you." He grabbed hold of Royce's forearm, and pulled him toward his own bed. Tom was in it, lying face down, like a ruin, and Lou pulled back the blanket. "Go on, man."

Tom was bleeding. Royce's face and voice went very hard, and he pulled the blanket back up. "He's got an anal fissure, Lou. He needs to be left alone. It could get badly infected."

Lou barked, like a dog, a kind of laugh. "He's going to die anyway!"

Royce moved away from his bed. With Tom in it, he had no place to sit down. Lou followed him. "Come on, Royce. Come on. No more pussyfooting." He tried to put his hand down the front of Royce's shirt. Royce shrugged it away, with sudden annoyance. "Not tonight."

"Not ever?" asked Lou, amused.

"Come on, Royce, give it up man," said Harry. He grabbed Royce playfully, about the waist. "You can't hold out on us forever." He started fumbling with the belt buckle. "Hell, I haven't eaten all day."

"Oh yes you have," said Lou, and chuckled.

"Harry, please let go," said Royce, wearily.

The belt was undone, and Lou started pulling out his shirt. "Let go," warned Royce. "I said let go," and he moved very suddenly. His elbow hit Harry in the mouth, and he yelped.

"Hey, you fucker!"

"You turkey," said Lou.

And all the poison rose up like a wave. Oh, this was going to be fun, pulling off all of Royce's clothes. Gary, and Charlie, they all came, smiling. There was a sound of cloth tearing and suddenly Royce was fighting, fighting very hard, and suddenly the Boys were fighting too, grimly. They pulled him down, and he tried to hit them, and they held his arms, and they launched themselves on him like it was a game of tackle football. I thought, there is a word for this. The word is rape.

"Alice!" I shouted up to the camera. "Alice, stop them! Alice? Burn one of them, stop it!"

Then something slammed into the back of my head, and I fell, the floor scraping the skin of my wrists and slapping me across the cheeks. Then I was pulled over, and Lou was on top of me, forearm across my throat.

"Booby booby booby booby," he said, all blubbery lips, and then he kissed me. Well, he bit my upper lip. He bit it to hold me there; he nearly bit through it with his canine teeth, and my mouth was full of the taste of something metallic: blood.

The sounds the Boys made were conversational, with the odd laugh. Royce squealed like a pig. It always hurts beyond everything the first time. It finally came to me that Royce wasn't gay, at least not in any sense that we would understand. I looked up at the camera, at its blank, glossy eye, and I could feel it thinking: these are men; this is what men do; we are right. We are right to do this to them. For just that moment, I almost agreed.

Lou got up, and Charlie nestled in next to me, fat and naked, white hairs on his chest and ass, and he was still beaming like a baby, and I thought: don't you know what you've done? I tried to sit up, and he went no, no, no and waggled a finger at me. It was Lou's turn to go through him. "Rear Admiral, am I?" asked Lou.

When he was through, Charlie helped me to my feet. "You might as well have a piece," he said, with a friendly chuckle. Lou laughed very loudly, pulling on his T-shirt. The others were shuffling back to their beds in a kind of embarrassment. Royce lay on the floor.

I knelt next to him. My blood splashed onto the floor. "Can you get up, Royce?" I asked him. He didn't answer. "Royce, let's go outside, get you cleaned up." He didn't move. "Royce, are you hurt? Are you hurt badly?" Then I called them all bastards.

"It was just fun, man," said Harry.

"Fun!"

"It started out that way. He shouldn't have hit people."

"He didn't want to do it. Royce, please. Do you want anything? Is anything especially painful?"

"Just his ass," said Lou, and laughed.

"He'll be OK," said Charlie, a shadow of confusion on his face.

"Like fuck he will. That was some way to say thanks for all he's done. Well? Are any of you going to give me a hand?"

Harry did. He helped me to get Royce up. Royce hung between us like a sack.

"It's that fucking poison you make, man," said Harry to Charlie.

"Don't blame me. You were the first, remember."

"I was just playing."

They began to realize what they'd done. He was all angles, like a doll that didn't work anymore.

"What the fuck did you do?" I shouted at them. He didn't seem to be bruised anywhere. "Jesus Christ!" I began to cry because I thought he was dead. "You fucking killed him!"

"Uh-uh, no," said Gary. "We didn't."

"Pisshead!"

Charlie came to help too, and we got him outside, and into the showers, and he slumped down in the dark. I couldn't find a rag, so we just let the lukewarm water trickle down over him. All we did was get him wet on an evening in November.

"It's cold out here, we got to get him back in," said Harry.

Royce rolled himself up onto his knees, and looked at me. "You were there."

"I wasn't part of it. I tried to stop it."

"You were there. You didn't help."

"I couldn't!"

He grunted and stood up. We tried to help him, but he knocked our hands away. He sagged a bit at the knees, but kept on walking, unsteadily. He walked back into the waiting room. Silently, people were tidying up, straightening beds. Royce scooped up his clothes with almost his usual deftness. He went back to his bed, and dropped down onto it, next to Tom, and began to inspect his shirt and trousers for damage.

"The least you could have done!" I said. I don't know what I meant.

Lou was leaning back on his bed. He looked pleased, elbows sticking out from the side of his head. "Look at it this way," he said. "It might do him some good. He shouldn't be so worried about his little problem. He just needs to relax a bit more, try it on for size. The worst thing you can do with a problem like that is hide from it."

If I'd had an axe, I would have killed him. He knew that. He smiled.

Then the lights went out, without warning as always, but two hours early.

There was snow on the ground in the morning, a light dusting of it on the roof and on the ground. There was no patter. Royce did not talk to the cameras. He came out, wearing his jacket; there was a tear in his shirt, under the armpit. He ate his breakfast without looking at anyone, his face closed and still. Hardly anyone spoke. Big Lou walked around with a little half-grin. He was so pleased, he was stretched tight with it. He'd won; he was Boss again. No one used the showers.

Then we went out, and waited for the train.

We could see its brilliant headlight shining like a star on the track.

We could see the layers of wire-mesh gates pulling back for it, like curtains, and close behind it. We began to hear a noise coming from it.

It was a regular, steady drumming against metal, a bit like the sound of marching feet, a sound in unison.

"Yup," said Charlie. "The drugs have worn off."

"It's going to be a bastard," said Gary.

Lou walked calmly toward the cameras. "Alice? What do we do?" No answer. "We can't unload them, Alice. Do we just leave them on the train, or what?" Silence. "Alice. We need to know what you want done."

"Don't call me Alice," said the camera.

"Could you let us back in, then?" asked Lou.

No answer.

The train came grinding into the platform, clattering and banging and smelling of piss. We all stood back from it, well back. Away from us, at the far end of the platform, James stood looking at the silver sky and the snow in the woods, his back to us, his headphones on. We could hear the thin whisper of Mozart from where we stood. Still looking at the woods, James sauntered to-ward the nearest carriage.

"James!" wailed Charlie. "Don't open the door!"

"Jim! Jimmy! Stop!"

"James! Don't!"

He waved. All he heard was Mozart, and a banging from the train not much louder than usual. With a practiced, muscular motion, he snapped up the bolt, and pulled it back, and began to swing open the door.

It burst free from his grasp, and was slammed back, and a torrent of people poured down out of the carriage, onto him. His headphones were only the first thing to be torn from him. The Stiffs were all green and mottled, like leaves. Oh Christ, oh Jesus. Uniforms. Army.

We turned and ran for the turnstile. "Alice! God-damn it, let us in!" raged Lou. The turnstile buzzed, angrily, and we scrambled through it, caught up in its turning arms, crammed ourselves into its embrace four at a time, and we could hear feet running behind us. I squeezed through with Gary, and heard Charlie behind us cry out. Hands held him, clawed at his forehead. Gary and I pulled him out, and Lou leapt in after us, and pulled the emergency gate shut.

They prowled just the other side of a wire mesh fence, thick necked, as mad as bulls, with asses as broad as our shoulders. "We'll get you fuckers," one of them promised me, looking dead into my eyes. They trotted from door to door of the train, spring-ing them. They began to rock the turnstile back and forth. "Not electric!" one of them called. They began to pull at the wire mesh. We had no weapons.

"Hey! Hey, help!" we shouted. "Alice, Scarlett. Help!"

No answer. As if in contempt, the warm-up lights went on.

"We're using gas," said Alice, her voice hard. "Get your masks."

The masks were in the waiting room. We turned and ran, but the cameras didn't give us time. Suddenly there was a gush of something like steam, in the icy morning, out from under the platform. I must have caught a whiff of it. It was like a blow on the head, and my feet crossed in front of each other instead of running. I managed to hold my breath, and Royce's face was suddenly in front of me, as still as a stone, and he pushed a mask at me, and pulled on his own, walking toward the gate. I fumbled with mine. Harry, or someone, all inhuman in green, helped me. I saw Royce walking like an angel into white, a blistering white that caught the winter sunlight in a blaze. He walked right up to the fence, and stood in the middle of the poison, and watched.

The gas billowed, and the people billowed too, in waves. They climbed up over each other, in shifting pyramids, to get away, piling up against the fence. Those on top balanced, waving their arms like surfers, and there were sudden flashes of red light through the mist, and bars of rumpled flesh appeared across their eyes. One of them had fine light hair that burst into flame about his head. He wore a crown of fire.

The faces of those on the bottom of the heap were pressed against the fence into diamond shapes, and they twitched and jittered. The whole wave began to twitch and jitter, and shake, against the fence.

It must have been the gas in my head. I was suddenly convinced that it was nerve gas, and that meant that the nerves of the dead people were still working, even though they were dead. Even though they were dead, they would shake and judder against the fence until it fell, and then they would walk toward us, and take us into their arms, and talk to us in whispers, and pull off the masks.

I spun around, and looked at the mound, because I thought the dead inside it would wake. It did seem to swim and move, and I thought that Babylon would crack, and what had been hidden would come marching out. The dead were angry, because they had been forgotten.

Then the mist began to clear, blown. I thought of dandelion seeds that I had blown like magic across the fields when I was a child.

"Hockey games," I said. I thought there had been a game of hockey. The bodies were piled up, in uniforms. They were still. We waited. Harry practiced throwing stones.

"What a mess," said Gary.

There were still wafts of gas around the bottom of the platform. We didn't know how long we would have to wait before it was safe.

Suddenly Lou stepped forward. "Come on, let's start," he said, his voice muffled by the mask. He pulled back the emergency gate. "We've got masks," he said.

None of us moved. We just didn't have the heart.

"We can't leave them there!" Lou shouted. Still none of us moved.

Then Royce sat down on the grass, and pulled off his mask, and took two deep breaths. He looked at the faces in front of him, a few feet away, purple against the mesh.

"Alice," he said. "Why are we doing this?"

No answer.

"It's horrible. It's the worst thing in the world. Horrible for us, horrible for you. That's why what happened last night happened, Alice. Because this is so terrible. You cage people up, you make them do things like this, and something goes, something inside. Something will give with you, too, Alice. You can't keep this up either. Do you have dreams, Alice? Do you have dreams at night about this? While the Wigs are at their parties, making big decisions and debating ideology? I don't believe anyone could look at this and not feel sick."

"You need to hear any more?" Lou asked the cameras, with a swagger.

"I mean. How did it happen?" Royce was crying. "How did we get so far apart? There were problems, sure, but there was love, too. Men and women loved each other. People love each other, so why do we end up doing things like this? Can you give me a reason, Alice?"

"You do realize what he's saying, don't you?" asked Lou. He pulled off his mask, and folded his arms. "Just listen to what is coming out of his closet."

"I am not going to move those bodies, Alice," said Royce. "I can't. I literally cannot move another body. I don't think any of us can. You can kill us all if you want to. But then, you'd have to come and do it yourselves, wouldn't you?"

Lou waited. We all waited. Nothing happened.

"They'll—uh—start to stink if we don't move them," said Gary, and coughed, and looked to Lou.

"If we don't move them," said Harry, and for once he wasn't smiling, "another train can't come in."

"Alice?" said Lou. "Alice?" Louder, outraged. "You hear what is happening here?"

There was a click, and a rumbling sound, a sort of shunting. A gate at the far end of the platform rolled back. Then another, and another, all of them opening at once.

"Go on," said Alice.

We all just stood there. We weren't sure what it meant, we didn't even know that all those gates could open at once.

"Go *on*. Get out. Hurry. Before one of the Wigs comes."

"You mean it?" Harry asked. We were frightened. We were frightened to leave.

"We'll say you got killed in the riot, that you were gassed or something. They'll never know the difference. Now move!"

"Alice, god-damn it, what are you doing, are you crazy?" Lou was wild.

"No. She ain't crazy. You are." That was Royce. He stood up. "Well you heard her, haul some ass. Charlie, Harry, you go and get all the food there is left in the canteen. The rest of you, go get all the blankets and clothes, big coats that haven't been shipped back. And Harry, fill some jugs with water."

Lou didn't say anything. He pulled out a kitchen knife and he ran toward Royce. Royce just stood there. I don't think he would have done anything. I think he was tired, tired of the whole thing. I mean he was tired of death. Lou came for him.

The Grils burned him. They burned Lou. He fell in a heap at Royce's feet, his long, strong arms all twisted. "Aw hell," said Royce, sad and angry. "Aw hell."

And a voice came cutting into my head, clear and blaring. I was crazy. The voice said, "This is radio station KERB broadcasting live from the First Baptist Church of Christ the Redeemer with the Reverend Thomas Wallace Robertson and the Inglewood Youth Choir, singing *O Happy Day*."

And I heard it. I heard the music. I just walked out onto the platform, reeling with the sound, the mass of voices inside my head, and I didn't need any blankets. O Happy Day! When Jesus wash! And Los Angeles might be gone, and Detroit and Miami, a lot of things might be gone, but that Sunday night music was still kicking shit, and if there wasn't a God, there was always other people, and they surprised you. Maybe I'd been fooled by history too. I said goodbye to the cameras as I passed them. Goodbye Alice. Goodbye Hortensia. See ya, Scarlet. Butch, I'm sorry about the name.

They were making funny noises. The cameras were weeping.

I walked on toward the open gate.

For America

THE UNCONQUERED COUNTRY

A LIFE HISTORY

I watched a family of about eight persons—a man and a woman, both about fifty, with their children about one, eight and ten, and two grown-up daughters of about twenty to twenty-four. An old woman with snow-white hair was holding the one-year-old in her arms and singing to it, and tickling it. The child was cooing with delight. The couple were looking on with tears in their eyes.

The father was holding the hand of a boy about ten years old and speaking to him softly; the boy was fighting his tears. The father pointed to the sky, stroked his head and seemed to explain something to him.

FROM THE TRANSCRIPTS OF THE NUREMBERG TRIALS AS REPORTED IN *THE QUALITY OF MERCY: CAMBODIA, HOLOCAUST AND MODERN CONSCIENCE*
BY WILLIAM SHAWCROSS

PART ONE

THE NEW NUMBERS

Third Child had nothing to sell but parts of her body. She sold her blood. A young man with a cruel warrior's face—a hooked nose between two plump cheeks—came to her room every two weeks. He called himself her Agent, and told a string of hearty jokes, and carried a machine around his neck. It was rather like a pair of bagpipes, and it clung to him, and whimpered.

Third rented her womb for industrial use. She was cheaper than the glass tanks. She grew parts of living machinery inside her—differentials for trucks, small household appliances. She gave birth to advertisements, small caricature figures that sang songs. There was no other work for her in the city. The city was called Saprang Song, which meant Divine Lotus, after the Buddha.

When Third was lucky, she got a contract for weapons. The pay was good because it was dangerous. The weapons would come gushing suddenly out of her with much loss of blood, usually in the middle of the night: an avalanche of glossy, freckled, dark brown guppies with black, soft eyes and bright rodent smiles full of teeth. No matter how ill or exhausted Third felt, she would shovel them, immediately, into buckets and tie down the lids. If she didn't do that, immediately, if she fell asleep, the guppies would eat her. Thrashing in their buckets as she carried them down the steps, the guppies would eat each other. She would have to hurry with them, shuffling as fast as she could under the weight, to the Neighbors. The Neighbors only paid her for the ones that were left alive. It was piecework.

The Neighbors had coveted the lands of Third's people for

generations. Then the people of the Big Country, for reasons of their own, had given weapons to the Neighbors.

Third's nation had called itself the Unconquered Country. It had never been colonized. Then the Neighbors came and conquered the Country. They conquered the South at first, with its cities and City People. The North still fought. Its mobile villages moved into the hills.

Third had been a child in a rebel village, hidden in a valley. She lived there until the end of her sixth summer. In the middle of the village, on a wooden pole, there flew the white and yellow flag of the Unconquered People. The women had worked the rice, while men kept watch in the hills, with old guns from other wars.

The name "Third Child" had been a spell, to make sure that there would be no more children born to her mother and father. The spell worked. A month after Third was born, her father was killed. By a tiger, it was said. There were very few tigers left. They had become beasts of portent. They ate people.

Third looked ordinary, to herself and others. She loved numbers. Her cousin, who was a man, had a position as an Accountant. Third would sit next to him in rapt and silent wonder, as the yarrow stalks clicked back and forth, counting in fan-shaped patterns. Her cousin was charmed that she was interested, sweet and silent as a child should be. He showed her how the yarrow worked.

Numbers were portents too. They were used as oracles. This was a practical thing. Rice shoots were counted; yields were predicted; seed was stored. Numbers spread out in fanlike shapes, into the future.

Third could read them. She saw yarrow in her mind, ghost yarrow she sometimes called them, and they would scurry ahead of the real stalks. They moved too fast for her to follow, flashing, weaving. They leapt to correct answers, ahead of her cousin.

If anyone asked Third how much rice was in a bowl, she would answer, "enough." It was always polite to answer that there was enough rice, even when there wasn't. But if anyone had pressed for more detail, Third could have answered, "Six hundred to seven hundred grains." The yarrow stalks in her mind would click, telling her how much space ten grains took—as represented by so many lengths cut into a stalk—and how much space there was in a bowl. The ghost yarrow opened and closed, like a series of waving fans, beautiful, orderly, true.

As Third carried food to her mother in the fields, the yarrow would move. They told her the number of rice shoots, and the rate of their growth. She would have an early sense of the harvest, and how many days were left until they all could rest. She could not follow the waving fans, but she could feel her mind driving them. It was a pleasurable sensation, this slight sense of forcing something ahead. She could make them go faster if she wanted to.

It was how she saw the world; it was as if the world were a forest of yarrow, moving all around her, as if numbers were leaves, rustling in the wind.

Third did not talk much. This was considered delightfully demure. She helped around the house, she found helping about the house very easy, and even her mother, who was used to her, had to exclaim at the tidiness of Third. Her second sister was chagrined. But the eldest sister was proud of her. Everything was always tidy around Third. The mat, the vase, the wooden cup, the brazier, the clay pot full of sour sauce: they were in place. You knew Third had been at work because it was beautiful. Organized according to some unseen principle that even the number-blind could recognize as possessing quality.

"Our little princess," her eldest sister would call her. Only princesses in stories had time for arranging flowers. Third worked quickly. This house had no flowers, but it looked as if it did.

The rebels had an interest in education. They sent a teacher to Third's village, and she was a woman of great application. She stayed eight weeks and two days, and then she had to go back to the war. It would be, as one always had to say, enough.

She was to teach the children how to read and to count. Third was averagely bad at her letters. This was mostly due to shyness. To read, you had to stand and speak, and this she had never been called upon to do. The language of the People was not pictographic, but it was tonal and each sound-sign had to show shifts in tone. It was ferociously complicated. Third was interested in the architecture of the signs. Their shapes kept turning in her mind into proportions that as yet had no meaning. The teacher would force her to speak, to say something.

"I like that," Third said, pointing to an arch in a sign and following it with her finger.

"But what does the sign sound like?" the teacher would insist.

Third would go quiet and downcast, feeling that she was doing wrong. The question made no sense. Sign sound like? A sign sounds? Small brown face and black button eyes were clouded with withdrawal and remorse.

Oh, my People, the teacher would think, looking at her, despairing. There was so much to do. She could not be angry.

It was at mathematics that Third was noticeably backward. Numbers for her were always part of something else. They could only exist in relation to other numbers, in relation to real things. They could not be uprooted and made alone. They were related, like people.

"What number is this?" the teacher would ask, holding up a card.

"Number as what?" Third would murmur. She tried to read the digits as she read the yarrow. Their proportions carried no meaning.

"Number of anything," the teacher would answer. "Just the number. By itself."

Third would stare back mournfully at her, and the teacher would pass on to another child. The teacher taught the children by day, under a screen of bamboo, so that they could not be seen from the air.

"One day," she told them, "the Neighbors will be gone. The Neighbors will be gone, and the foreigners will be gone, and the People will need to work, to build. You will have to build. You will have to work, to count, to read."

What the People needed to be, what they had to become, were fighters. That was what the teacher knew. Third was self-contained, beautifully mute, as was expected of children of the People, and this made the teacher very impatient. The People must stop being quiet. To stay themselves, to hold back the Neighbors and the Big People, who wanted to swallow the Unconquered.

The teacher turned Third into a symbol. The symbol was this: when this one small girl learns to count, I will know I have done some good. Third became a target. It was a kind of love.

She made Third stay after the others. She held up cards. "What number is this? What number is this, Third? Look. Tell me the number."

Third, seized with a panic that she was doing wrong, would not move, would not speak. She had never done wrong, and her teacher was trying so hard, paying her special attention. And Third hated it. That made her feel even more in the wrong.

She went off at night, creeping out of her house, to pound the mud with her feet, and fling the yarrow stalks in her mind at the sky in anger, going over and over them, trying to find some link with the marks on the horrible cards. Even then, Third did not cry.

Then one day, the teacher had an inspiration.

It was after class. The other children were back out in the fields, shaking the muddle out of their heads. Third was alone with the teacher again.

"Well," the teacher said. "Today we try a different approach." And she brought out the yarrow stalks.

No, thought Third. Leave those alone.

"Now, Third, look. One. One stalk. Not many stalks. Just one stalk by itself," said the teacher, and smiled, and watched. "That is one."

It was like a door beginning to open, and it was as if Third slammed it shut. Third was in terror, though she did not know why.

"Now, Third. Two. Two yarrow stalks."

Lips pressed together, Third jammed all the stalks back together in a bunch.

"No, no. Two. See? Only two."

Blindly this time, Third reached for the yarrow, and the teacher took hold of her hands, and pushed them away. She picked up the yarrow stalks and hid them behind her back. Third tried to reach around her, one quick, tiny hand after another. The teacher had to use both hands to fend her off. The yarrow stalks were left behind her on the mat. Third sat back. The teacher relaxed. Third leapt forward, and grabbed a fistful of the yarrow, and the teacher laughed.

Third made a fan, one yarrow stalk between each finger. Still chuckling, shaking her head, the teacher grabbed the yarrow and used them as levers to prize apart Third's fingers.

"Sit there," the teacher said, and pushed Third back. "Now. One. Two. Three." She laid the stalks down, but far apart, in parallel lines that Third knew could never meet. Third. Three stalks together made three parts of a whole. These did not. Third understood, and she did not want to. As if tearing through flesh, the teacher was rending the numbers apart. She was making them alone.

Third turned and tried to run. The teacher yelped with laughter, and grabbed her, and hugged her, controlled her by hugging her.

"You won't get away that easily," said the teacher, grinning.

Third wanted to hit her. She wanted to yell and scream and get away, but she could do none of those things. She was frozen. She was going to have to count.

"Give me numbers," whispered the teacher.

"One . . . two . . . three," Third said, looking down, in a tiny and wan little voice.

For some reason, the teacher was disappointed.

"Oh," the teacher said, and dropped her arms, and gave Third a little pat. "Good. That was simple, wasn't it? Now you can count. And after that is four and five." The teacher laid down more stalks. "See? Four and five. Say 'Four and five,' Third."

"Four and five," murmured Third, and everything around her seemed bated, like breath.

"Now say them all together, all the numbers."

Let me go, Third's eyes pleaded, but the teacher pretended not to understand. The teacher kept it up, all the way to ten. In the end, it was the teacher who had to leave. Third was left alone, under the screen, quick night having fallen. She was afraid to move.

Something terrible had happened to the numbers. They wouldn't work. Third tried to drive the yarrow in her mind, but as soon as they touched on any one of the new numbers, they were snagged by something. They stopped, and had to start again, grew confused, or were left naked, hanging, and Third realized she had never really understood how they danced their way to answers. They were going away, like friends.

She walked to her cousin's house, taking tiny steps. She was frightened that if she ran, she would disturb the numbers more.

They were eating at her cousin's house, but Third gave no words of greeting and did not take off her shoes. She walked very carefully to her cousin, and dropped to her knees next to him and folded herself up into a tight, supplicant little ball. She was shaking.

"Third Child, cousin?" he asked, alarmed, meaning, What is wrong? He thought her mother had died.

"The numbers. The yarrow," she said, her words like little parcels.

"Ah!" said her cousin, and began to smile.

"Show me how they work!"

"But you know how they work." Third said nothing. Her cousin cradled her up next to him, and kissed her forehead, and held her to his plump bosom and his crisp plaid shirt. "Your teacher," he said, "says I must not."

He could feel her wilt.

"You will get used to the new numbers in time," he cajoled her, shaking her slightly with affection. It was touching how important small things seemed to children. "You will see. They are new, modern numbers, and we can use them to fight the Neighbors." But his face was darkening, for under his hand, the child was trembling.

Third's eldest sister came looking for her. "Little princess!" she said in alarm. "What has she done to you?" They began to understand that something had been broken.

Sometimes at night, the old numbers would return, like the ghosts they were. Like ghosts, they were disordered, limping. The things they whispered made no sense. They were sad in the way that ghosts are sad, trying to fight their way back to life, back to sense, irredeemably marred.

Third welcomed them, and hoped for them and wanted them to work. She pitied them, and finally, she grew weary of them. She could still use the real yarrow stalks as well as other children did. That was, after all, enough.

She did not remember the exact day that the teacher left. She only remembered the hateful nugget of gladness she felt when the teacher was gone. The teacher was going back to the war. When Third heard the teacher had been killed, she was glad.

There was the rest of the summer. It seemed a long time then. It rained. The marriage of Third's cousin was arranged. He would be wed after the monsoons, and Third would help with the flowers.

His family had a house-birthing for him. His new house was born, and was led baby-wet and making soft, breathy noises from house to house. It stumbled on its fat, dimpled white legs, and it wore strings of bangles as it was paraded. The People sang it songs, and patted it, and the children rode on its patient back. Third's cousin would train it as it grew, to shelter his new family.

The houses of the People were alive. They lived for generations, with wattles and wrinkles and patches of whisker, like ancient grannies. They wore roofed porches from their heads, like reed hats. They knew their families and cared for them. It was said that they remembered even those who had died long ago, and grieved for them. It was said they had a special cry for the dead, to greet their family's ghosts.

Third was under her house when the Neighbors came. She was feeding the hens. In her language, hens were called Great Fat Ladies in White Bloomers. Third fed them slugs she had collected from the paddies. She counted their eggs and she knew which Ladies were fattest. She knew their future from their weight.

It was the first cloudless day. The old house above her sighed and shifted on its haunches. It fed on light. The borders of its shadow were sharply defined on the ground.

Suddenly there was a warbling. It was from the men on the hill, and the house stood up.

It lurched to its feet, swaying, and the wicker cages between its legs snapped and flew apart. There were crashes of falling crockery overhead. Third knew her second sister had been beside the charcoal stove. She heard her second sister scream. Third ran outside to see.

All along the valley, the houses began to hoot in panic. The flood warning, the warning for a flood, over and over. The hens scattered, in wavering lines.

Low overhead, and silently, came Sharks. Sharks, it was said, had been human once. Sunlight reflected on their humming wings, and they were long and sleek and freckled with big brown spots like old people get on their hands. Third saw their round and happy faces. She saw them smile. As they passed, wind whipped into her face, and she turned.

An attack. Third knew what to do in an attack. She was to hide in the deepest part of the house, and wrap herself in white blankets. But the porch of the house now towered above her head. Her sister stood on it, wailing, beet-red, scalded by the stove.

"Sister, get inside!" cried Third. The old house trumpeted with relief, and snatched Third up with its trunk. It thought there was a flood, thought it had to keep Third from trying to swim, from drowning, so it lifted her up high over its round and featureless head, and began to march for the higher ground. The ground was still moist. There was no dust. Third could see everything.

She saw the stampede of houses, as they gained speed, throwing their great feet forward into a lumbering trot, their heads bobbing with effort. She saw the fields beyond, the women running, but she could not see her mother, and she saw the Sharks. They puffed out their cheeks and they blew, and where they blew, everything died in a line, like a furrow.

The rice went brown, crumpling up like burning paper. A Great Fat Lady collapsed in a rumpled heap like a big balloon losing air, her feathers curling up, melting away. Third knew where the path of destruction was proceeding. She knew who was going to fall next, who was running to intercept the lines of death. She tried to call to them. "Madame Goh! Madame Goh! Stop running!" she piped, and heard the frailty of her own voice. She looked for her mother. She looked for her sister.

The old guns on the hill leapt forward and settled back, and there was a boom and batter that made Third scream and cover her ears. Parts of the opposite hillside were thrown up as chunks of rock and the spinning heads of trees. The Sharks whistled, cheering, as if at a football match, and swept low over the guns. After that, the guns were silent. The Sharks rose up in the sky, reflecting light like dragonflies. They were almost beautiful for a moment. Then they turned and descended on the village. As they leveled off, Third knew she was directly in their path.

Third's eldest sister jumped down from her cousin's house as it lumbered forward. She dodged between the houses on her long stick legs, in her red gingham dress.

"House," she called as she ran. "Old house. Kneel down! Kneel down!"

She jogged backward beside it, jumping up and down, trying to reach Third. The house was too panicked to notice, and Third was clogged with terror. Third saw the faces of the Sharks, the row of smiles, the number of teeth. They batted their eyelashes at her, and giggled. They puffed out their cheeks like the Four Winds, and blew.

Third turned her head, and felt the withering blast of antilife pass her by. It scraped her ankle, and the flesh over the bone rose up in protest, bubbles of oil seething under a patch of skin. She felt the backwash of air as they passed. She felt a wing throb, almost gently for a moment, on the top of her head. There was tinkling, musical laughter, a sprinkle of notes that almost reassured Third Child. Then she looked down.

Her elder sister lay in a puddle. The gingham dress had gone orange. Her skin was a sickly, translucent yellow, puckered up and crinkled and soft. Her pigtails had gone altogether; strands of hair blew in the dust.

Overhead, the Sharks made a rude, farting sound. They sashayed in the air, bumping their middles from side to side, as if they had hips. They were mocking humankind.

* * *

The Neighbors followed soon after, in the cavernous bellies of winged transports. There were ninety of them, in three parties. They did not look different from the Unconquered People. They had the same sleek brown skin and they were not ugly. They wore green coolsuits against the heat, and had bands of metal strapped to their index fingers that spurted fire and light where they pointed. They also carried the ceremonial bayonets that were the mark of a true warrior. The Sharks hovered overhead holding the fluttering banners of the Neighbors in their teeth.

Third's mother sat in the darkest part of the house, Third and her second sister on her lap. Rocking them, going "Sssh, Ssssh, Sssh," to soothe them. The eldest sister still lay in the dust outside: the second sister wailed inconsolably. For Third everything was muffled, even the pain in her ankle. Third was silent. She must have gone for a drink of water, for at some point she was standing in front of the window by the tub. Through a wavering curtain of hot, rising air, she saw two village men being led out into the paddies. All the sound was muffled, too, except for the buzzing of flies.

One of the villagers was her cousin. He had a soft round face and a thick mustache. He wore a crisp plaid shirt that his mother would have beaten clean that morning, and the loose black leggings of the People. The trousers had an airy slit up the inside leg, and one of the Neighbors ran the blade of his bayonet up along it. Her cousin stepped back, scowling, too anxious to be angry. Third saw one of the Neighbors tell a joke, laughing, and flick his cigarette into the water.

Both men were pushed down onto their knees. The other villager, a wiry and nervous uncle, began to plead, jabbering. A Neighbor knelt on his shoulder, and pulled his head back, hard, by the hair. The uncle held up the thin palms of his hands against the bayonets.

Third's cousin knelt, fists folded, calmly glancing over his shoulders at the familiar hills, as if he did not care about them, not yet sure, unable to believe, that he was going to die.

Third did not remember his murder. She remembered the face of the man who did it. He was tiny and thin and wretched, with outlines of gold around his tobacco-stained teeth. His cheeks were deeply scarred by pockmarks, and he was grinning a rictus grin. It took over the lower half of his face, and Third understood that he was grinning in order to frighten, because he felt evil, and he thought that this was what evil looked like, and that evil made him important.

Suddenly her cousin was on his side, his face still soft and confused. Once he and Third had gone out together to look at the stars, and he had lain on the ground like that. Third had fallen asleep with her head on his chest. Blood spread across his chest now, in the orderly patterns of the crisp plaid shirt.

He was the Accountant. No one else would know so well how the yarrow worked. Third's mother eased her away from the window.

The Neighbors came for a visit. They took swigs of water from Third's cup. "We are your friends," they told Third's mother, and requisitioned the rice she had not hidden. They told her to save her menstrual blood. Third's mother dipped and bowed to them, hands high over head. She smiled. When they were gone, she pulled Third to her, and hugged her, and her hands were trembling. Third listened to the Neighbors under her house, chasing her White Ladies. They were taking them away.

"They are going to do something with our blood," said Third's mother. "They want to weaken the male power of our men."

They slaughtered ten of the old houses. Third's own house began to make a new noise, a wheedling noise, tightly constrained. The walls shook delicately. Third's mother risked looking out of the window, and saw them hacking at the carcass of their cousin's house. The new little white house lay by its side. The Neighbors began to erect new, dead houses that could not walk to other valleys.

"There is nothing for us here," said Third's mother. In the night, she parceled up the stove, and a pot, and their rice, and she led her children away from the village.

They had to leave their old caring house behind. They tethered it to a stake. It knew it was being left, and couldn't understand why. As they crept away it began to bellow after them, tugging at the line that held it. Deserted houses sometimes died of love.

"Go!" whispered Third's mother, and pushed her, and gave her another nudge when Third turned around. "Keep going! Don't look back even if I fall down." They heard the Neighbors call to each other. They sounded like dogs barking. Third and her family flitted into the shadow of the trees and waited until their house fell silent. Then they moved on.

They went, like everyone else, to the city. Third's mother carried them most of the way on her back.

There would have been flowers at the wedding of Third's cousin. Years later, she still found herself looking forward to it. All the village girls would have been linked together by a chain of flowers. Third would have tended the bride.

The villagers grew the flowers, lotuses, along the borders of the rice paddies. The flowers were not picked, except for special occasions. In the mornings the lotuses would be open wide; by noon they would be shut. There had been a medium in the village who claimed she had the soul of a prince who was in turn possessed by the soul of a sorcerer. Third had once seen her eat a glass cup to prove it, crunching it in her mouth. Each house had a shrine to the Buddha, which was exchanged each month with a different house.

The People sang when they spoke. The language was tonal; melody carried meaning. The numbers sang too. The yarrow would be cast into patterns that were tones. They seemed to speak. They turned into songs.

They were feast songs, work songs, cooking songs, cast by the yarrow. Everyone sang them. Long afterward, Third would find herself humming them. She no longer knew what they meant. She had forgotten the words and the numbers. But they still murmured to her, like voices in memory.

Her name was a spell, a number, and Third's mother only had to say it, to remember tigers. As they fled from the village, Third and her family were in terror of tigers. Where they slept, Third's mother made a fire against them.

In the middle of the night, Third felt hot breath on her cheeks, and opened her eyes. Looming over her, as large as she was, was the face of the tiger. There was blood on its muzzle, and its great green eyes stared into her, piercing her like shafts, brushing, it seemed, her very soul, making it go hushed and cold. Third did not move. There was nothing she could do. The tiger snuffled her once more and then, having eaten already, silently padded away on its big orange feet. Third looked, and saw that her mother and sister were still alive.

Third couldn't sleep after that, so she tried counting the stars. It was so slow. One. Two. Three.

Suddenly there was a great rising out of her of numbers. A rage of numbers, the old numbers, angry and dislocated. They reached up out of her for something, some answer, some reason. They almost seized it. The size of the world. The number of the People. Third felt her breath and heart constrict. The numbers withdrew like a flock of birds into the sky. She could almost hear them cawing. She saw the pattern they made. It was the pattern of the future, black wings and tiger stripes.

In the morning, she stood up when her mother did and told her nothing about it.

PART TWO

THE CEREMONY

The city of Saprang Song had paved streets, over two thousand of them, and plumbing, enough for a million people. By the time Third was an adult, eight million, half of the People, had crowded into it.

The old city was made of stone and steel: the new city was made of flesh. The Neighbors had introduced a new kind of mobile home. It was slow and stupid, a long beige tube, with ribs in its ceiling, and a single window, and a single door. When it was closed, the door looked like the bottom of a mushroom, all gills. When it opened, a flap of flesh came out like a tongue, steps to climb.

The houses were supposed to spread out, across the countryside. Instead, the refugees discovered that the houses could climb, on legs that looked like the cooked wings of chickens. They had long hairs like wires at the tip. The houses could cling to each other's backs. As the refugees swarmed, the houses rose up in haphazard towers, tall lopsided heaps of housing, waves of it, with no streets between them. They looked like a piled mass of Conestoga wagons.

The People had to walk up and over each other's houses to get to their own, or squeeze through narrow passageways past houses turned into tiny shops or brothels. They shouted at each other to be quiet, and fended off new, creeping houses with brooms. Lines of laundry, gray and faded, hung between the towers, and the air was always full of the smell of cooking and the hearty blare of media entertainment. Sometimes the ribs of the lowest houses would break from the weight, and the towers would collapse in a fleshy avalanche. In the monsoon rains, the water would drain down the towers in steps, like waterfalls, and flood the lowest layers. The houses would go very diseased, soft and bruised and seeping. The very poorest people dried the dead ones, and lived in the husks. Or they ate them.

They fought with municipal beasts that prowled the streets eating garbage and the unloved dead.

Third was going to sell her left eye. It was common practice. There were dealers. They would prize it out of her, without any drugs for the pain, and freeze it, and sell it for transplants or machinery. It was illegal, of course. The dealers had stalls in the markets that could be moved quickly when the Neighbors came.

There were many people waiting in line. The old woman in front of Third already had a puckered pouch of skin where one eye should have been. She was going to sell her second eye in order to buy her granddaughter a wedding coat. She was very calm and gracious and proud, in immaculate black. "You must not imagine I was always like this, oh no," she said, smiling, wagging a finger. "I was a high lady in my village." They all said that, but the gentle, precise way she spoke made Third believe her. "Now my granddaughter will be one as well. That is her mother, there, my daughter." A woman in a glossy pink jacket stood well away from the line, pretending not to see them. "Isn't she pretty? She is so embarrassed. Make sure she gets the money, please?"

"You. Next," said the dealer, looking harassed and chubby in his white shorts and bright printed shirt. He led the old woman away with his young son to help. He drew a black drapery on rings, like a shower curtain, around her. When the old woman emerged, both eyes were closed, and her skin was white and greasy with sweat, and she reached out into the air for Third, and tried to speak, but the sound was slurred and distorted, like a tape at the wrong speed. She grabbed Third's arm, and Third felt a jolt from her, like electricity, from the quaking of her bones.

Third fainted. She lacked food and blood, and she'd been standing for hours, and waves of nausea seemed to pour out of the old woman. When Third awoke, on asphalt, on crushed and sour cabbage, the woman was gone. A soldier, in the uniform of the Neighbors, was leaning over her.

"The Peace of God," he said. He was of the People, from the country, and with country courtesy he bowed, his hands pressed together as in prayer, at the level of his mouth and chin. That meant the soldier considered Third to be his equal.

She plainly wasn't. Third grunted and sat up. "Peace of God," she murmured, and did not bother to bow. She tried to stand up, to regain her place in line. The soldier helped her to her feet, but kept a grip on her arm, and would not let her move back toward the dealer's stall.

"Perhaps you would like something to eat?" he asked, grinning stupidly, with a battery of green, misshapen teeth. He was very ugly, with no chin and a large Adam's apple, and creases across his neck.

"Yes," said Third, immediately, whatever it was he wanted from her, though she was still feeling queasy. "In there." There was a small shop that sold dried insects in glass jars. Some of them were coated in sugar.

"No, no, you cannot eat there," he said, and pulled her with him.

"But that is what I want," she protested, looking wistfully back at the window full of insects. What sort of crazy man was this? Did he want a prostitute? She, Third, was no prostitute, he must see that. She was Dastang Tze-See, which meant Desperate Flies in Filth. Desperate Flies filled their wombs, as she did, with other forms of life. No man would go near them. There were silly, nasty stories of men finding Sharks in wait inside them. He had seen her in the line, he must know that. So what did he want?

He took her to a proper food wagon where families ate, with a sign and a man in an apron, and he bought her roast pork and bean sprouts and rice, and she nearly fainted again, from the smell, and from wonder.

She crammed her mouth full of it. The skin on the pork had actually been rubbed with salt, and it was crisp and moist with fat, and the bean sprouts were hot and fresh and clean tasting, and the rice was hefty and drenched in soy.

"Is it good?" the soldier asked.

Third shrugged with equivocation, her cheeks round and shiny with grease. It was not wise to appear too grateful. The soldier watched her as she ate, still smiling. If only, she thought, he would stop grinning and hide those teeth. Poor people should never smile. She was considering whether she had the strength to run away from him, when he said, "I have to go now."

She looked at him, eyes slightly narrowed, still chewing.

"I must return to the barracks. Look, meet me here tomorrow, this time, and we will have another meal."

"All right," said Third with a shrug.

"You will be here? You will not go back to that line?"

Third worked a piece of pork loose from between her teeth. The line was her business.

"I'll give you money, you won't have to."

"I'll be here," said Third, scowling.

"Tomorrow, then," he said, and turned sideways to move through the crowd.

"Hoi!" Third called after him, and he looked around. "Why are you doing this?"

"For the sake of the People," he said, no longer smiling, and gave her another equal's bow.

The next day he was there, waiting for her. That made him even more of a mystery. He bought her the food and then began to tell her about himself.

"I am not very good with numbers," he said, and smiled as if he had made a joke. "I was not much good at school. But I am good in the army."

He is not very intelligent, Third decided. That is why he smiles. For some reason, this made her smile too, and feel indulgent.

"Before that," the soldier said with innocent assurance that she was finding this interesting, or in some way necessary, "I was a priest."

In the real days before the war, all young men had been priests instead of soldiers. He must have chosen to become one. Why, wondered Third, is he telling me all this?

"I had the shaved head. The yellow robes. And I did not work, I was given food. When someone died, I sat with them and listened to the story of the one who had died. We sat like this for hours." He showed her how he sat, his hands on their shoulders, rocking. "I wrote the story down, and put it in the temple so their history would be known." He smiled again.

"I would put one third of the food I was given in the ghost boxes to feed the dead. Many of the priests did not do this, they kept the food for themselves, but that is wrong. The food is meant for the dead. So they will not feel alone."

Does he believe it? Does he believe in ghost boxes and life histories? What does he want from me? The answer when it came was so simple that Third felt foolish for not understanding before.

He wants, she understood, a wife. Oh, poor man. That's it, he has been a priest and his time is up—all young men were priests for two years, and then they married, and now is his time to marry. She found his adherence to the pattern touching. It was almost mathematical. And sad. For this man was ugly.

His name was Crow. Crows were omens of death. The family had been given a cursed name as a punishment, and so they were outcasts, except now, when soldiers were needed. As a priest he would have been shunned. Willing and smiling, she saw him, willing and smiling. No one of any station would want a family history written by someone called Crow.

"You have not told me your first name," she said. Only after she said it did she realize that it was exactly what she should have said. That was the pattern. You know the last name, and only ask the first name later. When you are courting.

He told her, and she had to close her eyes with embarrassment, shut out the world. Oh, it was not possible, poor, poor, ugly man.

His name, in a certain light, meant Nourisher of the East. It could also mean, more simply, Dung. Crow Dung with the constant smile.

And I am ugly too, she thought. Oh, she knew that too. She was short and bowlegged, with a thick waist and thick wrists. He wants a wife who is not beautiful, and he wants one of no social standing.

He wants a wife to be grateful. And yet . . . there was something else. He was a country man. Perhaps he was also kind?

A kind man, however ugly, who wants a wife is an opportunity. Very well, Crow Dung, she thought. I am sick of hunger. I am sick of noise and people's sheets hanging out over my window. But this is being very hard. I also think you have virtues. I will see.

"I am a country girl," she told him. "The city confuses me. But I have, I am told, great skills. The thing a woman needs in housework is proportion. That, I have always had. My family used to call me Little Princess, because princesses have time to arrange flowers. I had no time, but I was quick enough to arrange all things. That sounds like I am boasting."

Third looked down, shyly. She was surprised at how easy it was for her to become a country girl after all this time. She had thought she was playacting.

"But I love beauty. And I love things to have a place. And I love the space between things." She found she was telling the truth.

"I often think the stars have a place. When I put the mat and the bowl and the jug of sauce on the floor I think: these also have a place. Like the stars." And she smiled.

Oh, Third, she thought, you are shameless. Crow Dung grinned and grinned.

Right, she thought.

The next morning, her Blood Agent came. "I have fallen heir to great fortune," she told him. "I do not need you."

"What about my ten percent?" he asked.

Third saw his ten percent ever so much more clearly than he did. She threw it over him, her blood, very exactly ten percent of what she usually gave him. He stumbled backward, squawking. He knew very well the blood of Dastang Tze-See often had disease, though he still sold it. His bagpipe creature made sucking noises, sensing its feed. It took ten percent too.

Well, she thought, watching him go, now we will see. I can always get another Blood Agent. But she still had the marks on her arm.

Crow Dung did come courting, with heavy formality. "I come to visit the young Mademoiselle," he said, bowing in his army uniform. He was so proud of being in the army. Third thought he looked ridiculous.

He had brought her a gift. "I saw this," he said and passed her a gift box made of glazed and woven reed, "and I thought: someone in my position cannot arrive without something to show for himself."

Why don't you ask me about the marks on my arm? Third thought. Why don't you ask me how it is that I am alive? She looked at the gift box, and her lip curled, and she passed it back to him. "I don't want it," she said.

Third had a beast in the back of her head, and it was born of hunger and filth; filth and disorder and shame, like a sharp stench. The beast said, I must have this. The beast said, I will not get it, I have never got anything without ripping something out of myself. She confused Crow Dung with people like her Blood Agent. She did not realize that she was hateful to him.

Whenever he visited she insulted him. "You are a common soldier. Some sergeant, you say. I cannot be seen with you. I am of good family. It is wrong. Why do you keep coming here?"

And Crow would keep smiling. Is this some kind of joke to you? she thought.

When he was not there, when she was no longer bitter and anxious and ready to be aggrieved, it came to her that perhaps Crow understood. He understood why she was angry, though she herself did not. Either that, or he was too stupid to notice. I must, she told herself, stop thinking of people as stupid. Who am I, Dastang Tze-See, to call anyone stupid?

She ate her meals alone. She ate a kind of curd that was made from sewage, processed by microorganisms. It was called War Tofu, and was odorless and absolutely tasteless.

She was cold at night, shivering like a dog having dreams, under a single thin blanket.

Oh, Lord Buddha, send him back, and I will beg his forgiveness, she would say, to the night sky that had no stars.

And he would come back, and she would rail at him, and Crow would smile and bow. She was behaving exactly as a country girl should.

Then he asked her to the Ceremony.

This was so unasked for, so wonderful, that Third could not help but throw him out in a fury. Ceremony? How could she go with him, Crow Dung, to the Ceremony? She was already asked, she had many friends, he was to go away and silently ask himself where he thought he was.

It was so beyond hope that anyone would take her to the Ceremony.

The People had a Prince. The mention of his name was enough to make the bottom edge of their eyes sting with salt tears, for the Prince was from the old days, when the Country was Unconquered. He was fat and healthy, with fine white teeth, and he was kind and clever. Even the Neighbors could see his fine qualities. That was why, thought Third, they put him back on the throne. Under their noses, he prayed for the deliverance of his People. Third kept pictures of him from the papers on her walls. She prayed to him. She loved him, not in the way you love a man, but in the way you love yourself and the things that make you. She was fierce on the subject of the Prince.

And Crow had asked her to the Ceremony, where she would see him.

She thought she was not worthy. She thought she was ugly and dark-skinned and could not dress suitably. When Crow asked her, she wanted to hide, hide her head and run from the house.

"I am going with someone else," she told him. She was so poor her nervous hands had nothing to play with.

"That someone is very honored," replied Crow.

I hate you, thought Third. Why are you so honeyed? You are like a windup doll.

"I am, I hope, a friend," continued Crow. "So, please, I hope you will find this to your taste and that you will wear it to the Ceremony with your friends."

He laid out on the floor of Third's house—oh, in the old days, she would not have had a house by herself, and if she did, he could not have been there alone with her, it was all a shadow show, but he wanted to believe. It was he who wanted to believe. He laid out on the floor a new dress. It was black, deep black, fine black, not the sort of black that goes patchy when it rains, good black. And it had gold leaves on it. Third almost wept.

"Why did you do that? I did not ask you to do that!" she raged. "I don't need your dresses."

"Of course. Oh, that is evident," replied Crow. "But it would be such an honor for me if you wore it."

Third felt like weeping on her knees. "I will consider," she said. She had two dresses that had long ago forgotten what color they were. When Crow was gone, she held the dress up to the light. The light caught on the leaves. There were twenty-one of them. An auspicious number. The dressmaker knew and probably wondered if anyone else knew or cared that the dress was an oracle. I care, Third said to the silent dressmaker. Then she felt panic. How will I tell him that I will go with him? I have been so rude. I have sent him away, will he come back?

He did, but with no gifts. That is good, Third thought, you have given me enough. No gifts. It is time I treated you with some respect.

And so she bowed when he entered. "Mr. Crow," she said. "We find ourselves in strange situations, with no guide. And I think: here is one of the People, who serves in the army because he thinks this is right. Now this is an honorable thing. And I should not despise his rank. Or fear it. And I think: my fabled friends are as nothing to this one man who cares so much for his People and for his work. I should not be hard. And so I make an easy decision. One that is happy for me. I tell my friends: there is a special person who must take priority at this time. Next year this might not be the case. Perhaps I will not have the opportunity next year. Life is such that we are only given the opportunity to do the right thing once. And it is our duty to do the right thing."

And so she went to the Ceremony.

The Ceremony was in the Old City, with its streets of stone. A foreign city, she thought as she walked through it. She hated right angles. So many broad avenues met at right angles, and she knew that foreigners must have made them. But suddenly the streets went small and sheltering again, and she thought: we built in stone once too. So she did not hate the stone any longer. She and Crow walked to the central square.

The square was the most ancient part of the city of Saprang Song. There were umbrella pines all around it, and temples. The temples were made of volcanic rock or brick, with thin and delicate spires and smiling stone faces that were images of the Buddha. In the middle of the square was a concourse of green, tended grass with a gravel track around it, and bleachers along one side. It was used mainly for horse races now. Once a year, it was used for the Ceremony . . .

A temporary stage had been built in the center of the green. A small orchestra in formal evening wear sat on it, miserable with the heat. Rows and rows of priests, in yellow, with freshly shaven heads sat in pride of place, just in front of the stage. Behind them, on the grass or in the bleachers, were the prosperous people of the city. They sat on blankets with picnic hampers, and they wore the clothes of the Big Country. They had beautiful children, little girls in pink or orange trousers with white socks and shiny black shoes, who ran laughing, holding ice creams. The women sat serenely on rugs, like princesses, their legs folded under them, their hair in smooth oiled domes with shiny tin stars on it.

Third only had one shirt, which she had to wear with her new dress. The shirt was cheap cotton, with faded blue flowers, frayed around the collar. Her dull, unoiled hair, pulled back severely and tied with a bit of colored yarn, was that of a peasant. She clutched her meager little beaded purse and walked without looking around her, blind with shame.

"Sergeant! Sergeant!" a voice was calling. "Sergeant Crow!" A man, sitting on a folding chair, wearing sunglasses and a uniform and a black beret, was waving to them. He was smoking a cigarette in a holder made of bone, his teeth clenched about it as he called again. He wore polished boots to the knee.

As they approached, Crow bowed, grinning, and bowed again, hands held high above his head. "Colonel Tam Dah. Sir!" Crow said in an unpleasant, barking, official kind of voice. "Madame Tam Dah!" he said to the colonel's wife. She inclined her head slightly, with an unperturbed smile. She looked away from him and through Third, smoothing down her trouser suit and adjusting her sunglasses.

"We find this Ceremony most important for the People," the colonel said. "A sense of continuity is most important, don't you feel, Sergeant. Under the circumstances."

The circumstances, thought Third, are that the Neighbors hold us and that you City People have joined them. No wonder you lower your voice.

"Certainly, Sir. The wisdom is apparent," Crow said briskly. Even in his new green coolsuit and slicked black hair he looked wretched and small, dipping and bowing. Third moved from one foot to the other. The colonel's wife tapped her knees with the tips of her fingers. A pair of earplugs were whispering music to her. On top of the hamper was a bar of broken-open chocolate. In a moment, politeness would demand that the colonel ask Crow to watch the Ceremony with them.

Then Crow said, "I must make excuses, Colonel, Sir. But we have seats in the bleachers, and we must make our way to them."

"Of course, of course," said the colonel, already looking elsewhere. He gave a lax wave of dismissal with his hand as it hung over the arm of the chair.

"It has been delightful, Sir. Delightful, Madame," Crow assured them.

As Third walked away, she heard the wife say, her voice too loud because of her earplugs. "Hmm! The Crow and his Turtle."

Third stormed up the steps of the bleachers ahead of Crow. She pushed her way past a seller of sparrows in cages, and trod on the toes of people who stood up to let her pass. If I am a peasant, I will act like a peasant, she thought. She sat down without smiling and greeting the people next to her, without looking at Crow when he joined her. She answered him with fierce, short grunts.

"Look, Third, people from the Big Country," he whispered. Third had never seen Big People before. They had been given special places under a canopy by the stage. They arrived all together, lumbering like houses, tall, clumsy, with enormous booted feet, and they did indeed have skin the color of plucked chickens. Their wives, towering columns of crumpled cotton, dropped down onto their deck chairs, relieved of their own weight. They were all so large, it seemed, swollen with power, sprawling on the chairs, chewing gum. They frightened Third, and made her angry. What are they doing if they don't want to be here, she thought. We don't want them. They don't understand. They don't believe. This is our country. One of them had orange hair and was covered in speckles, like a fish. Or a Shark.

Suddenly there was a sound like the sea, and all the People stood up and roared. It must be the Prince. Third looked wildly around her and finally saw, in the air, coming out of the north, a van, held aloft by four giant swans, and there was a man in it, and Third felt something unexpected catch in her chest. Yes, yes it was him, and he looked just like her pictures. He smiled and waved, and flung up both his arms over his head, like the Spirit of Happiness. The van swept low over the crowd, and he threw out handfuls of white lotus blossom. His suit and his tie were white. The swans were white, their long necks held straight out, their wings whistling. They began to pump backward, furiously, and the carriage was lowered toward the stage. Guards ran out to steady it. The orchestra struck up a cheerful, seesawing song that the Prince had composed himself. Before the van was quite down, he launched himself over the side, like a fat, happy schoolboy. "Up! Up!" he shouted, and suddenly, from behind the stage, a flock of balloons was released.

They were silver, thousands of them, one for each year of the Country's history. They all seemed to be blown toward the bleachers. They wriggled their way through the air, toward the People, and each of them, in silver, was a sculptured portrait of the Prince, and each one of them said, with the Prince's voice, "An offering. An offering to the Buddha. A holy offering." At the ends of each of their tethers, which were segmented metal bands, was a three-fingered hand. The hands reached out, and the People eagerly surged forward, reaching over each other's shoulders to place earrings or rice cakes into them. Third reached out with one small brass coin. The balloon's hand felt warm and rubbery. "Thank you, sister," the balloon said. Third's face was reflected back at her from the Prince's own.

"To Heaven! To Heaven!" said the Prince, and the balloons sucked in air, and swelled, and slowly, en masse, began to rise. The Prince urged them on with great windmill circlings of his arms. The priests, who had been still, leapt to their feet and began to bash gongs and bells and cymbals. The balloons interwove with each other, flashing with reflected sunlight against the pure blue of the sky. Spots of sunlight flittered across the crowd, dazzling them, making them yelp. Then rising above all the other noise, slow and heavy, there began a song.

It was an old song, one Third could almost remember, one she thought everyone had forgotten. The woman next to her reached across and took her left hand. All the People linked hands, as if they were flowers at feast. Crow took her hand too. Oh, she thought, we are not defeated, we are not broken. We are still the Unconquered People. A beautiful young girl of the People ran onto the stage, her face crumpled with the effort of not laughing, and kissed the Prince, and the People cheered. Many good things are real, thought Third. I am going to have a husband. I am going to have a life. The balloons dwindled until they looked like a host of daytime stars. They would rise so high, and then rupture, but their souls would go on.

The Prince looked up and waved. "Bye-bye," he called to them, like a child. Crow, faithful with his broken smile, was looking steadily at Third.

Three months later, the wars began again.

PART THREE

A BIRD, SINGING

The big men changed their minds. Who could say why the Big People did things? They gave weapons to the rebels this time, who were still in the hills like an unhealed sore. These weapons could do something new. Blowing Kisses, it was called.

A nurse led Third through the corridors of the hospital. The way the sounds and whispering reverberated made Third feel ill. Lined up on pallets all along the halls were the new wounded, muttering, often to themselves. They looked very calm, without a mark, except for strange bruises, as if someone had brushed them with ashes.

Crow was on a bed, in a ward. There was nothing wrong with him that Third could see, except for a patch of skin on his forehead like the skin of a rotten apple. Wanly, he smiled when he saw her, and held out his hand. It was a monk's hand, with slender, flute-playing fingers. Third looked about her in dazed confusion. The nurse had to help her step over people to get to his bed.

"They *found* you," murmured Crow.

"A lady came and told me you were here, and led me."

"Blessed lady." His hands still reached out for her, but she did not approach.

"What is wrong with you?" Third demanded. She could see no wounds.

"There is a hot little egg in the middle of my head, and it is hatching. I can hardly see you. Come closer. Sit on the bed."

Third, who had hardly known what to do or say before, was now overwhelmed with mortification. There were people about them everywhere. It was bad enough having to talk in front of them. Nevertheless, she jumped up onto the very foot of the bed, her legs dangling so far from the floor. She coughed to clear her throat, and began to talk of innocent things. "I saw your aunt as you asked me. She is very well. She gave me tea. She has bought herself a dog. One of those small nasty ones with a face like a China dragon. Stupid thing, to have a dog, you have to feed it."

"I hope you will be friends," said Crow.

"She treated me well enough," Third said, with a shrug. "My wedding coat is nearly finished." She had become a seamstress, working in the night, and she was saving scraps of cloth for it. "It is all white. It has a white dove on it, and it has a white portrait of the Prince."

Crow settled back and let his hand fall. "Tell me about it," he asked.

"That is all there is to tell, just that," she replied, embarrassed.

"It has a high white starched collar and the winged shoulders," he said. His eyes were dim and loving, looking through all the hospital, at the coat, seeing it clearly, or perhaps another coat that he remembered.

"Yes, that's it," said Third in a thin voice, though it wasn't.

"That is good. That is a very country coat. But you must not let anyone see it. Not with the Prince's portrait on it. The rebels hate him. They will hate you. Promise me you will hide the coat."

Third was not pleased. Hide her coat. What was he talking about? "The rebels are People too."

"They have changed. When they ask, do not say you almost married a soldier. When they ask, say you married a fighter for the People, and that the foreigners killed him. It will be true."

"What nonsense!" said Third. "What is wrong with you? I can see nothing wrong with you." She looked about her at the other wounded. There seemed to be nothing wrong with any of them. "When will you be out of that bed?"

"Soon," said Crow.

"There!" said Third. Her legs ached from hanging over the floor. Angrily, she moved farther onto the bed.

When she looked back, Crow was holding his hand over his

head, watching his fingers wave, like wind chimes in a light breeze. He began to talk even worse nonsense.

"Hearts go up like balloons," he said. "Hearts ring like voices, echo like clouds. Cobbles underfoot. Always stumble. Drains. When looking upward. There is a bird singing."

"What are you saying?" Third whispered, looking around her. She wriggled farther up the bed and finally took his hand. He grabbed it fiercely.

"There is a *bird singing,*" he insisted, his face shuddering as he began to cry. "They are pulling off its legs and wings, but it is still singing."

"Ssssh! There is no bird."

"There is! But no one can see it!"

"It is this place," said Third, miserably. "All this noise. It is confusing." Badly frightened now, she squeezed his hand, and covered it with her other hand.

"When I was a boy," he began. "Strange cities. Always there. Always there. Never left me."

Was he trying to tell a story? You had to listen when someone finally spoke. Third peered at him anxiously. He stared ahead, as if moving at high speed. Then he began to chant.

It was a priestly mantra. The words meant nothing, they were deliberate nonsense. Meaning would distract. "I ing a na. I ing a na. I ing a na," over and over very softly.

"That's better. That's better," Third told him. His voice faded away altogether, and he went very still, his wet eyes still on her.

She had never realized before that he was beautiful. She had never seen his body. His legs were hot under the white sheet, and his chest was bare down to the waist, smooth and brown and surprisingly fleshy. His lips were only slightly parted over his crowded, crooked mouth, and a tear still crept down his face. She looked at his hand, and played with his long supple fingers. Even the hand looked more substantial now, veined and broad and masculine.

She coughed to clear her throat. "I have been thinking," she said. "This city is no good for us. It is a bad place, with all these Desperate Flies crowding in because of the war. We could go back to my village. There is much orderly planting there. It is in the west, away from where the war is now. There is a lot of land there, because all the men have been killed. We could get married there. All the girls will be in a chain of flowers. They will sing the song of the true knight who climbed the mountain. They will steam fish with ginger." It seemed to her that Crow nodded, slightly, yes.

"We could look for my old house," she said. "They don't die, the old houses, they are like oaks. I'm sure it will know me. It is stupid to keep a dog when you can have a house. A house is a shelter." For some reason she felt tears suddenly sting her eyes. That was foolish.

"Ah, well," she said, and let go of his hand, patting it. She pulled around her work bag, and took out her quilting. "We can talk about it later. I will stay here."

A lady came toward her, in white, big breasted, in the squeaking white shoes of the Big People, and suddenly she looked to Third like one of the other White Ladies, a giant hen.

"You had better go now," the hen said, warily.

Third could not help but grin. She had to cover her mouth.

The woman looked very displeased, perhaps insulted, and she strode, still squeaking, briskly round the side of the bed, and felt Crow's forehead. Crow, who had been smiling at her with Third, seemed to freeze with embarrassment at being touched by another woman in her presence.

"I will do that for him," said Third, shyly. She lifted up his hand, which was still warm, to pull the sheet up under it, to hide Crow's body from this woman. Abruptly the woman snatched the hand from her, and held it by the wrist.

Then she leaned over, so that Third had to look at her terrible face with its strained smile. "There is no point to you staying any longer," she said.

"Tuh," said Third, and made a gesture of throwing the hen a bit of slug.

"It is best that you go now, really," said the woman, who was actually shaking from fatigue. "Come along now." She tried to take Third's elbow to ease her down the bed. Third pulled away.

"We are talking about family business," said Third, haughtily. "We do not want to be interrupted."

The hen put a hand on her own forehead, and closed her eyes for a moment. She sighed and said, "He will be doing no more talking."

"Then let him sleep," said Third and picked up her quilting. "I will stay here."

"He is dead," said the woman. "I'm sorry. We need the bed."

"Don't be silly," said Third. "He was talking to me a moment ago. Go away and leave us alone." She turned away from the woman, and took up her needle and thread.

"All right," said the woman, wearily. "You can have a few more minutes." Third heard her squeaking away.

She turned to Crow, who seemed to nod his head in approval. The tear on his face still moved. It touched the pillow and was gone, absorbed. Suddenly, even though it was daylight with people all around them, Third laid her head on his bosom. "I am like the cat, sometimes," she told him. "When things are near me, I pretend I do not want them. I think I do not care for them, in case they are taken away. Most things get taken away. It is like that when people are hurt. When they are near, I give them no sympathy, in case they take advantage. It is only when I leave the room, that I can weep for them. Do you understand?" It seemed to her that he did. His chest was still. She sat up, and moved the sheet a little higher. "Tell me about when you were a boy," she asked him, patting the fold of the sheet. He didn't answer. She sat and thought nothing, only nothing, for a very long time.

Until the hen came squeaking back. "This time you must go. This is really too bad. There are people on the floor!" Third looked at her, unblinking. The woman suddenly shouted. "There are sick people. You must leave!" Third would not move. "My dear woman, I know this is terrible, but there are others. Please go. Please." The woman looked around her helplessly, and then left.

Third stared at the body. It was very still, like statues of the reclining Buddha, but it was going ugly again. The teeth were sticking out farther from the mouth, and the eyes, under heavy lids, were dry and crossed. A fly picked its way across the lips. Third, distracted, waved it away. It came back.

There was a bustle behind her, and the woman was coming with a man now, a doctor, and she was abject and pleading and servile, saying that she had asked, that she had tried everything. The doctor, aged and respectable, sat on the bed next to Third. He expressed his condolences and said that he did not know why it was that fine young men had to die, except that it could not possibly be the will of God. Could she see, though, that the bed was needed for other people's loved ones? Would she go? "Up, up, my daughter," he said, trying to coax her.

Third suddenly snarled, and tried to hit him with her dogged little fist. He ducked and it missed. "First Sister was withered by Sharks! Second Sister . . ." she yelled, and choked and tried to hit him again. Her second sister now lived by prostitution, sitting in an airport window, arranging her hair so that the sores would not show. Their mother had starved herself to death when they were children, giving them her food so that they would have enough. One always had to say there was enough. "Go away! Go away, and leave us alone!" The doctor leapt down from the bed, slipping on his leather soles. Third flung her quilting after him as he scuttled away, and she sat and wept, not knowing why she was weeping, and hid her face.

Suddenly it was dark. There was soft moaning, and the clatter of instruments on moving trolleys, and the sound of flies. All that Third thought was that it was late, time for her to go. She jumped down from the bed, walked down the passageway between the beds, and nodded politely to a nurse as she passed. Somehow she found her way down the stairs and through the hallways, to the large, heavy main glass doors. It was not until she saw them, swinging, saw her own reflected image like a ghost in the blackness beyond, that she realized, or else remembered, that Crow was dead.

She gave a little yelp, and covered her mouth, and turned and ran. She had not looked at him properly, knowing he was dead, to remember his face. She had not asked the nurse what would happen next, what the funeral arrangements would be. In a panic, she ran down the corridors, which all looked the same, which all echoed, which all were crowded with dying men who looked the same. "Crow! Crow!" she called for him, though it was stupid, he couldn't answer. She ran up steps, she remembered steps, to the room she thought he would be in, but all she found there was an empty bed among the full ones. She ran to another ward. "Oh, no. How stupid. Oh, no," she said to herself in a breathless voice. In that room all the beds were full of different people. Wrong room, back again to the first one. But all the beds in that room, too, all of them, were full. Right room, wrong room. She saw a nurse, one she didn't recognize, and grabbed her arm.

"Many pardons. Many pardons. Can you tell me where my husband, Crow, Nourisher of the East, is?"

The nurse, tired beyond endurance, simply shook her head and pointed toward a doctor in the shadows.

"Doctor," said Third, "Doctor, my husband is dead. He died here, and now I can't find his body, and I have to make arrangements!"

The doctor, one she didn't recognize, took her arm. "You are the next of kin?"

"Yes, yes," she said, trembling like a bird.

"Then don't worry. Go home and try to sleep. We will contact you about the arrangements later. Come now, this way. I will show you the way out."

"Thank you, sir. Many pardons," said Third and looked back over her shoulder, hoping by accident to catch one last glimpse of Crow.

The main doors swung again, and this time Third seemed to catch the reflection of many ghosts. They crowded the main hall. The doctor nodded to her and light flashed on his spectacles. Light danced on the doorway as it settled shut: Third was outside on the hospital steps, and the sky overhead was full of light and a crackling sound.

Fireworks. Why, thought Third, why are there fireworks?

"Oh, Crow," she whispered, as the sky was spangled. "How could you leave me? What do I do now?" Green and red opened up in the sky, flower-bursts of light, loose and shimmering. She had never known him as a man. That was what it was for, finally, the wary approach, the angry rebuff, the gradual drawing together. It was meant to end with her lying next to that beautiful body. That was what she wanted.

She realized then that she loved him. For his beautiful body, for his broken face, and for his heart, what was inside him. Oh, Third, fool, it is too late to realize that. What good is that now? Like the cat.

It was not enough. Was it all for nothing? Third watched the fireworks.

Then she understood life histories. Why people told them. They wanted to save something. Suddenly, as badly as she had ever needed anything, Third needed a priest. She saw the spires of a temple, dark against ocher sky. She ran.

Across the hospital square, past a fountain, as if the fireworks were bombs, and she were dodging them. She ran up the temple steps to the great carved doors. They flickered in the pink-white fireworks light.

They were locked. Third tried to shake them, and felt the heavy bolts behind them. "Peace of God? Peace of God?" she called, panting, in a weak voice.

When had the temple doors ever been barred? Suddenly angry, she slammed her fist against them, pounding, and heard how small the noise was in the rolling darkness behind them.

"It's closed," said a voice behind her. An old man was squatting on the steps, hunched over a bowl of rice, twisting round on his haunches to look at her. Third stared at him.

"The temple is closed," he repeated.

"Are you a priest?" Third demanded, avid.

"What? No, oh no. All the priests have fled. Haven't you heard? They refused to join the army, and the Neighbors started putting them in jail. Where have you been hiding?"

"Where did they go?"

The old man laughed. "Ho! Even if I knew, I wouldn't tell. One of them set himself alight in the main square. You must know that. Where they have the Ceremony. The Neighbors will not let anyone bring flowers to that place. They will not let anyone mourn."

"There must be priests somewhere. Have they all gone, all the temples?"

"Ah." The old man shrugged. "Who can say?"

Third ran from temple to temple, all across the city, and they were all closed. The fireworks erupted overhead. Victory, the Neighbors were claiming, in only two months' time. The summer streets were full of laughing people. A parade of street players jostled past Third. They carried huge lights that blazed into her face. Their aloof painted faces smiled as rockets whined overhead. An old woman picking over fruit glanced at Third, blinking with heavy-lidded, reptilian eyes. No one knew who Crow was, no one knew he was dead, no one knew of the grief that Third carried within her, like a pouch of pus. "Have you seen a priest?" she asked, and people passed, pretending not to hear. There were soldiers, celebrating, waving their weapons in the air. You will die, Third thought, coldly.

It grew late. Third saw a man bowed under a machine, carrying it on his back, delivering it. He wore scraps of cloth that had been sewn together to look like an important person's suit of clothes. The fireworks stopped, the streets began to clear. A line of students meandered arm in arm toward Third. They wore white T-shirts splattered with rebel slogans in red paint. They wound themselves, laughing, around a fire hydrant.

"Forget your priests," they told Third. "The priests can't help you, they just sit on their yellow backsides." They burbled a mocking imitation of a holy chant. "Pieces of God. Pieces of God. Pieces of money." They wheeled drunkenly away, like a straggly white worm.

Very suddenly, Third was alone in the middle of the wide avenue. She heard the sound of wind move across the cobbles. She knew, with the sensation of claws sinking into her back, that she would not be able to mourn. There was no way left for her to mourn. It had been taken away. She looked up at the sky. How nice it would be, she thought, to be a balloon and simply drift away, to somewhere else.

"Hi!" piped a shrill little voice. It was an advertisement, standing suddenly in front of her. "I'm the Coca-Cola girl!" It thrust a glass of fizzing soft drink up toward her.

"No thank you. Go away," said Third.

Advertisements came alive at night, and were allowed to climb down from their signs. They were slightly flattened, like cartoon figures, with sharp creases along the edges of the arms and legs and heads. This one was a little girl, with pigtails, and wide Mickey Mouse eyes, and a red gingham dress, and three-fingered hands. She broke into a song.

> *Coca-Cola gives you life*
> *Gives you hope*
> *Gives you strength*
> *To carry through the day!*

Third turned and walked quickly away from her. The advertisement was programmed to sing, to someone, and there was no one else. She followed Third down the steep slope of the avenue, skipping. Her shiny black shoes went *pop-pop-pop* on the cobbles because they were suction cups. Third covered her ears, and began to run. The advertisement ran with her, dancing. "Busy people like you like Coke because it gives them instant energy to face the brisk life of the city," the advertisement pleaded, wishing perhaps it was able to say something else. "One glass of Coke gives you all the major vitamins and minerals, including C and the B group so necessary to cope with stress. Stay healthy! Stay happy! Drink Coke!"

"Go away!" shouted Third.

The advertisement staggered back a step. Then she began to sing again. ". . . gives you life / Gives you hope / Gives you strength . . ."

Give me my husband, thought Third. There was scaffolding, unassembled, beside a building. Third picked up a length of pipe and spun round and smashed the advertisement as hard as she could.

She hit it on the shoulder. The arm broke off. It was full of red, rather dry meat, and did not bleed. Third squawked in horror at how easily it broke apart. The thing kept on singing ". . . gives you life . . ." Third hit it again and again, to make it quiet, to stop it singing, to knock it away from her. Its skirt slipped off and the naked little legs kept on dancing with nothing above them. The slightly flattened head lay on the ground, its cheeks still the color of peaches, and it was still singing. Third kicked it, and it spun around and around like a plate, skittering down the hill. Third could hear the sound of the wind again, hollow. She drew in shaky breaths, feeling ill, and finally wanted to go home.

She had to walk back across the Old City, and through the heaps. She knew each heap by name—the Scarecrow, or the Fist Raised Toward Heaven. It was the time of the dogs. They barked, wild and unchecked, as she climbed up and over the roofs of other people's houses, toward her own. Once she was inside it, it turned its light on, and there it was, bare and gray and streaked and smelling of fungus. She groaned and fell facedown on the bed.

She heard the sound of many children playing and a band playing the Prince's song. Oh, she thought gratefully, oh, I'm falling asleep. As soon as she thought that, she was wide awake, with the iron knowledge that Crow was dead. Crow, she thought, I'm sorry I cannot mourn. It must be a terrible thing to lie unmourned. You must wander unsatisfied. She lay unmoving for a very long time, eyes open. Perhaps this is what it is like to be dead, she thought. Outside a cat was mewling, caught in a trap. People ate them now. Then Third remembered. There was one thing Crow had asked her to do.

She lit a candle and took out her wedding coat. It was lumpy, misshapen, made of scraps, unfinished. She saw that now. Everything in her life had been like that. She knelt and cut open the floor of her room, and the house shivered in pain, and she lifted up the lip of flesh. The hollow in the floor began, immediately, to seep moisture. She wrapped the coat in a plastic garbage bag, so that it would not be stained, and she laid it in the hole, smoothing it down so that it would not wrinkle. She managed to squeeze a tear out of herself, like liquor from an unripe wound, and she closed the flesh over the coat, and covered that with matting. It would heal shut.

Then Third stood up and walked, dazed, out of her house, she did not know where. Direction chose her.

She found herself at the edge of the main temple square. The umbrella pines rose and fell like waves around her. The bleachers were there, for the horse races, but where the stage had been, there were only blowing bits of paper and a patch of white ash. Lights bobbed idly about it. It was guarded. Third was turning to go, when she heard, within the wind, the sound of a cry.

The cry was small and plaintive and sweet. It sounded like Third felt, as if something had been lost. It was coming from under the trees nearby, a whistling that rose up at the end, like a question, like no other noise Third had heard before. She ducked under the branches. There was something on the ground, a bundle, and the light caught it. It was a bird that was making the noise, its feathers puffed out in the wind, a young bird. She knelt beside it, her throat clenching like a fist. The bird was a crow.

"Crow!" she said and picked it up and finally, gently, softly, the tears came, in an easy film down her face. She rocked with it, back and forth. "Crow. Crow. Crow."

Suddenly the lights were harsh in her eyes, and she turned away.

"What are you doing here?" demanded one voice.

"Why are you crying?" demanded another.

They were Neighbors. Third could only see their shadows behind the lights.

"I am crying because of this bird. It had been blown from its nest. It is so small."

"You are not supposed to be here. Get out."

Third stood up, and bowed to them, and ran. She held the bird to her face and breathed on it. A crow was an omen of death, but a crow that sings was something more. There is a bird singing. He had said that.

Weeping, consoled, Third was sure that Nourisher of the East had found his way back to her.

Part Four

The Crow That Warbled

The Crow That Warbled grew into a great, ragged-feathered beast, with gray-green scaly legs and claws, and a beak that seemed too large and heavy for its head. It was too big to be kept in a cage; there were perches in all the corners of the room, and linen cloths under its feed tray, and a sand box. In one corner of the room was a shrine, with paper flowers that Third had made from cigarette boxes. In frames made of twisted wire were drawings she had made of the Dead: her mother who had starved; her first sister who was withered; her second sister who sat dead and undiscovered for half a day in an airport window. There was a drawing, too, of Nourisher of the East, looking as plump and healthy as the Prince.

Third had never been told where the funeral was. She was not, after all, the next of kin. She did not know where Nourisher of the East had been cremated, or where the ashes were. When she visited his aunt, the people in the next house smiled and said she was not at home. The fifth time she came they said, still smiling, "In all fairness, we ought to tell you that, for you, she will never be at home."

"Tell her," Third replied, "that all she has is ashes. I have the soul."

She had the Crow That Warbled. She called it Husband. She bathed it regularly in the cleanest water she could find, and dried it in white cloths, laughing and teasing, and it would tilt its head, as if wondering if she were mad, and that would make her laugh more.

She set it free, over the heaps, from her high window. The Crow That Warbled would hover, high, in the same place for ten or fifteen minutes at a time, and it would sing, and the songs it sang were the songs of the People. Third knew it was a spirit then. How else would it know to sing the morning song at dawn, or the feast songs, or the songs for the Dead? The poor people, in their dangerously shifting heaps of housing, all looked up toward it. They understood the miracle. The wild children who lived like animals in packs under bridges, crept out of the shadows to listen. Old women would hum along with the songs, rocking on slippery mushroom steps, remembering. When it was tired, the Crow would flutter down among them and look pointedly at the rice in their bowls. They would chuckle and give Crow some, for they knew it was a ghost, and it was utmost politeness to feed a ghost. They would duck and bow at its arrival, their clasped hands high over their heads in respect. But the Crow always returned to Third. The People would look up at her window then, and wave. She was mistress of the miracle. And Third, for the first time, smiled back.

It was strangers who didn't like the Crow, people who wore the clothes of the Big Country and carried lacquered canes, people who were lost and panicked in the heaps. The Crow would drop on them to say hello, for it thought it was human. It would come singing the song of hospitality, a black Crow, bringer of Death. The strangers would scuttle away, quietly, pursued, holding on to their hats, afraid to run or shout, because that would mean they thought they would die if the Crow touched them, and City People were not supposed to be superstitious. They believed, nonetheless, and would try to swipe at Crow with their canes. The people of the heaps would point at them and laugh. They would follow in a crowd to see the end of the comedy. The strangers would think they were being chased by the poor. Their faces said that all their most anxious fantasies seemed to be coming true.

People started coming to Third for cures. She found that by laying hands on them, she could send them away at least thinking they were better. She began to grow herbs in window boxes for remedies. People gave her messages for dead relatives, for the

Crow to carry. They bowed to her, hands high over their heads, and called her Widow.

Third had to wear spectacles now. A doctor at the hospital, to which she kept returning, got her a job at his brother's factory. She peered down a microscope, watching crystals grow. The work ruined her eyes.

The crystals were sliced continually as they grew, and Third had to make sure that the pattern on each slice was the same, like rock candy. She found it difficult to keep count of how many she inspected. The machine presented them in groups of ten, and all she had to do was remember how many groups. This confused her.

"I never learned my figures," she said, smiling behind pebble spectacles. "I am very ignorant." There was no shame in admitting this to an educated man.

"Just make a mark with this pencil, one for each group," said her supervisor, who blamed the war.

She kept track of her change in the market by remembering the color of the coin. Then the money was devalued, and everyone began to use paper. So she began to remember the faces on the paper instead. She couldn't read the names of the faces, so she gave them the names of people in her old village, and kept their titles. One was the landowner, one was the doctor, one kept the seed grain. That way, she had a rough idea of what she was owed.

Then they changed it all around by saying that the value of each note was now what it would be if it had an extra zero on the end of its number. They could not afford to reprint their money.

The day this happened, Third stood weeping in the market, shaking the one note in change she had received from a market dealer. When he looked worn, bored, anything other than guilty or caught out, she became hysterical. She was not even shouting words, just tones of anger. All her money for the week was gone. An older gentleman took her arm, and whispered to her, calmly, trying to make her understand that the money was worth more now. Many people gathered around, to try to explain. They could not all be thieves. Third was mollified in the end. She left with her one note.

But she did not understand. She felt betrayed, as if nothing would ever make sense again. She went home and asked the Crow. The Crow was silent, but it seemed to be a significant silence. The answer was not here, he seemed to say. It lay elsewhere. Everything that made sense was going elsewhere.

So she lived. In the evenings, she sewed, jabbing her fingers with the needle because she couldn't see. The Crow perched beside her, and seemed to watch with interest.

She collected old advertisements. Her babies, she called them. Some of them might have been. They were old, about to die. She hung them on the wall, faded green, rusty red. When she fell asleep, over her sewing, on the floor, they came alive. Their skin was peeling off, and they could no longer sing except in worn, whispering voices. The Crow would try to teach them new songs, but they shook their heads. That was beyond them. They danced around Third as she slept, in the moonlit room, like dreams. In the morning, they would be back on their signs, frozen still and silent.

Third even began to get to know her house. It had not been imprinted to care about who lived in it, but Third dusted its corners, and swept away its old itchy skin, and talked to it until it came to know her and the rhythm of her tread. She knew when it slept, and sat still herself then, to let it rest. Friends told her that it grew fretful and sighed when she was not there, in the market, at work.

There was always work, at the factory, in the heaps, at her quilting: work as the pot bubbled on the stove in the home Third would have made for her husband, work, until, after only two or three years, she became stolid and drab, her skin toughened somehow and polished-looking like old leather. People called her Old Woman. She was twenty-seven years old, but Third did not know that. She and numbers were permanently estranged. So if people called her old and treated her with some extra consideration, that was fine. She elbowed her way through the stalls, singing the old songs in a loud shrill voice, pulling a squeaking wooden wagon behind her, a small bowlegged woman in spectacles and a very faded cotton shirt. She counted faces instead of numbers. Everywhere she went, she expounded the miracle of the Crow That Warbled.

"He goes back to the Land of the Dead, to where everything is as it should be, as it was, where the People still are Unconquered," she said.

The People of Saprang Song could hear the war, its dull roar, its high-pitched hum, but the battles never seemed to reach the Divine Lotus, as if the city were charmed. Over it, over the heaps of the People in them, the Crow That Warbled hovered, singing the old songs.

Part Five

No Harm Can Come

The rebels won. The news was spread by the packs of ragged orphans who lived wild. They ran through the heaps, and were for once admitted without qualm into the rooms of the People. Outside Saprang Song, in the burned paddies, the army of the Neighbors and their servants had been destroyed.

The City People celebrated. They built bonfires in the squares and in the narrow passageways between the heaps. They banged on pans to make something like music, and blew through paper on combs. The rebels were the People, like themselves; the People had won. They hung their white sheets out of their windows as a sign of victory. They gathered under Third's window and called for the Crow That Warbled. It hopped excitedly among them, from shoulder to shoulder. They bowed to it, laughing with toothless mouths. They sang with it. They grew drunken and bold, heaping up the banners of the Neighbors on the fire, wrapping themselves in white to jump over the flames. "Unconquered, Unconquered, Unconquered," they chanted, hopping up and down in unison. This was not an old song, or an old dance. Third didn't like it. She slipped away unnoticed to her bed.

Almost everyone but Third slept late the next morning. Daylight came and there were none of the usual sounds of the heaps.

Third was awakened instead by the sound of things falling. She heard laughter, loud. She got up, and stumbled bleary-eyed to her window.

She saw pots and plastic buckets cascading down the side of the lower heaps, and two men wearing nothing but their underpants dancing round and round a rice barrel. They chanted like children, "All fall down." Mr. Chiu, a Chinese immigrant, had opened up his house as a tiny shop. He stood outside it now, still in his nightshirt, distraught, biting his thumbnail. The shop was being ransacked. Third ducked low behind her window.

The men tipped the barrel over, and Mr. Chiu cried, "Gentlemen! Gentlemen!," and the rice fell with a hissing sound. The men staggered back from it, laughing. They were soldiers, soldiers for the Neighbors addled on battle drugs, traitor People who had taken off their traitor uniforms in order to pass as patriots. All of this will stop, thought Third, with a sudden jab of military feeling, now that the Neighbors have gone. One of them wheeled around and pointed his fingers at the jars in Mr. Chiu's window, and the plastic containers burst into flame, belching out black smoke. Mr. Chiu gave a little scream and scurried into his house to push the burning jars out of his window with his bare hands. The soldiers plumped down on the rooftop, and woozily began to pull on shirts and trousers. Their feet caught in the cuffs, and they set each other off on fresh bursts of hacking, senseless laughter. The clothes were Mr. Chiu's own.

This will not be a day to be out on the streets, Third thought. "Crow, today we will stay inside. Until everything is settled, and the Neighbors are gone." Crow seemed to understand. With cowboy cries, the soldiers pushed themselves off down the slopes, tobogganing on their asses, bumping at each level. One of them waved Mrs. Chiu's most private garments over his head. Mr. Chiu stumbled out through the smoke, weeping, cursing, under the white celebratory linen that was now turning black.

There is no food in the house, Third suddenly remembered. Worse. There is no water. Mrs. Chiu was trying to coax her husband back inside. He shouted up at the towers, cursing the People, the harm they had brought him, cursing them for not helping, and he flung a tin up toward them.

Chiu will give us no food, not now, Third thought. I have to go to the market. If I go now, while it's early, I may miss the worst of it.

"Stay inside," she warned the Crow. "Today is not a good day. Today will not at all be like last night." She took her squeaking wagon, and crept down the heap, on the side away from Mr. Chiu.

There was an old market that opened early for wholesalers. It had once been well outside the city. The heaps had encroached upon it, shifting. Each day they surrounded it in a different shape. Third came upon it unexpectedly, up and over the roof of a house. She saw the two long sheds in the middle of the square and a mass of black, people in black, rebels, a rebel encampment, and she tried to dart back. Instead, she slipped, and slithered down the side of the house. She landed on the market pavement, with a great clatter, just next to a rebel boy and an old truck.

The boy howled, and spun around. There was a ripple of laughter from the other rebels. Third made a show of laughing too. The rebel boy did not offer to help her up. He stared at her as if she were a ghost. He had a tattooed face and several wristwatches along one arm and wires trailing out of his ears. Third stood up, smiling. "Peace of God," she wished him. "Grateful praise to long-awaited victors." The boy's rough country face did not light up with a courteous smile. It stared back at Third, and then shook with a scornful chuckle. He turned back to the truck. It shrank from him, great folds of flesh blinking over the twin lenses of its windshield. He climbed into its cab and shouted an order, a wrong order. The truck whined miserably, and twisted in place, refusing to obey. The boy shouted again. This time, the truck did what it was told, and backed up at high speed, into the wall of houses, breaking through the mushroom flesh.

There was desultory applause from the rebels; this boy was not held in high regard. Third saw them, slumped on the stone, sprawled against each other, exhausted, with leaden, unmoving faces. There were girls among them, and they were young, almost children.

The boy jumped out of the truck, slamming shut the metal door that was hung like an earring through its flesh, and it yelped in pain. Inside the broken wall, a woman and two children crouched amid the smells of cold soup and beds. The boy stepped back, his face contorted with rage, and he howled, and he suddenly seemed to fill with light. His eyes glowed with it; it shone orange through the flesh of his cheeks, and lit up the roof of his mouth. It blazed, blinding out of his eyes, and the truck was suddenly engulfed in fire.

"Get out! Get away!" shouted the woman in the house. The truck obeyed; it jumped forward on its wheels and stood still, juddering and coughing in pain and panic. Third ducked away from the heat. Suddenly the truck roared forward across the market square directly at the rebels. They jumped up, or somersaulted backward out of its way, and it crashed into a wooden support, pulling down a corner of the shed, taking part of the tin roof with it, tipping up and rolling over onto the unliving container that was bolted to the shell of its back. It could not turn over. Its rows of knuckled legs pedaling helplessly, its burning wheels whirring in the air as it steamed and crackled and spat, shivering, whinnying like a horse.

Third began to walk toward a gap between the houses; it was full of hanging laundry; she could hide behind it. She had to leave her wagon behind; it would squeak and draw attention. She began to think she might escape, when she heard the sound of sandals flapping behind her. She went very still and waited. "City Woman!" a voice said, triumphant.

She turned as they crowded around, craning their necks to see her, with dead, blunted faces. Shadows of smoke wafted across them. Third could smell their sour clothes. They had encrusted teeth and lumps just above the eyelid where parasites dwelt. "Peace of God," she said, warily.

"God, pah!" said one of the boys, spitting at her feet, to a murmur of laughter. Even the spittle was tinged with black.

"I came back to the market, and saw that it was empty, so I am leaving," Third explained.

"Market!" exclaimed a girl, indignant, and began to strut,

hands on hips. "We have had no market, City Woman, in five years. We had to eat worms. Would you like worms to eat, City Woman?" Then Third understood; this was a brave, naughty girl. She saw again, under the bandanas and weapons and salt-stained black, how young they were, rude children, and she lost her fear. She became outraged.

"I ate worse, girl," she replied. "I had to sell my blood. My mother starved to death. I am nearly blind from working in their factories. So don't you spit at me when I give you holy greeting, and call me City Woman, because I am one of the People. And the People show manners and respect!"

Some of them giggled at this old-fashioned display of authority. "And who is your husband?" challenged the girl, coming closer.

"My husband was a fighter for the People and the foreigners killed him!" The words came out of her without thought; she was bursting with rage, stretched so tight with it that tears oozed out of her, because she finally understood, looking at the foreign weapons, why it was true. "I am a Country Woman!" she shouted. "I had to flee here for my life! From the Neighbors!"

This was not what the rebels expected. They looked at each other, scowling and bemused, and scuffed their feet on the stone. "From what village?" demanded the girl.

Third told her, proudly, fiercely. And for good measure, she cuffed her about the head. The girl did not strike back.

"It's one of ours," said an older boy, grimly. "Mata!" he said, which meant "We have made a mistake." It was a swear word. He bowed, suddenly, hands held high, and said in another voice, the voice he would have had if there had been no troubles, "We are sorry, Mother. We have offended without cause."

"Yes you have!" snarled Third, water shaking itself out of her eyes. The other bowed, murmuring.

"We will escort you back," the older boy said. "The streets are not safe. There are too many bad elements. We must deal with them. But we mean no harm to any of the People." He was some kind of leader among them, with a weary face, his hair tied up in a bun at the back. "We are fighters for the People too." He tried to smile.

Ten of them went with her, pulling her wagon as she stalked on ahead of them, still angry.

"We put out sheets to welcome you," Third said, flinging a hand up in the direction of the white hangings.

"We thought people would meet us. We thought there would be parades," said the youngest, and was nudged into silence.

"You came too late. We sat all night at fires, singing because you had won," she told them bitterly.

She pointed to the fires as they passed them. They skirted mounds of garbage. People lived there too, in shacks made out of garbage. They passed a quagmire of sewage called the Slump. The rebels craned their necks in wonder at how high the heaps had risen, swaying slightly in even this faint morning wind, pinkened slightly by the dawn.

"There are so many!" one of them said. "It can't be done! What they tell us, eh? We won't be able to."

"All the real People will leave," repeated the leader. "They will leave because they want to leave. The others will not be real People."

Third was thinking furiously. Leave? All of us? Is that what they mean to do?

Then, against a blue sky, between the Scarecrow and the Fist Raised Toward Heaven, she saw the Crow That Warbled, flying toward them. She gave a little cry and covered her mouth. She knew what was going to happen.

The Crow was singing as it came, a clear morning song, one that praised wifely duties and domestic content. He was greeting their guests.

"Go back!" Third shouted at it. "Crow, go back! Get away!"

The rebels saw it, too, the omen of death. The older boy lurched forward, his face curling with disgust, choking with it. He had seen so much of death that images of it were clear to him. The youngest boy hissed, and picked up a smoldering blade of bone from a fire, and threw it at the Crow. The bird landed in the narrow passage-way and hopped toward them, twittering, cocking its head in a sideways question, bouncing toward Third, with whom it was always safe.

"Crow, go back," she pleaded.

"Go back!" the rebels repeated. The Crow hopped up on Third's shoulder and the rebels drew back, and the Crow said hello to them in a cheerful, bobbling note. Then it hopped onto the head of the youngest child. He squealed and went still. The Crow leaned over, upside down, its claws clenched onto his hair, to peer into his face. The boy screamed and could not move. One of the others swiped the bird from his head, and it fluttered to the ground. The rebels kicked it, and suddenly it let out an ugly squawk of fear, the sound of a real crow.

"He is not Death," Third was saying, but she could not make the words loud enough. "Crow! Sing!"

There was a scattering of feathers. The Crow hopped twice, away from them, and into the air, and its wings made a hearty flapping noise, and it rose up, veering between the rows of hanging sheets, and all the windows were full of the faces of the People, and it was like the Ceremony. The Crow rose up above the sheets, higher than all the towers, to where it always hovered and sang, to where Third thought it would be safe, when the older rebel made a horrible noise, his head full of suppurating memory, "Uhhhhh!," as if he were vomiting, he pointed his finger at the sky, steel clamped around it. Third could follow the tongue of light through the air, see it curve with the nightmare slowness of foreshortened perspective, and her mouth gaped slowly open be-cause she couldn't breathe, and she saw the light flick at the bird, and disappear.

The Crow That Warbled burst into flame. It flew, on fire, or-ange and red and white, higher than ever before, deeper into the sky. It rose, then dipped, swerving, then found its course again, straining toward heaven. It hung in the sky, still for a moment, and then fell.

It fell, the speed of the air extinguishing its flame. It struck a heap and rolled off it into the air again, thumping into another house, sliding down its side into the box of herbs in Third's window. It flared up again, setting the rosemary alight, scenting the air. There were screams from the People.

Third was still. Third was silent. She wondered very calmly what would happen now that the Crow was destroyed. She was not at all surprised when out of the portal of a house, rocking back and forth down the steps, came a tiger. It sat on the roof of the house below, tamely, and licked its muzzle, and waited.

Everything was muffled, except for the sound of flies. Third's cousin lay at her feet, still in his plaid shirt. The blood was black and congealed now, old. He held up the yarrow stalks toward her.

"But you know how they work," he said as he had once before, long ago. Third shook her head. She didn't know, not any longer.

Where the rebels had stood, the murderous little Neighbor grinned. His pockmarked face was close to hers, his teeth edged in gold, his eyes gleaming. "You see? You see?" he seemed to be saying over and over like a bad joke that needs no explanation. "Go away," murmured Third. She felt an arm go around her shoulder.

The arm was pale yellow and withered. Third turned and saw her elder, trusted sister. She was bald, and her face was like an old fruit that had exploded. The eyes had expanded from the sudden heat and burst, the lips had burnt back from the teeth.

"Take off your spectacles, Third," her sister told her. "Not now. Slip them off while no one is looking and let them fall. Only City People wear glasses. They will kill you for them. That's right. Slowly. Casually." Her sister cradled Third toward her, pressing her against the gingham dress. She was still taller than Third, on long stilt legs. "Oh, I have missed you so much, sister. I have wanted someone to talk to so much. Now we will talk all the time. I will go with you now, and take care of you. We all will. All the Dead."

"Ah, yes, so that's it," thought Third. "I see. I see." Crow was like a gate that had broken open. The Dead could come through it. She let her glasses, a scant presence in her hand, drop. Everything was blurred, as if seen through tears. She saw a blurred woman wave her arms, shouting at the rebels.

"It is no good, everyone must leave now," the rebel was saying.

"But where will we go? How can we leave?" the woman demanded. Quiet, fool, thought Third. They have weapons. And they are crazy.

"Back to the country. Go back to the country so you can be People again, not this City Filth, where you are all whores of the foreigners, with their trash. You go now!"

"But I have to pack my things!"

"You will need nothing. Everything will be provided."

"My children!"

"Your children belong to all the People. The People will care for them."

"Madness! Madness!" shouted the woman, realizing, staring at them.

"You will all leave before midday," the older rebel announced. He was a mere wavering of black to Third. "All leave the city. It is diseased and we are going to burn it!" He threw up his hand, and blasted the sky, and there was a noise like thunder back and forth across it. The People fell silent. They began to be afraid.

Enough, thought Third, and turned, and began to walk.

"Where are you going, Mother?" the oldest rebel asked.

"I am going home, to my village," she replied, and she thought of her advertisements on the wall, and the drawing of Crow. She had made it look like the Prince.

The rebel grabbed her arm, and turned her around. "You see?" he challenged the People. "This woman does what is right. You can too. She is a real Person. Show that you are."

"Do what they say," advised Third, glumly, and began to walk again. The rebel walked with her.

"Do not go like that," he murmured, pressing close. "Go back to your house. Take some food."

"There is no food in my house," replied Third, thinking of the paper flowers.

The rebel pushed a rice ball with a sliver of dried meat wrapped around it into her hand. "Take this." He gave her his tin cup. Without looking at him, Third snatched them; without another word, he darted back to the others.

"You see?" Third's sister said, not marching, but sauntering beside her. "You are charmed. We protect you." Only the Dead, thought Third, were clearly visible. The living were fading.

It was still quiet, still early. Bands of rebels, chatting, quite ordinary, were wiring up loudspeakers while children looked up admiringly. Somewhere in the distance, a scratchy broadcast voice began. Third could not understand what it said.

Rebels began to go from door to door. Women stood in doorways, listening to them and scowling slightly, holding shut their morning robes, pulling back hair from their faces. Get moving, Third thought, delay will cost you. She heard shouting from inside houses as people disagreed. They took time to pack. Third walked more quickly. There was a crowd in front of a small shop. Third turned sideways through it, and heard the shopkeeper's fat wife say, "You want it, it costs more today."

People began to run. Blankets full of things were being lowered from windows. Excited children ran about on the heaps blowing toy horns. Third looked up and saw a man on the very top of a heap. He was rocking back and forth on his heels for balance, trying to coax his house down, on a leash. "Autumn? Where is Autumn?" a woman called out over and over in panic.

"You won't get out this way," said Third's sister. Third turned, and began to walk toward the Old City. She cut through stables, where cars slept at night, and climbed up stone steps and out of the treacle-smelling darkness to paved street.

The Old City was full of people. A woman pushing a baby carriage full of tins rammed into her, and without another word shoved the carriage into her again, until Third got out of the way.

Third couldn't see. The living jostled past her. In front of shop windows, clothes dummies lay naked and Third thought, with a lurch, that they were bodies. Third looked at the clouds, to rest her eyes. She could see things that were far away, the broad patterns.

She was looking at the clouds, stumbling, when she heard a dull, spreading roar, at once crackling and moist, like a spill of watermelons. It started behind her, to her left, and moved around her in the same way the sound of breaking surf moves along a beach. She turned and saw the heaps collapsing.

She saw a tower pitch forward from its middle, and the houses on top of it separated, scattering, their spider legs kicking as they seemed to almost float down through the air. The main body of the tower nudged another, breaking it in the middle, sending houses somersaulting through the air, spilling furniture, hurtling into other houses, dislodging them, bursting apart. The houses above these, without support, slid helplessly down, other houses still on their backs. It was a contagion, each house linked to another. They collapsed, and broke, and gathered into a massive spreading weight, a roiling wall of flesh. It smashed into the first of the hard stone buildings, rearing up and slapping down on its roof, scraps spilling all over it, and very suddenly came to a stop. Boom, like that. The noise stopped, and there was a mound of flesh held back by the stone, pressed in layers like the kebabs the Arabs cooked. The sun, through mist, seemed to perch on top of it. A sound came from within it, very faintly, like the squealing of seagulls.

Third turned away, and marched. She walked with her eyes closed as much as possible, humming a song. Opening them, closing them, she saw the dismantlement of Saprang Song in flashes.

She saw a Chinese family burned. They were cheering the rebels, lined up on the roof of an emporium, waving flags, and the rebels burned them, aunts and nieces and grandfathers. Before Third could look away, they were set alight. They stood rigidly within the fire, still holding up infants, like an old family photograph, blackening.

Something stick thin, leaning on a gleaming metal pole, lurched in front of Third. "Can I take your arm, dear?" it asked. It was a woman. She was wearing a blue hospital coat, and the pole supported a pumping, artificial heart.

"Ask someone else," Third replied. "I can't see."

Something bumped into her, and apologized with two voices. It had wrinkled skin like an elephant, only it was blue: crumpled pajamas. Two men missing legs were hopping together for support.

Third dimly made out the shape of the hospital building. The rebels were making the patients march as well. Third found herself suddenly in a line of marching things, all down around her knees, hunchbacked, bobbing, and all talking at once, very softly and clearly. "I am a delicate piece of lifesaving equipment," said a little beige box on muscular, human legs. Another, armored like a beehive, black, waddled ahead of it. "I can take over cerebral functions for all blood groups," it announced in a hushed voice. "Please treat me with care."

Suddenly a rebel stepped in front of Third. "You are going the wrong way, Old Woman," he said.

"I can't see!" exclaimed Third. She could see well enough that the line of machines led to another mound of flesh. There was a shadow on top of it, black. It had a sharp green grin. "Please treat me with care," said the little beige box as the shadow brought something, a garden hoe perhaps, down on its head.

"You go that way, to the Bridge," said the Rebel, trying to block her view. "Across the River, that way there." Third leaned around him, curious. She wanted to see. There was a white coat talking, a doctor.

"But these things save lives, they can save the lives of your friends, why are you doing this?" wailed the doctor. Without breaking the rhythm of his swing, the shadow brought the hoe down with a crack, on the doctor's head as well.

The rebel grabbed Third's arm and pulled her away. "She can't see!" he called out to his comrades. Then he murmured, thin-lipped, "You didn't see anything. Did you?"

He led her to a wide avenue that went down the hill to the Bridge, and there they were, the People, a dappled mass of them, black-haired heads and many-colored shirts. Some of them wore coolsuits and hiking boots and knapsacks; some of them carried parasols and twirled them. Some of them sat on the balconies of buildings, as if at a festival, drinking from tins and eating sandwiches. The People, always polite, always patient, talked in lowered voices about practicalities, without complaint.

"Once we are across the Bridge, we will be all right."

"Sssh, ssssh, darling, later. We need to save the food for later, all right?"

"Oooof! It's hot. Why couldn't they wait until spring?"

Third felt her sandal come off her foot. She spun around, but it was lost under a forest of legs. "My shoe! I can't see it. Can someone get it for me?" Third asked. People looked down around their feet, and shook their heads.

"I'm sorry, Mother. I can't see it," said a City Woman, very prettily. Third could see the blurred back-and-forth motion of her hand, and the wide white fan with red patterns. Her little daughter looked up at Third in silent dislike. Third could see her black eyes.

"Where are we going, Mummy?" the child asked in a discontented voice.

"You are going, Child," said Third, unbidden, leaning down, "to the Unconquered Country." The little girl buried her face in her mother's side. "Oh no, you must not be frightened! It is very peaceful there. Everything is as it should be, there."

"What do you mean?" the mother asked, sheltering her daughter.

Third bowed and made a gesture that enough had been said, and, smiling rather smugly, turned away. It was not for everyone to know. The sun seemed to swell, directly over the middle of the street. The People shuffled forward, a step at a time.

Suddenly the crowd heaved itself up in front of Third. They were on the stone steps of the Bridge. Third climbed them, as if they led to the altar of a temple, feeling a sudden gathering grandness, as if she were being married. Overhead, the great gray workings of the Bridge loomed like a gate. Third could see them clearly. She fixed her eyes on them, as she was carried forward in slow procession by the crowd. Then, at the very hottest moment of the day, under a merciless sun, in the middle of the Bridge, it came to a stop, and did not move again.

The asphalt underfoot was just on the point of melting, a sort of black putty, and Third had to move from one foot to the other, to save the bare one burning. There was nowhere to sit down. The People, pressed together, could smell each other's bodies. Balancing on the railing of the Bridge, holding on to a suspension cable, was a rebel girl, scowling with the heat, blinking. Just below her was the body of a dead soldier. The People backed away from it as much as they could, wrinkling their noses. Third squeezed her way through them, smiling, and sat down next to the corpse. Her knees touched it.

"Hello, Third," said the corpse. Third looked down and saw that it was Nourisher of the East.

"Hello," she whispered to him.

"Listen," he told her. "You will be on this Bridge for two days. People will die. It is most necessary that you get water. You can survive two days without food, but no water in this heat for two days and you will not be able to stand up, and the rebels will kill you." He told her how to get water. Third could not accept it at first, would not have accepted it from anyone else. "Wait," he said, "until it is dark." The rebel girl leaned back and drank deeply from a canteen.

Water was a joke at first, to the People on the Bridge. They were so thirsty, and down below, a hundred feet away, was the river. They could hear its roar; they could smell the spray. They drank the last of their warm sticky lemonade. People lost control of their bladders and bowels and could not wash. Infants began to shriek for water. It was only two hours later that Third saw someone jump off the Bridge. He was a young boy. He clung, hunched, to the railing for a long time, before finally letting himself slip off the side. His friends crowded round the edge to look, and then silently turned away.

People began to crawl along the railings to get out. Third nodded at them, benignly. She was not agile enough to climb, and they shaded her from the sun. For most of the distance, there were no cables to hold on to, and the people seesawed their arms, until they fell off, landing on the people beneath them:

much angry shouting. A man in a brightly colored short-sleeved shirt fought his way through the crowd. "Anything to drink?" he kept asking, smiling, perplexed. He had a fistful of paper money. "All of this, for a bottle of Coca-Cola. Here, look. All of this for you." A young woman, smiling, shook her head. The man could not believe it. "Look, what is a bottle of Coca-Cola worth?" The woman still shook her head. "It could buy you a nice house, a car!" he said, with a yelping, nervous laugh. He looked at Third. "All my life," he said, "I spent making money." He moved on. Some time later, Third saw the money blow past the railings, like leaves.

Surreptitiously, she took the corpse's hand. She wanted to ask Crow if the fire had hurt. She wanted to ask him if he knew that she had made a house for him, and lived the life she would have had if he had lived; that she had been happy. But it was difficult to ask such things, and besides, she already knew the answers.

"I came back," Crow said. "I could have kept on flying; the flesh had been burned away. But I chose to come back."

"Bodhisattva," said Third, realizing. Gratefully, she closed her aching eyes and slept.

Suddenly it was cooler, dark. "Now," said Crow. Through the girders of the Bridge was a tangle of stars. Amid them, the rebel girl squatted out over the railings, her trousers down around her knees. Third crawled forward with her tin cup. She held it out under her.

The girl squawked, and clenched, and stopped herself.

"Please," said Third. "It's only water. It's the only way. There is nothing wrong."

The girl looked helpless and harassed; finally she had to let go. The water spilled gently out of her; it rang in the tin cup, filled it generously. It seemed such a natural, friendly thing to do, sharing water. Third very elegantly raised the tin cup and sipped it. It was surprisingly cool and mild, only slightly salty. She nibbled her rice ball for a moment, then held it out toward the girl. The rebel hesitated, but was very hungry. Finally, she broke off a piece of it, and gave Third a wisp of a smile.

The girl was from Durnang province, to the north. Most of her family were still alive, but scattered. She had never been to school; she had fought with the Ghost Wolf regiment instead. She asked Third why she held the hand of a dead traitor.

"Because he was of the People, once," said Third. "There is no difference. The Dead are the living." The girl did not believe in the Buddha. That was Shinga Iary, she said, Consoling Nonsense. Third repeated the words.

"We must get off this Bridge," said the girl.

"How?"

"We could just walk out, over them," said the rebel. "If there's trouble—pow. Come on."

Third looked at the People, all lying in orderly rows. "No," she said. "You go. I'll stay." She watched the girl stumbling out over the backs of the People. Where she passed, there was the wailing of a baby.

Why did I do that, Third wondered. She knelt down again beside the body. She picked up the cold hand. Whose are you? she asked the hand. It looked so small. Did anyone mourn for you? Did anyone love you, like I loved Crow? She looked at the expanse of fallen faces, blue in the moonlight.

There is a part of me that loves them, she realized. That is why I stayed, because they are my People. That is not Shinga Iary. She sat through the night, holding the dead hand.

The next day ground on, hotter and hotter; like a mill. The faces of the People were the faces of the Dead—bloated and unmoving and lopsided, with open mouths. An infant was lapping the asphalt, ceaselessly, with its tongue. Third stroked its head to make it stop.

You are all Dead, she thought, we are all crossing over. The thought made her feel peaceful and at home; all of her friends were Dead. In the city behind, brown clouds of smoke were rising up. In the sky overhead, birds still wheeled on currents of air, and clouds still subtly changed shape, breaking up the light, casting huge shadows through it. Third lay back. I could be a child again, she thought.

"My name is Third," she murmured to the clouds, "and I was born in a village called No Harm Can Come . . ."

Her voice trailed off. Why did it seem that there was no point going on? She felt warm, cushioned. She rolled her head and found that her special teacher was sitting next to her.

The teacher was younger than Third now, but she was still smiling. "Give me numbers," the teacher said.

Third found that she did not hate her. All of that was so long ago. The woman's face was thinner than Third remembered, and the smile more uncertain. You were trying, Third thought, poor thing, you were trying to help.

"I don't have any numbers," said Third, shaking her head.

"Oh, but you do," said the teacher, rocking forward on her knees, holding out her hands on either side of her. "You have faces instead of numbers."

So I do, thought Third, and smiled back at her. That is what I have. Thank you.

In the sky overhead there was a daystar, moving. The Big People put machines in heaven. High up, there was cold metal and safety. The Big People slid between the stars, it was said, in a network, like a spider's web. That was as close as they would ever get to Heaven. Slide, Third told the Big People, slide and leave, leave the world to us again.

She closed her eyes and dreamed, dreamed of great arches made of white stone in the sky, and the arches made her happy, like being in a temple. They held up the sky and the stars, and there was a road, a bridge across a gulf. The bodhisattvas came back along it, out of love, to lead the People. She saw them, wearing gold hats like the spires of temples.

Night. Death. Dawn. Cool breeze, smelling acrid, the odor of burned tires, and an ocher sky with a heavy orange sun.

"Now," said Crow. "Get up." The corpse's head had disappeared under a sheen of jelly; and translucent, wire-thin worms twisted in its mouth. "The worms are the truth," Crow said. "They are words."

"We are numbers," said Third. Her sister was beside her, and helped her stand up. Third felt very weak; she couldn't lift her feet, so she pumped her knees back and forth to get the blood flowing, as her sister held her arm.

"You have had great fortune, Little Princess," her sister said. "You did not starve, or wither. You were loved, but you never became a soldier's wife or a City Person, so you can lose no one else. You have lived the best life possible in the Land of the Faithful."

There was a jabbering of orders from far ahead. The People sat up, blinking, prodding relatives, helping them, groaning, to stand up. A mother tried to wake her baby; there was something wrong with the way its mouth hung. The mother shook it, and began calling its name. "Stand up," said Third, a hand on the woman's shoulder. "Take him with you. It is time."

The ghost numbers rose up, thousands of them, as if ruptured from balloons, reaching up for some reason, some answer. The number of the People. The size of the world.

They found it. Third could see the high white clouds, and there was a bridge across a gulf, and the People were crossing it, Third's first sister who had been withered, her second sister who had finally died in her airport window, an old man Third suddenly recognized from her village. She gave him a friendly wave. There was a man, too, whose face she could not quite see, riding on the back of a tiger.

There came a sudden booming, a crackling. Fireworks? Why should there be fireworks? Third turned in time to see the spires of all the temples on the hill rise up on clouds of dust, like rockets. They were lifted up, and listed to one side, straining toward Heaven, hanging in the air for a moment, and then fell, uninhabited stone. Ah yes, even that made sense. The temples were being killed too, to join them. The temples would be there waiting too, and the villages, and the houses. The houses would greet their families with their cry for the dead.

Third felt something feather-light descend on her back, and something dry and bony wrap itself around her neck, and she felt her mother's face press close to hers. The skull was only lightly covered by a dry crackling of skin. "I carried you once, daughter," she said. "Now it is your turn to carry me."

And in the sky was a bird made of fire. It burned, leading them, and it sang, a strange sad song that rose up at the end like a question, for everything that had been lost, an orphaned song, for an orphaned people. The bird was not struck down.

"We are going home, child," whispered Third's mother. "Third Child, we are going home!"

for John Lennon,
for Philip K. Dick, for Walter

— AFTERWORD —

A Fall of Angels was written about 1976 as a show of strength. *Fan* was written in 1988 or '89. Both *O Happy Day!* and *The Unconquered Country* were finished in 1984, a year in which I could do no wrong.

It has been very strange rereading them, as if I had run across my younger self. There is the embarrassment of reliving youthful inadequacy; grief for departed energy; a kind of sympathy for the awkwardness and sincerity and pomposity of youth.

There is also the embarrassment of old friends. Here they come, like certain kinds of fan. Here comes Teenage Megadeath, envisaging the slaughter of millions and imagining that this is an effective protest. Here comes the Expository Lump, covered in spots and determined to back you into a corner to detail at length his brilliant ideas. Here is Unperceived Sources, all agog with Star Trek and unaware of it. Here comes Style, all done up in German Expressionism, or Brechtianism, or whatever mainly visual or musical trend has caught his attention, his hypersensitivity to fashion. These are among the usual embarrassments of writing Science Fiction, a genre that is at its most flaming, its most colorful, the less you know, the ruder your taste.

A Fall of Angels was going to be published at the time. Hilary Bailey, editor of *New Worlds,* liked it, but that incarnation of the series folded before it could appear. I had been terribly spoiled— the very first story I had written had been published by her as well.

I thought all my stories would be published. I gave *Fall of Angels* everything I had.

Never give a hundred percent. Bob Dylan said it, and I thought it was a terrible credo for an artist. Picasso said the same thing, but explained why. A full expenditure of artistic strength is actually ugly, like someone at a party trying too hard. People like feeling that there is plenty left over. Retyping, tweaking *Fall* for this edition, I had to relive just how much of myself went into it, the research, the endless rewriting, the boiling down. I remembered sitting on the grass in Regent's Park and writing the moment when Z mourns B and for just a paragraph or two something new happened; I was able to lament on behalf of someone else in their voice, not my own. I remember the discovery that every line of dialogue has an unspoken thought behind it, and ties in with the preceding line—either intimately as a reaction, or as denial, talking across it, ignoring it. It even taught me how to write simply about complex facts, which stood me in good stead when I found myself a public information officer. Writing *Fall* hurt, but in the way that training for a sport hurts; it also felt good.

A Fall of Angels did not sell, but it did give me months of something to look forward to. At least once a week I had the feeling I might hear something about it. I sent it to Brian Aldiss, like whom I imagined I would write. He was kind and helpful, but . . . he warned me of its length.

I knew of course it might not sell. I was still not prepared for the reality. The disappointment when I realized that it simply would not see print stopped me giving as much for a very long time.

However, the manuscript became a kind of calling card. I would leave it with other fans, or people who had achieved something in the arts, and it was enough to raise eyebrows if not investment. It meant I continued to think of myself as a writer.

Right now, *A Fall of Angels* is still the favorite among my own stories, not for its efforts at hard SF but for its intercutting of high SF with the down to earth, and its determination to tell a story without violence or anger. It really should not come as a surprise that you were sweeter, kinder when young. Somehow it still does, rather as though you had grown more rebellious and adolescent as you grew.

It is an odd feeling to see it published now, like watching a handicapped child grow up to become suddenly independent.

There is no such sensation with *The Unconquered Country*. It was bedecked with awards, and wrote itself after years of obsession with the subject. Bedecked with awards it might have been, and a Nebula nomination as well, but it fell out of print in America. *O Happy Day!* was about prurience and its role in politics, in entertainment, in life. Well, write about what you know. It was also about what I had seen in nascent sexual politics, at least in Britain. I too had been given political kisses. It was published in the first (!) *Interzone* anthology. *Fan* was a story I shut away out of a kind of rage—against what I am not too sure. I was angry with it, and was determined, particularly after a Writer's Block session, to let it lie. The writers in the group were concerned about this. Their expressed concern (especially Lisa Tuttle's and Bobbie Lamming's) was enough to be filed alongside the story in the same drawer. Someone had liked it, and wanted to see it live. Again, rereading it, I was surprised to find how much I liked it too.

How does the quotation go? The things that hurt me can scarcely be distinguished from the things that helped me. It is a shaggy, unreliable activity writing. There is no greater pleasure, as long as you have faith that someone, somewhere will see what you mean and forgive the things you don't.